An Australian Bush Track

J.D. HENNESSEY

with an introduction by KEN GELDER *and* RACHAEL WEAVER

 **Grattan Street Press**

Published by Grattan Street Press 2018
Series introduction, introduction, note on the text copyright
© Ken Gelder and Rachael Weaver 2018.

Grattan Street Press is the imprint of the
teaching press based in the School of Culture and
Communication at the University of Melbourne,
Parkville, Australia.

THE UNIVERSITY OF
MELBOURNE

Cover image, *An exploring party looking for a sheep run* (1847) by Alexander
Denistoun Lang, sourced from the National Library of Australia
(nla.obj-135291075).

An Australian Bush Track originally published in 1896 by Sampson Low,
Marston & Company Limited in London.

Grattan Street Press
School of Culture and Communication
John Medley Building,
Parkville, VIC 3010
www.grattanstreetpress.com

Printed in Australia

NATIONAL
LIBRARY
OF AUSTRALIA

A catalogue record for this
book is available from the
National Library of Australia

SERIES INTRODUCTION

The Colonial Australian Popular Fiction series brings the excitement and diversity of colonial Australian fiction to the attention of contemporary readers – and there is certainly some remarkable fiction to read here.

Encompassing both novels and short-story collections, the series will include a range of popular genres that flourished during the colonial period: the bush sketch, the Lemurian novel, crime and detective fiction, the colonial romance, the Gothic tale, the convict novel, the goldfields adventure, and the bushranger novel. Some of the authors were bestsellers in their day, and their work can still take us by surprise. We aim to make colonial Australian fiction accessible to contemporary readers – and we hope the design and layout of these works will be helpful here.

But we also want to honour the original forms of these works. So we have reprinted from first editions or from the original serialisation of a work in newspapers or journals. Each publication includes a short introduction written by academic specialists, which provides a brief biography of the author (or authors) and offers critical insight into the work and its contexts. We would be particularly pleased if some of our publications eventually became set texts in university or senior secondary courses. We believe these vibrant works from our turbulent past have much to offer all readers of Australian literature. Some of them – especially those exploring the colonial frontier – can be confronting in the intensity of their racism and the level of their violence against Aboriginal people. But it is important for contemporary Australians to experience the legacies of colonialism in all their dark complexity. By doing so, we can begin to understand our historical condition and work towards a more reconciled future.

The Colonial Australian Popular Fiction series is an ongoing collaboration between the Grattan Street Press and the Australian Centre, both based within the School of Culture and Communication at the University of Melbourne.

Ken Gelder and Rachael Weaver

CONTENTS

INTRODUCTION

Ken Gelder and Rachael Weaver

John David Hennessey was twenty-seven when, in 1875, he emigrated from England to Australia. Trained as a Methodist minister, he worked in a number of regional parishes in different parts of Queensland. Later on, he moved into printing and journalism, launching the monthly *Christian Messenger* in Brisbane in January 1883. Hennessey was keen to increase the influence of homegrown Christian journalism, and in 1886 he moved to Sydney to establish the *Australian Christian World*. But he was also financially ambitious, claiming on the eve of his departure from his Brisbane congregation that 'it was possible to establish a religious Press in Australia which would be a commercial success'.[1] Hennessey's aim was nothing less than to make Christian newspapers central to the business of colonial nation building. 'The leading men of the colonies,' he argued, 'were ready to stand by them in their enterprise, and they did not intend to fail.'[2] This bold declaration draws together some of the elements we shall find in Hennessey's 1896 novel, *An Australian Bush Track*: commercial investment, a solid colonial masculinity, and the resolute striving for success. Soon after he arrived in Sydney, Hennessey turned the *Australian Christian World* newspaper into a fully-fledged publishing company and floated it on the stock exchange for £1 per share.[3] This, too, is important to know as background to *An Australian Bush Track*. One of its intrepid protagonists, Bright Hartley, has an 'almost unbroken record of success' in financial investment; he

---

1 'Congregational Reunion', *Telegraph* (Brisbane), 16 February 1886, p.5.

2 Ibid.

3 'Prospectus', *Sydney Morning Herald*, 17 July 1886, p.5.

is described early on as 'adventurous and speculative'. We can think of the novel itself in exactly the same way: an adventure narrative that is literally a work of speculative fiction, fantastic and otherworldly, but at the same time all about fortune-hunting and the pursuit of wealth – which then means thinking speculatively about creating a company, calculating its share value, its capacity to turn a profit, and so on.

In the event, the *Australian Christian World* was unceremoniously liquidated in December 1891. Hennessey left Sydney and – with his second wife – set up a farm at Wynnum on Moreton Bay, Queensland. By this time, his journalistic attention had turned to agriculture and new farming techniques. In January 1894 Hennessey launched the monthly *Australian Field*, writing instructively about the experiences of a 'New Chum Farmer'. An article in Sydney's *Australian Star* thought that this lavishly produced journal captured 'the enterprising spirit of the age'; it was able to boast a national circulation of 10,000 per issue.[4] A year later, in Sydney, Hennessey established Hennessey and Harper Co., Ltd., a literary agency that also contracted advertisements and offered printing services. He began publishing fiction around this time, too. His first novel, *The Dis-Honourable: A Mystery of the Queensland Floods*, was initially serialised in the northern New South Wales weekly, *Richmond River Herald and Northern Districts Advertiser,* 18 August 1893–6 April 1894. Hennessey used the pseudonym 'Carey Grove' to disguise his identity for this serialisation, no doubt because the story was 'published by special arrangement with Hennessey's Intercolonial Press Association', another operating title of Hennessey and Harper Co., Ltd. Other serialisations followed – for example, in Queensland's *Bundaberg Mail* – showing how Hennessey used different district newspapers

---

4   'A Success in New Journalism', *Australian Star*, 1 June 1894, p.8.

across the colonies to his advantage. His 'Intercolonial Press Association (or Agency)' then published *The Dis-Honourable* in Sydney in 1895. But Hennessey also found a publisher in England with Sampson Low, Marston & Company, and was soon part of Low's much more globally circulated Indian and Colonial Library series.

His second novel, *Wynnum White's Wickedness*, was serialised in rural newspapers in 1895–6 and published by Sampson Low in 1896 as *Wynnum. An Australian Bush Track* went down the same path, so to speak, beginning its serialisation in January 1896 in the weekly *Western Grazier*. 'The right of publishing this Novel in the Wilcannia District', this paper notes, 'has been purchased by the Proprietors of the Western Grazier.' Even so, *An Australian Bush Track* was also serialised in newspapers in Queensland, New South Wales, South Australia and Victoria at more or less the same time. We can see here just how important the rural press was in circulating the literary works of emerging Australian writers. While his fiction was being serialised, Hennessey also began syndicating newspaper articles under the title 'Agricultural Notes for Practical Men', developing his reputation as a reliable source of information for farming communities. His identity as 'The New Chum Farmer' soon became well-known across the colonies; capitalising on this, his company Hennessey and Harper collected and published his articles under the title 'The New Chum Farmer, with hundreds of practical hints on agriculture and dairying' in 1897. Heavily invested in growing the prosperity of the nation-to-come, he began publishing the weekly *Australian Federalist*, championing the cause of federation. His novel, *The Sea Cliff Towers Mystery*, was serialised here from the first issue in June 1898; he also continued his agricultural articles, this time under the more gender-inclusive title, 'Agricultural Notes for Practical Men and Women'. The Brisbane *Worker* had satirised the *Federalist* as the 'Sweateralist' because it paid its staff below union rates.[5] Nevertheless, Hennessey was a single-minded champion of federation, arguing that it would 'foster a national sentiment in which we are sadly deficient as Australians'.[6] After Federation, he moved to Victoria and continued writing and publishing popular fiction. He died at Dromana in 1935.

An Australian Bush Track is an unusual colonial novel, bringing together two quite different narrative strands: a masculine Lemurian adventure fantasy, and a story about an 'Australian Girl'. The Lemurian novel emerged in the late nineteenth century, giving us a very singular kind of fantasy: the discovery of a 'lost world' and a 'lost race' in the obscure reaches of a nation's interior. Perhaps the most globally famous Lemurian novel is H. Rider Haggard's *She: A History of Adventure* (1887) in which white explorers follow instructions written on a mysterious artefact that take them into the African wilderness, where they discover an ancient tribe presided over by a powerful sorceress, Ayesha. In 1864, the English zoologist Philip Sclater had given the name Lemuria to a 'hypothetical continent' in the Indian Ocean, connecting it to the dispersed habitats of lemurs, a species of primate (from the Latin *lemures*: 'spirits of the dead').[7] Ernst Haeckel, the famous German evolutionary biologist, went on to identify Lemuria with 'Paradise', connecting this supposedly lost ancient place to a lapsarian condition.[8]

5   'The Sweateralist', *Worker* (Brisbane), 7 May 1898, p.2.

6   'A Last Word to the Electors from the Leaders of Federation', *Illawarra Mercury*, 28 May 1898, p.1.

7   See J. David Archibald, *Aristotle's Ladder, Darwin's Tree: The Evolution of Visual Metaphors for Biological Order* (New York: Columbia University Press, 2014), p.127.

8   Sumathi Ramaswamy, *The Lost Land of Lemuria: Fabulous Geographies, Catastrophic Histories* (Los Angeles: University of California Press, 2004), p.42.

The Lemurian narrative soon offered a kind of fluid or free-floating set of conventions that could be applied to almost any new territories that lent themselves to pseudo-scientific investigation and exploration. In Australia, it flourished for a brief moment in the 1890s and early twentieth century: just before, and just after, Federation. Examples include Carlton Dawe's *The Golden Lake* (1890), J.F. Hogan's *The Lost Explorer* (1890), George Firth Scott's *The Last Lemurian* (1898), Charles Junor's *Dead Men's Tales* (1898) and Rosa Praed's *Fugitive Anne* (1902). Junor dedicated his collection of stories to Rider Haggard and paid tribute to the Lemurian formula that the novelist had established ten years earlier: 'Unknown lands, containing races of nebulous antiquity, and with curious customs, and noble or diabolical traits of character, have been worked out.'[9] We can perhaps already see that the Lemurian novel routinely allowed for the expression of racist fantasies, ideologically and imaginatively tied to the imperialist project of the discovery/invasion of new worlds. In Hennessey's *An Australian Bush Track*, this is given an interestingly literal realisation when the adventurers find themselves in possession of a letter written by Captain Cook, dated May 16th, 1770. This is the moment Cook arrived at – and named – Moreton Bay, where the opening of the novel is set. Cook's letter tells of a boat full of Aboriginal people approaching the *Endeavour*. A boomerang is thrown, after which the boat mysteriously disappears. It seems at first as if this is an act of Aboriginal resistance. But the boomerang – like the mysterious artefact in Rider Haggard's *She* – turns out to be a delivered message. When it is translated, it leads the adventurers into the Queensland interior where – true to the form of the Lemurian novel – they discover a 'lost race' that is identified

9 Charles Junor, 'Introduction', *Dead Men's Tales* (Melbourne: George Robertson & Co., 1898), p.xi.

as more ancient than Aboriginal people; not local so much as intercontinental, the 'remnant of a great nation which came there from some part of the mainland of Asia'. They also discover an underground river and an inland sea, reproducing an earlier colonial fantasy fuelled by explorers such as Charles Sturt in the 1840s. A keyword in this particular colonial Lemurian novel is 'queer', used continually as a way of making place seem singular and strange – and, by the end of the nineteenth century (when the age of inland exploration was coming to a close), of reanimating the possibility for novelty in Australian adventure fiction.

Readers today will find the casual racism of this novel difficult to take. The lapsarian aspect of this genre – and its ties to evolutionary biology – meant that a 'lost race' was usually discovered at the moment of its degeneration; or, it was seen as an ancient form of 'superior' civilisation that was made to contrast with negative colonial representations of dispossessed Aboriginal people. *An Australian Bush Track* inclines towards the latter, not least because it also wants to bring its intrepid adventurers out to the edge of the frontier where they face some renewed Aboriginal resistance. By the 1890s this is also *post-*frontier, indicated by the presence – in the midst of all this – of a settled homestead with a family and a garden. John Holdfast (as his name suggests) is the 'ideal pioneer squatter' type with a firm grip on the land he occupies. Manly, strong, practical, skilled in bushcraft, he is also virulently racist; he joins the other men in the expedition into the interior and bolsters their chances of success. But this novel is not only about men. It also introduces an important female protagonist, Dorna Stoneham, who we can recognise as another key colonial character type: the Australian Girl.

The Australian Girl was an increasingly familiar figure in colonial literature towards the end of the nineteenth century, appearing in novels such as Rosa Praed's *An Australian Heroine* (1880) and Catherine Martin's *An Australian Girl* (1890). She is often identified with a bold, capable femininity, tied to the wellbeing of the colonies and, later, the nation itself. But she can struggle under the influence of patriarchy, and the question of who she should marry is also challenging. In *An Australian Bush Track*, Dorna Stoneham is one of seven daughters living on an island in Moreton Bay with their ill-tempered, violent father. Raised like 'boys' to help out on the farm, ride horses and sail boats, they are at the same time 'the best of the fine ladies in town'. Dorna almost immediately draws the attention of Hartley and the other male explorers with her unselfconscious beauty, strength of character and practical knowledge. 'If she's a specimen of Australian bush girls,' Dawson remarks, 'they're simply wonders.' Later on, she embarks on a journey that takes up a considerable portion of the narrative, putting an Australian Girl's adventure into dialogue with the novel's masculine journey of exploration. At Ipswich, she buys a whip and 'one of the latest improved hammerless revolvers': the shopkeeper, she writes, 'stared at me as though I were one of the New Women that people are talking about'. The New Woman was a *fin-de-siècle,* proto-feminist figure, popularised in fiction overseas by writers such as Olive Schreiner and the Irish feminist Sarah Grand – who had coined the term in 1894. The Australian Girl is often firmly distinguished from this figure, however; the New Woman's fashionable tastes, worldliness and decadence, are compared unfavourably with the Australian Girl's healthy freshness and simplicity ('this barefooted girl of Stoneham's').[10] As she travels through Queensland, Dorna deals with a number

10 On the New Woman and the Australian Girl, see Michelle Smith, 'The "Australian Girl" and the Domestic Ideal in Colonial Women's Fiction', in Tamara Wagner, ed. *Domestic Fiction in Colonial Australia and New Zealand* (London: Routledge, 2016), pp.76–77.

of suitors and tries to work out what her romantic future will be. She goes on to play a major role in the Lemurian expedition and in the violent, racist imperatives of settlement – firing her new revolver at 'troublesome' Aboriginal people when the party finds itself under attack. *An Australian Bush Track* is a fascinating novel that is unrepressed in its representation of colonial racism and the driving forces behind it: dispossession/land acquisition, the relentless pursuit of wealth and resources, and so on. Along the way it gives us a feisty Australian Girl who charts her own route through a speculative male fantasy, finally emerging – as John Docker memorably put it – as 'a colonial Woman on Top'.[11]

KEN GELDER is Professor of English and Co-director of the Australian Centre at the University of Melbourne.

RACHAEL WEAVER is an ARC Senior Research Fellow in English at the Australian Centre at the University of Melbourne.

WORKS CITED

Archibald, J. David, *Aristotle's Ladder, Darwin's Tree: The Evolution of Visual Metaphors for Biological Order*. New York: Columbia University Press, 2014.

Docker, John, *The Nervous Nineties: Australian Cultural Life in the 1890s*. Oxford: Oxford University Press, 1991.

Junor, Charles, 'Introduction', *Dead Men's Tales*. Melbourne: George Robertson & Co., 1898.

Ramaswamy, Sumathi, *The Lost Land of Lemuria: Fabulous Geographies, Catastrophic Histories*. Los Angeles: University of California Press, 2004.

Smith, Michelle, 'The "Australian Girl" and the Domestic Ideal in Colonial Women's Fiction', in Tamara Wagner, ed. *Domestic Fiction in Colonial Australia and New Zealand*. London: Routledge, 2016.

11 John Docker, *The Nervous Nineties: Australian Cultural Life in the 1890s* (Oxford: Oxford University Press, 1991), p.212.

A NOTE ON THE TEXT

This edition of *An Australian Bush Track* follows the first edition of the novel, published in London in 1896 by Sampson Low, Marston & Company, as part of Low's Indian and Colonial Library. The novel was initially serialised in the weekly *Western Grazier*, 11 January 1896–18 July 1896; it was also serialised in the *Gippsland Farmer's Journal*, 14 January 1896–25 February 1896 (ending at chapter VI); the *Daily Northern Argus* (Rockhampton, Queensland), 9 March 1896–27 June 1896; the *Bathurst Free Press and Mining Journal*, 20 April 1896–1 July 1896; the weekly *Yorke's Peninsula Advertiser*, 15 May 1896–20 November 1896; and the *Gympie Times and Mary River Mining Gazette*, 2 July 1896–25 February 1897 (incomplete).

The editors of the present text have sought to balance scholarly accuracy with readability. Some punctuation, capitalisation, spelling and hyphenation has been changed for the sake of consistency (e.g. 'to-night' to 'tonight'). Scholars seeking an unamended text of this edition should contact info@grattanstreetpress.com for details.

An Australian Bush Track

CHAPTER I

A MAN WHO BELIEVED IN LUCK

THE SHADOWS OF a summer evening were lengthening across one of the lower reaches of the Brisbane.

It had been an exceptionally high tide, and the great stretch of water, dotted here and there with mangrove islands, was almost level with the river banks.

Some of the adjacent low-lying lands were submerged.

The afterglow lingered in the western sky, and its light, broken by the shadows of tall gum and bloodwood trees, was reflected here and there in weird patches of colour upon the water. There was just – only just – breeze enough to keep the mosquitoes quiet.

On the south side of the river a huge ocean steamer in ballast lay at anchor, the high water causing her great sides to tower above the bank, until passers-by on the neighbouring roadway might have thought that she had been stranded, and was shored up upon the land.

A coasting steamer had just passed up the river, and although she had turned the bend and was out of sight, the regular throbbing of her engines could be distinctly heard in the distance.

A schooner creeping past in perfect silence from the bay was beating up stream, making a long leg; she would soon have to 'go about' and make a short one, as what little wind there was blew in uncertain puffs from the west. Near shore, a yacht of a few tons had cast anchor, the slightest sound being audible as the crew made her snug. This being effected, they pushed off from the dainty little craft in a dinghy. The crew numbered two men and a boy; the latter sat in the bows while one of the others sculled leisurely towards a landing stage running out a short distance into the water at the foot of the garden, which belonged to a commodious and well-to-do residence.

The whole scene was suggestive of repose.

A flight of black swans, high above reach of fowling-pieces, moved slowly towards their feeding ground on the shores of Moreton Bay. Not infrequently, large fishes threw themselves out of the still water in their gambols, the heavy splashes they made when falling back into the river being distinctly heard. It must have been nearly a mile from shore to shore.

The occupants of the dinghy, however, had not far to row, and as on reaching the jetty they found the water to be within a few inches of the planking, they pulled the boat up upon the landing stage and, throwing their belongings over their shoulders, the two men sauntered leisurely up the garden walk to the house.

The place presented a semi-tropical appearance.

Clumps of graceful bananas moved their broad pendulous leaves languidly in the fitful evening breeze.

Pineapples were growing luxuriantly in the fruit garden, while near them were English apple and pear trees laden with fruit. In the matter of flowers the kindly earth seemed to have become a mother, for they grew in profusion everywhere – English and Australian and those of other lands – the very air was odorous with roses and carnations and mignonette, mingled with the perfume of tropical flowering shrubs.

'I hope you are in no hurry for dinner, Hartley,' said one of the two new arrivals as they came upon the owner of the residence, stretched full-length on a cane lounge under the wide verandah portico.

'Not for half an hour or so,' was the reply.

'That's right,' said the previous speaker; 'it would be too bad to go in and leave that afterglow and its reflection on the river, with no one to look at it.'

'People talk about the scenery of the Swiss lakes,' he said, looking down the river, 'but when you catch this part of the Brisbane River in the gloaming, with a full tide, it is one of the most romantic spots in existence. It's not grand, you know, but it's downright interesting. See, now, how it changes!'

'Do you often get it like this, Hartley?' asked the third man as, following his friend's example, he stood and gazed at the truly wonderful scene.

'I don't think that I have seen it half-a-dozen times just as it looks tonight, and never so beautiful as now,' replied Hartley, quietly.

'But we've had it much like this, twice in four days,' said the first speaker.

'You have,' said Hartley, sitting up and dropping his legs over the side of the lounge, while he felt leisurely about in the pockets of his loose jacket for his tobacco pouch. 'You have; it's your luck!

'It's strange now,' he continued, as his two friends sat down and got ready for a smoke, 'some of the biggest strokes of luck, and queerest adventures too, which have befallen men in any part of Australia have happened to the newly arrived. I don't attempt to explain it,' he continued, 'but facts show that the newer things are the more capricious is the luck. It has repeatedly happened, for instance, that when experienced miners have failed, and after months of heart-wearying toil have thrown up a "claim" for a duffer, some raw new chum has come along and positively stumbled into a fortune. I could give you instances of such things by the score,' continued Bright Hartley, stretching himself and putting his hands into his trousers'-pockets with a self-satisfied air, as he looked through a cloud of tobacco smoke, first at the river, and then at his friends.

It was as much as to say 'I, Bright Hartley, was one of the lucky new chums.'

'Ah! that may be *in regard to mining*,' drawled out the long individual, who, with his feet elevated upon the rail of the verandah, now lay back in a large cane chair, smoking.

'Mining be hanged!' said Hartley, facing around; 'it has been so in business, and in the learned professions, and politics, and in everything else. Australian luck is a thing which positively revels in surprises. You meet with men in all positions in life in the colonies, of whom, when you come to know them, you wonder how on earth they got to be where and what they are. It certainly was not their talents put them there, so, you see, it must have been their luck. You have an illustration of it in the very matter which you told me of last night, and I may say that it is because I attribute it solely to your unsophisticated good luck that I have a leaning towards it.'

'Go on,' said the long man, who saw that Hartley had more to say, and wanted encouragement.

'Well, I will make the application then,' continued Hartley. 'You two fellows came to Australia simply because you were at a loose end. After roaming and shooting and yachting, and all the rest of it, over half the world, you profess to find nothing new under the sun. I suppose, now, that you, Buchanan, would give one of your fingers to have a really original adventure to talk about when you get back to England, and Sir Charles here aspires to literature, and talks of writing a book. Time is no object to either of you; you want adventure, and the queer thing about it is that for a hundred years or more the key to an adventure seems to have been awaiting you two English innocents down in Moreton Bay. It's most extraordinary! Stoneham has known all about this matter for years, without mentioning it to a creature until you two come across him, and fairly stumble into what seems to me to be one of the queerest and most mysterious affairs in Australian history. You actually discover an unpublished and hitherto unknown letter, written by Captain Cook in 1770; you unearth a mysterious aboriginal apparition, and come here to me with ancient gold pieces in your possession, and an uncut diamond worth a king's ransom, taking the whole thing as a regular matter of course, and half-suggesting, notwithstanding the gold and diamond, that Stoneham has been trying to have you, because he is not able to produce a photograph of Long Tom!'

'That is the result of our having been had before,' said Sir Charles Dawson, laughing. 'Some of your colonials would fill us to the brim with absurd stories if we would let them, in the hope that they might afterward meet with some of their nonsense in a book.'

'I don't deny that,' said Hartley, excitedly, 'but this thing is altogether different. Why, if what you have actually shown me only got into the hands of the newspaper men, they would cable it, word for word, to Europe, and you would set all the scientists of Christendom by the ears. The whole thing is so extraordinary that I have hardly thought of anything else all day. You see, you have facts before you, which all allow to be stubborn things. First of all, there's the letter, which, if it is not genuine, must be accounted for in some other way. I'll swear that neither Stoneham nor any other man down there could have written it. Then the gold pieces are certainly ancient, and the stone is genuine – I know a diamond when I see it, even if it is in the rough.'

'Then do you advise us to accept Stoneham's offer?' said Buchanan with a yawn, as though it did not matter very much which way it was.

'Yes,' said Hartley, deliberately. 'I have thought it carefully out; it will give you fellows something new to talk about on your return to Europe – that is, if you come back again, for there is always a spice of danger about interior travelling anywhere; and you will find it the same here, although we have no big game such as you meet with in the jungles of India and Africa. If I had not so much business on hand, upon my word, I'd feel inclined to make one of the party. Three or four months ought to do it, and then you will know how much truth there is in Stoneham's story.'

'And supposing that we do not come back again?' said Sir Charles, with a smile.

'You are neither of you married,' said Hartley, 'and if you should happen not to return, the girls you leave behind you will soon console themselves with other men. But what's the use of talking nonsense. It's only the good who die young.'

The speaker was Bright Hartley, of Brisbane, Sydney, and the Barcoo, and sundry other parts of the world in which he had possessions. He was one of the few Australians whose lives show an almost unbroken record of success. It was not so much his business of a general merchant as his outside speculations which had been so singularly fortunate. He always bought in and sold out at the right time. He had in turn gone into mining, sugar-growing, and station property, with equal success. It was a proverb among his acquaintances that Bright Hartley's touch turned earth to gold. Men generally attributed it to his luck, and while Hartley would laughingly allow that he had been born under a lucky star, and was a strong believer in individual good fortune, he rightly claimed that foresight, sagacity, and secrecy had much to do with the satisfactory result.

Hartley was undoubtedly superstitious. There were men whom he regarded as unlucky, and with whom he would on no account have joined in any business transaction; and, among other superstitions, he had a belief that his good luck would leave him the moment he married.

'You see,' he would say, 'a man must tell his wife, if he has one, and that spoils it all. I'll make a big coup some day, perhaps, and then tie up everything in Government debentures, and bank shares, and house property, and risk it and get married.'

In the meantime, however, he made up for his celibacy by innumerable harmless flirtations, some of which, by the way, were with other men's wives.

Bright Hartley was a fair man, rather below the average height, with blue eyes, and tow-coloured hair. He was as tight and round in his garments as is an average, middle-aged alderman, and was conversant with all sorts and conditions of Australian people, places, and things. He knew how to manage a sugar plantation or sheep station, or work a goldmine, and had seen a bit of cattle duffing on the Barcoo; but he also could tell you how Miss So-and-So's stays came to be laced so tightly that she fainted at the last Government House ball. In fact, he read the whole secret of colonial life as from a book. There was nothing of any interest, bad or good, which he had not seen or heard about; and yet he had not a wrinkle on his brow, and could not be induced to own up to being anything over forty.

That he was adventurous and speculative may be gathered from his conversation already recorded; and it should be said that, coming from such a well-informed and prosperous man, the advice he tendered had made a strong impression upon the minds of his two young friends.

'I can't make you out,' said the senior of the two Englishmen, Sir Charles Dawson, who with his friend and travelling companion, Captain Buchanan, were the 'innocents' Hartley had referred to. 'As a matter of fact, you are as hard-headed as anyone I have met with, and yet in this affair you appear to be most credulous. You cannot, surely, believe the whole of this most extraordinary story of Stoneham's to be gospel?'

'Come and let us have dinner, and after that I will talk to you,' said Hartley.

CHAPTER II

CAPTAIN COOK'S LETTER

DINNER AT THE Bungalow, as Hartley had modestly named his commodious bachelor residence, was an important function, and it was an hour and a half afterward when the verandah chairs were again occupied, and the conversation resumed.

'My special difficulty with this matter,' said Sir Charles, laughing, 'is this ancient black fellow. I thought that Australia was much too new for anything in the shape of superstitious lore.

'One expects when on the Rhine, or anywhere else in Europe, to meet with lusty old goblins, and banshees, and wraiths, and goodness knows what; but to have a hoary old demon down in Moreton Bay, dating back to the time of Captain Cook, is enough to take one's breath away. Look here, Buchanan,' he said, placing his muscular white hand upon the shoulder of the captain, a tall, gentlemanly man of four and twenty, 'we'll have to take Hartley's yacht and run down to Stoneham's, and get him to introduce us to "Long Tom" and "The Fishers of Moreton Bay"!'

'You might not wish to go a second time,' laughed Hartley.

'Well, I don't want to doubt the evidence of my senses. Old gold coins and a genuine diamond are very tangible witnesses; but to have them mysteriously connected with a jolly old ghost with a phantom canoe, supposed to be seen cruising about Moreton Bay, is a pretty big thing for an Agnostic like myself to swallow. But let us have another look at the letter.'

The three men went inside at this, and Sir Charles lifted an ancient-looking document up to the light.

'Ah!' he said, 'there's a 1767 watermark upon the paper. That favours the letter being genuine; but without questioning the facts, they may all be attributed to natural causes. Cook was no doubt deceived. Singular disappearances of vessels through the sudden rising of mists, etc., are by no means uncommon at sea, and why not in the bay. But read it out aloud for us, Buchanan, and then we can discuss it further outside.'

The captain drew a chair up to the table, and slowly read as follows:

HMS *Endeavour*,
Off Cape Moreton, Australia,
May 16th, 1770

Having met with a very remarkable incident yesterday, the fifteenth day of May, in the year of our Lord 1770, I feel it to be my duty to the possible future European inhabitants of this newly discovered continent, and also to His Gracious Majesty, King George the III, to place on record a true and circumstantial account of the singular and well-nigh incredible occurrence.

We descried yesterday morning at daylight a long stretch of low sandhills which terminated in a sand spit with a bluff rock on the foreshore. Rounding the cape, we cast anchor in eight fathoms of water in a broad, shallow bay. I have named the former Cape Moreton, and the latter Moreton Bay.[1] Later in the day I moved the *Endeavour* farther to the south-east on which the bay opened out, revealing a number of islands covered with green foliage, and also the mouth of a large creek or river. I went with the ship's longboat, accompanied by Mr Green, our astronomer, and Mr Banks, our botanist, and a picked crew, to explore some of the islands, in hope of adding to our collections of plants and animals, but being but partially successful we returned. I had been talking with the chief officer and Mr Green upon the quarterdeck when the former called my attention to a large native vessel, which seemed to have emerged from between the islands, and was rapidly bearing down upon us. We all remarked the unusual size of the craft. It was fitted with two masts, and carried large, triangular sides, seemingly constructed of some native cotton or grass, woven into cloth. There was high ornamental woodwork at prow and stern. It was now growing towards twilight, and partly on account of this, but principally by reason of the sails and high woodwork of the prow and stern, it was impossible to count the number of the crew. Several natives were seen, however, and at the stern,

---

1 Cook did actually name Moreton Bay on 16 May 1770, during the *Endeavour's* first voyage. His crew included the naturalists Joseph Banks and Daniel Solander, and the astronomer Charles Green.

guiding the vessel's course with a huge sweep, which answered for a helm, stood a native of stature and countenance never before met with by us in these seas. They slackened sail as they drew nearer, and the boatswain, by my direction, hailed her, calling out, 'Ship ahoy! what name?' In reply, a clear, wild, ringing sound came from the throat of the huge steersman, 'Dé Fuchers' is the best interpretation I am able to give of the sound, which we all distinctly heard. I may say that Dr Solander and Mr Green both support my opinion; but the second officer and others of the crew believe the words to have been 'The Fishers', which is, on the face of the matter, most unlikely, as, although they might have followed the calling of fishermen, it is impossible that they could have been acquainted with the English tongue. However, having thus called out, the native suddenly turned and threw towards us one of their weapons of warfare, called, I believe by them, a 'boomerang'. It came whirling through the air with great force, and seemed to have been purposely directed towards myself and the group around me. It was sharpened upon the edges, and the doctor narrowly escaped injury. Taking this to be an indication of hostile intention, and indignant at the weapon being directed at myself, some of the marines fired small arms in the direction of the periagua. I regretted this, as I was anxious to maintain friendly relations with the natives. But to our astonishment and consternation, immediately after the discharge of the firearms, we observed the native vessel to be gradually disappearing before our eyes. Many of the crew were watching from the ship's side, and a score of reliable witnesses are prepared to state, on oath, that she neither foundered nor was enveloped in mist, but dissolved before our eyes into air; the final disappearance being accompanied by a wild, sad scream, that sounded like a repetition of the previously spoken words. This untoward event has, I regret to say, filled the crew with the gravest apprehension and alarm, and I confess that my own mind is not without misgivings as to what warning the phenomenon may have been intended to convey. The weapon falling on the deck is constructed of a dark wood, and on one side is covered with letters or symbols of a singular form. Whatever may be the language, it is one that neither Dr Solander, Joseph Banks, nor myself can in any way decipher. The crew generally regard it with superstitious dread, and it has been hinted to me that it would relieve their feelings if I would throw it overboard.

Indeed, some of them, I understand, aver that unless it is thrown out of the ship we shall be wrecked before getting clear of the Australian coast. However, I shall not yield to them that far, but, partly to allay their fears, I have decided to have this statement, with an accurate drawing of the weapon and its inscribed characters attached, placed in a box and securely hidden or buried upon a small island of bright red soil, which can be discerned a few leagues from our anchorage. It will be represented to the sailors that the weapon or boomerang is in the box, which will lessen their fears, and in a few days, I hope, restore their equanimity. I intend to take the boomerang to Europe, in hope that its mysterious inscriptions may be deciphered and interpreted by some learned man, to the elucidation of the mysterious phenomenon which at present is inexplicable and awe-inspiring to all that witnessed it.

Given under my hand and seal, this sixteenth day of May, in the year of our Lord, seventeen hundred and seventy.

(Signed) JAMES COOK

Witness: JOSEPH BANKS

Attached to the letter was a further sheet of paper, on which was the drawing of a boomerang, almost full size, and engraved upon it were a number of singular characters, which could not be represented by any letters comprised in printer's type. Buchanan, who was the scholar of the party, said that the nearest approach to them which he had seen was in the uncial manuscript[2] of the Latin Bible, in the possession of the Bodleian Library, at Oxford.

The following translation of this remarkable inscription was signed by a professor of the Bonn University.

THE PATH OF ZOO-ZOO

*From the islands of the east, follow the broad flowing
waters beyond the snake-coils to its source.*
South of the setting sun, a cleft appears in the mountain.
Beyond is the great country of many little trees.
*Follow as the birds fly towards the setting sun of winter,
beyond the broad plains, over the white mountains, and
you reach the span longer than the arms of many men.*

---

2 An ancient Latin or Greek script, dating back to the 1st and 2nd centuries AD, where letters are disconnected from one another but words are not separated.

Beware of the great waters!
Beware of the white gates and the golden!
Beyond that fear not; your eyes will see, and your hands
may touch what all men love.

The men looked at each other, and there was a pause after the captain had finished, broken at last by Hartley.

'I was reading all that over before you came in,' he said. 'Now come outside and have a smoke, and I will give you the benefit of some information about the north-eastern interior of this continent, which I picked up out on my station on the Barcoo, and I think it will surprise you. That path of Zoo-zoo seems to me to have something in it, and if you don't go with Stoneham, I shall consider seriously whether I cannot make up a party to go there myself. I have a theory about that path of Zoo-zoo.'

Upon stepping outside upon the verandah, however, it became evident that Hartley's theory of the path of Zoo-zoo was not to be so soon disclosed, for a neighbour known as William Bronckhurst had pulled across the estuary in his boat, and having made her fast to the jetty, had sauntered up to the house, and now reclined at his ease, with a pipe in his mouth, on one of the lounges.

'Good evening, Hartley. How do you do, captain? Fine night, Sir Charles,' said the newcomer in a long, drawling monotone, without moving. It was evident that he had met the Englishmen before.

'Hallo, Bronckhurst!' exclaimed Hartley. 'What brings you round this way tonight? You should have come earlier, and dined with us. Got the boat down at the steps, I suppose?'

'Yes,' said Bronckhurst, who was a retired oyster-dredger, and one of the lucky holders of original

Mount Morgan shares, which had made for him a very respectable competency. It should be said, perhaps, that he was now located in a comfortable place on the river, his principal recreation being to cruise about the bay in a half-decker, fishing and shooting, and occasionally – especially on moonlit nights – to row across to the Bungalow and have a yarn with Hartley, if the latter happened to be at home.

'Look here, Bronckhurst,' said Hartley, abruptly, after the four had smoked for a few minutes in silence, 'did you ever hear anything about "The Fishers of Moreton Bay"?'

'I have,' replied Bronckhurst, with a good-natured laugh; 'but what of that?'

'Why, simply this. Sir Charles, the captain, and myself, have been talking over a matter which originated with Stoneham down at Smoke Island, and they laugh at me for a superstitious old humbug, because I tell them that, although what Stoneham says may be exaggerated, there is, at any rate, truth at the bottom of it. These chaps won't believe me; but if you tell us what you know of "The Fishers" they will no doubt pay more attention.'

'You must take all that Hartley says, *cum grano salis*,[3] broke in Sir Charles, laughing; 'but we really would be interested, and obliged to you, if you would recount what you may have seen and heard about these local legends. With the moonlight on the river, and the long shadows yonder of the trees, no time or place could be more suitable. I could credit any mysterious story, almost, tonight.'

'I cannot tell you much from personal knowledge of the facts,' said Bronckhurst. 'I have heard from Stoneham himself that he is acquainted with some queer things,

3 [Take it] with a grain of salt.

although he is a very reticent man. But there are few fishermen, or pilots in the bay, or indeed warders at the convict settlement on St Helena, that have something to say of "The Fishers of Moreton Bay". I confess that I know nothing personally about these things myself; that is as far as anything supernatural goes.

'You know Moreton and Stradbroke Islands form together a very big place,' he continued, turning round to the two Englishmen, 'and there is the remnant of a very remarkable tribe of black fellows living there. They are believed to be entirely distinct from those here upon the mainland, and have some singular traditions and customs. It's the belief of many of the oyster men and others that they know more about "The Fishers" and their doings than they will tell. But the mystery they say is, where the craft they talk of comes from, and how she disappears. They say that men will be netting on the bay at night, sometimes without any luck, when suddenly they see "The Fishers" canoe, or whatever you like to call it, bearing down upon them – occasionally in the very teeth of the wind – and then the fish will suddenly come down in great shoals in front of her, while at other times they will be gone in a moment, and then suddenly the craft will disappear. It is certain, as anyone living on the shores of the bay will tell you, that there are moving lights sometimes seen on dark nights, which no one can account for. I have seen them myself, and attribute them to the blacks; but the old hands among the fishermen generally keep at home on such nights. You ask one of them some day, when there is no fish in Brisbane Market, why it is, and he will very likely say, "Oh, Tommy was out on the bay last night," and you may guess his meaning if you can.

'A warder on St Helena once told me a queer yarn. It was Reardon, Hartley; and he is a decent fellow, as you know. We were yarning about the bay one night, and I asked him what he knew of "The Fishers". He said – for I remember distinctly – "I only once saw the craft myself, and I'll take my Bible oath that I had neither sleep nor drink upon me at the time, but I certainly saw the craft, and heard old Tommy's hail."

'I will tell you the yarn as near as I can in his own words,' continued Bronckhurst. 'He said that it was during one of those sudden thunderstorms, which occasionally sweep with such terrific violence across the bay. He was on duty. It was a moonlit night, but an immense greenish-black cloud came up from the south-east that blotted out everything. It was blowing with hurricane force; the strange thing was, that the horizon was plainly visible all round beyond the dense circle of clouds. It began to rain soon, pretty heavily, and the force of the wind sent the drops stinging against his face like small shot. The lightning, too, was very vivid. He was standing outside the lookout box on the north-east wall, as he thought that he heard a noise in one of the yards. He had his rifle, of course, in his hand, when suddenly there came two most vivid flashes of lightning. The whole bay seemed illuminated for fully a quarter of a minute, and within rifle shot of the island, right in the midst of the storm, he saw the craft. She had both sails spread, and was sailing along close-hauled in the very teeth of the gale. Long Tom was steering. Reardon said he did not know what impelled him, but he lifted the rifle, took steady aim, and fired. There was a ball cartridge in the piece, and everyone knows that Reardon is a good shot. All the answer he got was, "The Fishers". He looked about the same place during several following flashes of lightning, but the craft had entirely disappeared. He said that it was impossible that she could have got away by natural means, for he could see distinctly for miles during the flashes.

'There is one end of St Helena, I should say, where the old convicts will never, if possible, go at night. It's known as Long Tom's camp. Three convicts at different times have committed suicide there.

'Some of the old hands say they were there looking for some of Long Tom's property, and that he nabbed them at it.'

'Have you never tried to account for the origin of those stories yourself?' said Buchanan.

'Not I,' replied Bronckhurst – 'that is, not in that way. I attribute them to excited imagination, the result of lone-liness and singular and grotesque natural surroundings. Why, I have been on the bay myself at night when you could believe you saw anything. I would have sworn one night that I saw quite a number of people on a point which I knew had not a dwelling place within three miles of it; and what do you think it was? Dead mangrove trunks and roots, all broken off just about the same height from the ground, and a flock of shags or curlews or something perched one on each of them. To have seen the movement and heard the sound, and so on, you would have sworn that they were men.

'But, so long! Gentlemen, I must be off, or the tide will have run down, so that I won't be able to get the boat to the boathouse; and I want to leave everything snug for tonight, for I am going to Brisbane tomorrow.'

'Stop a while longer,' expostulated Hartley; but Bronckhurst had had his say, and being quite satisfied with himself, preferred to retire gracefully on his laurels. His going was usually as abrupt as his coming, for he was one of the men who allowed no consideration to interfere with their peculiar habits of mind.

'He's a queer stick, that,' said Hartley, as Bronckhurst took himself off, 'but a great fisherman.'

CHAPTER III

HARTLEY'S THEORY

N OW LET US hear this theory of yours,' said Sir Charles to Hartley, after they had listened for a few minutes to the splash of oars, as Bronckhurst pulled leisurely across the river.

'I would like first of all to say that Stoneham's position in the matter puzzles me,' replied Hartley. 'I have been thinking about it while Bronckhurst was yarning. Why should he tell you two so readily, and be so anxious for you to go in his company? I cannot get to the bottom of it, and feel confident that there is something personal to himself which he is keeping back, and also that he knows a jolly sight more about the affair than he makes out to you.

'However, this is my theory of the matter until something different suggests itself. Either wholly, or in part, the natives of Moreton and Stradbroke Islands are a remnant of a race which once inhabited some at present unknown part of the interior of Australia. For some unexplained reason, some of them made their way to the extreme eastern coast. In the course of generations they probably lost the actual knowledge of their origin, and even their more recent history may be to them very obscure. The writing which Captain Cook copied from the boomerang is, as far as I know, the only relic of any written language found in Australia. Unlike other ancient lands, we find here no inscriptions, nothing to prove that any of the original dialects have ever been reduced to writing. The inscription, then, points to the one-time existence of a prehistoric race, who were far more highly civilized than any of the present aboriginal tribes. This race possessed a knowledge of the art of writing, and probably a civilization equal to that of some of the more cultured nations of south-western Asia. We should naturally look for the remains of such a people in the north-central portion of the Continent, as indicated by the inscription on the boomerang.

'But, by the way, there is one thing about that inscription which is not clear to me. How did Stoneham get it translated by that professor of the University of Bonn?'

'Ah! Didn't we explain that to you?' said Sir Charles.

'No,' said Hartley.

'Stoneham explained it, I thought, very satisfactorily, and showed us a letter, which I borrowed,' broke in Buchanan. 'It seems he had Cook's letter and the drawing of the inscribed boomerang by him for some years – tried parsons, and doctors, and the curators of two or three of your colonial institutions; but no one could read the riddle until he met with a gentleman visiting Germany, to whom he entrusted the document. I have Professor Smythe's letter, which Stoneham lent me, somewhere amongst my traps. No, it's here. I must have put it in my pocket this morning.'

The letter was as follows:
University of Bonn, Germany,
March 20th, 1877

DEAR SIR,

I received your interesting letter in due course, with an accompanying document for translation. I must congratulate you on the occasion of my being able to furnish you with what appears to be a very accurate and literal rendering of the original. We have, as I dare say you know, nearly one hundred professors and lecturers in our university, and it was brought under the consideration of a number of men of high distinction as linguists before I could obtain an authentic translation. We are indebted to Professor Franz Schliemann for the translation, which I forward to you herewith. I may say that in two cases he gave alternative readings; but the sense seems to me so clear that I have not troubled to send them. He described it as a curious specimen of uncial dhatus.[4] Should anything noteworthy transpire as resulting from the translation, I shall be obliged if you will kindly furnish me with particulars, as the translation has been seen by a number of our professors, and has become a subject of interest to the whole community.

I am, dear sir,
Very truly yours,
CARL LUDWIG SMYTHE
John Gardner, Esq.,
Hotel de Hollande, Cologne

---

4 Possibly Sanskrit for 'relic', or 'primitive matter'.

'That sounds genuine enough,' said Hartley.

'Well, continue your explanation,' ejaculated Buchanan, who was evidently interested.

Hartley thought for a few minutes, and then proceeded. 'I am going to take it for granted that we accept Cook's letter as genuine, and also the translation of the inscription on the boomerang. Now, that inscription must be very old, and in Captain Cook's time writing was evidently, to these people, a lost art.

'One of their wise old men, probably generations before, had scratched the inscription upon the boomerang. It was the dim echo of some knowledge he had of a former home and treasure, which died out with the writer. The boomerang was probably regarded by the few remaining members of the tribe with sacred veneration. Its mysterious direction to the far-off fatherland may have been handed down for generations as one of the most valuable possessions of the tribe. Until at last they were startled by the appearance of Captain Cook's large vessel and the sound of his firearms. There is a well-known belief amongst many of the blacks that when they die they jump up white fellow. They may have regarded Cook and his people as some of the spirits of their ancestors returned in quest of the land and treasure, the memory of which in some hazy form still existed in their minds. The only offering which they could make to them was the sacred boomerang, which was thrown at the feet of Captain Cook. The noise of the firearms frightened them, and, under cover of the smoke, or aided by some mist or cloud, they vanished among the islands. That is the only possible theory of the thing which suggests itself to me. As for old Tommy, and the spectre craft at Moreton Bay, I cannot swallow them. It's all imagination, although by no means surprising to those who know the extent and contour of the land and islands in the neighbourhood.'

'But,' said Buchanan, 'what do you make of the two gold coins and the diamond?'

'They must have been brought when the original exodus was made from the interior,' said Hartley; 'and where they came from there are probably more.'

'All that sounds ingenious and plausible,' said Sir Charles; 'but it throws no light upon Professor Smythe's translation of the path of Zoo-zoo.'

'Will you read it out to us, Buchanan?' said Hartley. 'And I will give you my ideas as we go along.'

'By the way,' interrupted Sir Charles, as his friend commenced to read, 'I thought, Hartley, there were no sibilants in the aboriginal dialects?'

'Yes, that is so,' said Buchanan. 'Take the aboriginal names, and you will find the full-flowing vowel sounds predominating; as, for instance, "Woolloomooloo", "Mulwala", "Coogee", and "Bunaboonoo".'

'Well,' said Hartley, 'that bears out what I say about these people being the descendants of some distinct race of Asiatic origin. The sound of our English letter "s" is common enough in Arabic, Persian, Chinese, and other Asiatic languages. The very word first heard from the steersman who answered the hail of the *Endeavour* boat-swain contained a sibilant.'

'It certainly supports your theory,' said Sir Charles; 'but there's no need to pause any longer over that. We none of us at present know whether Zoo-zoo is a person, place, or thing.'

'I have been looking it up while you were away,' said Hartley. 'In Persian, a *Soonee* is a Sunnite; but there is no such word in English, although there is a somewhat similar word to describe a species of cetacean; but there is no etymological signification to throw any light upon it, except that zoology is the science of animals.'

Buchanan read on: '*From the islands of the east, follow the broad flowing waters beyond the snake-coils to its source.*'

'That's plain enough,' exclaimed Hartley. 'The islands of the east represent Moreton Bay. The broad flowing waters are the Brisbane River, and, by George! from the top of Mount Clutha, the twining and twistings of the river look just like snake-coils.'

'*South of the setting sun a cleft appears in the mountains,*' read Buchanan.

'That must be Cunningham's Gap,' said Hartley; 'and yet I question whether you could see it from the sources of the Brisbane. However, it does not matter, for "*the great country of many little trees*" can only refer to the Moonie scrub. What comes next?'

'*Follow as the birds fly toward the setting sun of winter.*'

'That, of course, means keep to the north-west,' said Sir Charles.

'*Beyond the broad plains, over the white mountains, and you reach the span longer than the arms of many men.*'

'There are plenty of broad plains over in that country,' said Hartley.

'But what about the white mountain?' said Buchanan.

'Ah! I think there is something in that,' said Hartley, smoking away vigorously.

'You don't mean to suggest that there are mountains covered with snow in the interior?' said Sir Charles.

'Yes, I do,' replied Hartley.

'Never!' exclaimed both listeners.

'There is nothing so very surprising about it,' said Hartley. 'For seven or eight months out of the year snow lies on Mount St Bernard, near Beechworth, in Victoria; and the mailman on the Dargo Track wears snowshoes in wintertime, and the snow is occasionally so deep that he will lose his way, because all his guideposts are covered. There are parts of New South Wales too, in the Snowy Mountains district, where high up there are deep fissures, in which the snow never melts all the year round.

'Now, don't think that I am exaggerating or romancing. I think it very possible that there may be white mountains in the north-central portion of the continent.'

'Australia is a queer country,' said Sir Charles. 'People in England would not credit it.'

'It's true, nevertheless,' said Hartley. 'I remember that one of the Barcoo blacks once told me a queer yarn about the north-west. We had been wool scouring, and the wool was uncommonly white. "Plenty dat feller up dere," said the black, and he pointed to the north-west. "What do you mean, Jimmy?" I said to him. "Nuthin', massa, big black feller tell. He gone bong (dead)."

'After a lot of cross-questioning, I gathered from him that he had heard from an old black fellow that some-where, many days' journey to the north-west, there were big hills with white wool upon them. It never occurred to me before, but he must have meant mountains covered with snow. No one could reach them on account of a great waterless region which was sometimes flooded in heavy rains. There was "plenty land", he said, beyond white hills "where dead black fellows corroboreed". You may take it for what it is worth, but there are the facts, and, to say the least, it's a queer coincidence.'

The three men smoked in silence for some time after this. What Hartley had said had aroused all sorts of imaginative pictures and suggestions. As Buchanan remarked, there certainly appeared to be something in it. Without more ado, the latter at once announced his willingness to make one of a party to go and see, and urged Hartley to go with them.

CHAPTER IV

SMOKE ISLAND

IN HIS OWN mind, Hartley was not nearly so complacent over this affair as he appeared to be, for he had a suspicion that there was more between Buchanan and Stoneham than was known to either Sir Charles Dawson or himself.

His guests had retired for the night, so he sat in his own room, and attempted to get a better understanding of the position of things.

'I cannot make head nor tail of Buchanan,' he said to himself. 'Dawson is as open as daylight, and has introductions which are unquestionable; but Buchanan is a problem – says little about his friends, and knows altogether too much for a new chum. I'd like to know where he was the other night when he brought Beauty home regularly knocked up; said he'd been lost, but he had done some hard riding somewhere. I wonder now whether he had been down to Stoneham's. It's singular they are both remarkably tall men, and not unlike in features. Then he is so dashed nonchalant over things – looks to me as though it were put on. He rides and shoots, and does every other confounded thing, even to playing the piano and singing. I'm hanged if I can get to the bottom of him. But I'll swear that he has had some previous knowledge of Stoneham. However, he is not a bad sort, only I like to know things.'

The fact was, Hartley was upset that they should have so completely got the start of him with Stoneham; for he knew more about that mysterious gentleman, and his general mode of life, than his guests had any conception.

Aaron Stoneham, the eccentric recluse, of Smoke Island, Moreton Bay, was a character that puzzled a good many people at the time of our story. A man of huge stature and great strength, hailing from the North of Ireland, he had settled some eighteen years before on the above-named island, and calmly announced to the curious that he did not care a curse about neighbours, and would sooner have the room than the company of the best of them. All kinds of scandal and rumours were current about him on his first appearance. He was an escaped convict, a defaulting Scotch banker, and some hinted at murder; but he cared no more for what people said of him than he did for the laughter of the jackasses, or the clatter of the locusts in the gum trees.

He took up the whole of Smoke Island from the Government at five shillings an acre, and said that he selected there to save fencing stuff, and secure decent company. The island stood about three miles out from the mainland, so it was evident that the decent company referred to comprised himself and his family – if he was possessed of one.

However, the few settlers on the adjoining mainland allowed that the new arrival, if unneighbourly, was smart, and must have money at the back of him, for he did a variety of things which filled them with astonishment, and even admiration.

There is nothing which more quickly commands the respect of the average Australian settler than the evidence of skill in dealing with nature and natural conditions. The man that can swing a powerful axe, or 'gentle' a horse, or manage a restive team, or hold his own with a gun or rifle, or successfully work an orchard or a farm, is the man he bows down to.

One of the first things which Stoneham did after arranging with the Government for the purchase of Smoke Island, was to buy a hundred acres of rich alluvial soil on the mainland just in front of his island, which was heavily timbered with valuable wood. It showed his smartness, for as soon as it was known that he had selected the island, half-a-dozen people thought of blocking him of a landing place on the mainland.

He at once enclosed this selection with a four-railed fence, a proceeding of itself sufficient to attract general attention. Most people in the neighbourhood were satisfied with a two-railed fence. Three rails to a fence signified that the occupant was in very comfortable circumstances; but a four-railed fence proved a man to be a bloated aristocrat, bent on treating his neighbours as though, like Bateman's bull, they could jump anything but a stockyard. However, Stoneham knew them better than they thought, for having completed his fence with the help of some black boys, he next warned of trespassers by affixing painted signs every few hundred yards, to the effect that any cattle, horses, or other trespassers found upon the property would be shot, by order of the proprietor. In a place where every man, in the matter of grass, and water and timber, tried continually to best his neighbour, this was more than human nature could stand; so, shortly after the appearance of the notices, two panels of the fence were found one morning sawn through, and a mob of cattle grazing in the paddock. That very day, however, Stoneham, with a double-barrelled gun under his arm, stalked into the only house in the neighbourhood which he thought likely to boast of the possession of a saw, and marched the frightened occupants out to the damaged fence, and stood by as the two of them repaired it. He then took his coat off and soundly thrashed them, and having impounded the cattle, to the wrath of the whole district, thereafter lived in peace.

He at once put up a strong-framed stable and shed inside his paddock, and kept a few horses there, with a strong vehicle for use when he occasionally went by road to town. The timber he utilized for building purposes on his island.

Notwithstanding his evident dislike of the whites, Stoneham somehow at once made friends with the blacks, who regarded him with great awe, and worked for him with unwonted industry. He brought a cargo of sawn timber, doors, and window-frames, and sashes, and tanks, and other of the more ornamental portions of a house, from the city by steamer, and after a month or two of hard work, with the assistance of the blacks only, had erected a fairly commodious dwelling. This he furnished simply, but comfortably; the best parlour even boasted a piano. Some good dairy cattle were landed, and a dozen horses, and some sheep, as one enterprising man made out with a telescope. And it became evident that Stoneham had come to stay.

Notices next made their appearance all round the island to the effect that trespassers would be summarily dealt with by the proprietor. What this meant a small camping-out party discovered to their cost very soon after, for, having landed on the island for the purpose of spending the night, Stoneham came down with a gun in his hand and half-a-dozen dogs at his heels, and simply tumbled them with all their traps off the bank into the water. There was a good deal of bad language, but no bones were broken, and no one was drowned. The loss of a gun or two, which Stoneham deliberately threw into the bay, had to be put up with; and Smoke Island soon became so notorious for its inhospitable receptions, that it ceased to be visited by any but the blacks.

In the meantime, Stoneham, with his aboriginal helpers, worked late and early; paddocks were cleared, and one of five acres ploughed and sown, an orchard was planted, and other improvements made, until the place acquired quite a homelike and settled appearance. He even had a small flower garden around the front of the house.

Two years passed in this way, and then early one morning Stoneham's yacht, or lugger, or whatever you might call the craft, lay alongside a big steamer at the anchorage, some twenty or thirty miles away from Smoke Island, and a ladylike woman with three young daughters, an old Scotch servant, and a heap of luggage, were taken on board, and sail was made for Smoke Island, and it became known on the mainland that Mad Stoneham had brought his wife and family out from Ireland. No one, however, not even the sugar-planter's wife at Blue Nose Point, attempted to pay a call. There was a mystery about them which half the neighbourhood were anxious to penetrate, but Stoneham's ugly temper and undoubted strength of limb were held in too great respect for anyone to venture to ask for information.

As the years slipped by, Stoneham was noticed to wear the look of a disappointed man; several children had been born to him, but they were all girls. Stoneham, of course, blamed his wife, as men mostly do; but Mrs Stoneham was a woman of some spirit and considerable force of character, and she disclaimed all responsibility.

'Well,' said Stoneham, 'it seems to be no one's fault except their own, so they will have to help me work the place as they would if they were boys', and he was as good as his word.

Stoneham's girls became the astonishment of the district, for on the very rare occasions they were allowed to run upon the mainland, it was seen that they were handsome, dashing girls who could, like their father, do any daredevil thing in the way of riding across country, or handling a gun, or managing a sailing boat; but there was still a well-bred superiority about them which made them to differ altogether from the selectors and others in the district around the bay. It was rumoured that they could sing and play and entertain as well as the best of the fine ladies in town.

It should be said that Smoke Island comprised an area of about seven hundred acres, and was in shape not unlike a pear, intersected for fully half its length at the smaller end by a navigable saltwater creek, which Stoneham made the port of his little kingdom, and near to which he had erected his residence.

The coastline facing the mainland was mostly formed of precipitous cliffs, which rose in places sheer out of the water; but there were also miniature bays, and white sandy beaches, and delightful nooks for bathing, while in the interior there were extensive views from a range of miniature hills with a cleared space on one of the highest summits, where the blacks said that in ancient days they made the smoke signals from which the island had derived its name. The island had a splendid supply of permanent fresh water. One large lagoon near the residence being specially noticeable for its depth and picturesque appearance.

Although Stoneham would have nothing to do with his neighbours of the selector class upon the mainland, he was tolerably friendly with a few people of the better class like Hartley, Bronckhurst, and others; but as may be gathered from the previous narrative, these knew little or nothing of his past history, or indeed of his present occupations, except that he had a snug and profitable island of his own without a mortgage, which in addition to livestock was well provided with fruit, vegetables, and general dairy produce – and a large family of wonderfully fine and clever girls.

Although Stoneham gave his wife and daughters to understand that he would not tolerate ordinary visitors, he seemed to take a pride in finding them well-bred horses to ride about the island on, and had one of the finest and fastest yachts upon the bay – worked, however, like everything else about the place, by the family. In fact, the way in which the Stoneham girls handled that yacht in a gale of wind would have made the commodore of a crack yachting club half-choke himself with envy and admiration.

It has been said that Stoneham had seven daughters, but at the time of this story there were but six of them resident at Smoke Island. Marjory, the eldest, had disappeared three years before in a cloud of mystery, and had been mourned by the whole family as dead.

It was supposed that she had been fishing from the rocks on the west coast of the island, and had fallen in and been attacked and devoured by sharks. That seemed the only possible explanation, for every one of the girls could swim as well as they could walk.

Stoneham, however, appeared to take little notice of the disaster, satisfying himself with strolling round, with his pipe in his mouth and his hands in his pockets, to see if anything was floating about belonging to the missing girl.

He was a strange man, and had many a time threatened to 'lay her wig on the green',[5] so possibly he thought that, as girls were fairly plentiful on Smoke Island, one would not be missed. It was remembered, however, that he had threatened the day before to put a stockwhip over the girl's shoulders because she had done something which had displeased him. Marjory had been no favourite, and she had disappeared; and, as far as he was concerned, there was an end of it.

There were many things going on upon and about Smoke Island, however, which Stoneham was not cognizant of, for the man's overbearing brutality and tyranny caused both mother and daughters to habitually deceive him when it suited their purpose; so it was not so very surprising that the whole of the girls took Marjory's disappearance remarkably quietly. They may have known more than they said about it; however, there was no inquiry. Stoneham only scowled when his wife tearfully suggested that there ought to be one, and said he'd like to catch any Government official inquiring about anything on Smoke Island.

He had been an engineer, or something of the kind, in former years, and had brought a large amount of

---

5 The mid-19th century Irish phrase 'wigs on the green' suggests a violent altercation, a physical fight in which wigs may be dislodged or pulled off.

technical skill and knowledge of mechanics to bear upon the management of things generally on the island. The girls had to help with the ploughing, and other similar farm work; but he had the best of agricultural implements, and thoroughly good horses, so that the work, for those early days, was exceptionally light. During the slacker months of the year he brought an old schoolmaster down to teach the girls, who, with the assistance of their mother, learnt something of everything possible to such a state of existence. But Stoneham's great pleasure was his yacht – of which, however, more later on.

The girls' sleeping quarters formed a separate wing of the house, which had been extended with the growth of the family, and here, a night or two after that on which Hartley had discussed the path of Zoo-zoo with his guests, the four eldest were gathered.

It was about eight o'clock on a moonlit night; one girl lay in a hammock, and three others were leaning against the verandah rail, looking away toward the mainland. The milking had been finished, and the cows turned out a couple of hours before, and the two younger girls had pulled over to the letterbox on the mainland to bring the mailbag; for although there were few letters, Stoneham was a diligent reader of newspapers, and liked to know something of politics, and the movement of the shipping.

The girls watched the returning boat, and listened to the regular dip of the oars.

It was a pleasant, dreamy picture which stretched itself away to the west in front of them. The mainland seemed heavily timbered, and beyond the tall treetops, upon a distant ridge, the crimson light of the sunset still lingered, and cast its dying hues upon the dark stretch of water. In the south-west heavy thunderclouds were gathering. And along the shore twinkling lights could be seen; someone had been burning undergrowth, and the glimmering fires among it had a picturesque appearance. There was a steady wind blowing from the north-east, right in the face of the gathering thunderstorm.

'Those clouds in the south-west mean mischief,' said Dorna, the eldest of the girls. 'That will just suit the old man.'

'You're not going to the anchorage tonight?' said Molly, from the hammock.

'I believe so,' replied her sister; 'there's something up – a China boat, perhaps, to be there with three dozen bags of rice for us, duty free.'

'Rice, indeed,' ejaculated Molly.

'Oh, don't bother! Perhaps there's opium, or cigars, or some other stuff,' said the first speaker. 'But we never ask the captain; that's his lookout. If we're late, you'll have to milk our cows tomorrow, for you can't sleep on the *Gadfly* when there's a Government launch or a customs boat about. And Jackey says that *Long Snoosem* is anchored up Black Wattle Creek, on the lookout for oyster pirates.'

'You'll be caught one of these nights.'

'I don't think so; but what if we are? They could never prove anything, even if they could overtake us, which they can't.'

'Bless you, Molly,' interjected Alice, 'if you'd sailed about with the old man as much as we have, you would not talk like that. No one loves him; but occasionally I do admire him, for he's the smartest man to handle a craft like the *Gadfly* that I should think ever lived. I would just like to see him have a regular close brush with some of those dapper customs officers; he'd lead them a pretty dance. You know they put it on an awful lot, with their gold braid and gilt buttons. It's the buttons that do the mischief! A very ordinary, meek sort of a little man will get quite fierce, and stiffen all over with official dignity, when he dons gold braid and buttons. I often think the old man must have been a terror when he was a ship's officer in uniform.'

CHAPTER V

STONEHAM'S 'GADFLY'

WHILE THE GIRLS were talking, Stoneham, with a couple of aboriginals, was busy with the *Gadfly* at the wharf; for Smoke Island boasted a commodious wharf and sheds and other buildings, which would have astonished a visitor unacquainted with the eccentric character of the proprietor. The eccentricity, or rather, perhaps, criminal tendency, of the man was also shown in the names which he gave to things about the place. Smoke Island, as we have said, had been so named by the aboriginals on account of its being used by them as a sort of station between the mainland and other islands; smoke being used to signal with instead of flags.

But Stoneham was responsible for the naming of his craft the *Gadfly* – a most singular name, it will be allowed, but one they had all got so used to that no one thought of its significance. Stoneham's pet saddle horse was named 'Lucifer' and a favourite bloodhound 'Satan'. The girls wondered sometimes how it came about that they had received ordinary Christian names.

The residence, which Stoneham had named Smoke Island House, was erected on rising ground, barely a quarter of a mile from the wharf, where he was now busily occupied. To all appearances, this wharf had been built of stone in the ordinary way. Such, however, was not the case. It was a perfectly natural wall of solid red rock, which extended for about forty yards in length, and had at least thirty feet of water by the side of it at high tide, and fully half that depth at low water. Steps had been roughly hewn in the rock, and a roofing projected out over the water at one end, giving the wharf all the appearance of a well-designed structure. Some fifteen or twenty feet back a substantial shed was erected, with heavy doors and fittings, and there was altogether a workmanlike finish about the place.

At the time referred to, however, a stranger might well have wondered as to what was going on, for the pulsations of an engine could be heard within the shed, from which a small cable was stretched to the midship hatchway of the *Gadfly*.

Had anyone asked black Jack or Tom what was going on, they would have said, 'Old man filling *Gadfly* with debble debble.'

The fact was that, unknown to anyone, and undreamt of by most people in those early days, this craft of Stoneham's was fitted with an ingenious electrical propeller.

It was no wonder that she could sail so close to the wind, and occasionally force her way in the very teeth of a gale. But the secret of the propeller had been kept in the family for it could be readily lifted when not required for use.

Stoneham was evidently in a bad temper as he bustled about making final preparations for the night trip, for he occasionally swore at the aboriginals – a sign that he was specially irritated; for, however he might treat his wife and daughters, or other white people, it was a singular fact that he rarely ill-treated or abused the blacks.

Men of the Stoneham stamp may be accredited with a selfish motive of some sort when they curb their tempers in any one particular direction. Mrs Stoneham often wondered why her husband made so much of the blacks; for he would occasionally be away for days together with them at Stradbroke or Moreton Islands, and gave no word of explanation on his return as to the cause of his lengthy absence.

It was on one of these excursions that the hiding place of Captain Cook's letter on Smoke Island had been disclosed to him by the aged chief of the tribe. Before Stoneham secured the translation of the inscription, however, he had questioned them long and closely as to their traditions touching the sacred boomerang, and the meaning of the inscription; but they either did not know, or would not tell him, anything further. Then he got the translation made in Germany, and as patience and perseverance usually bring their reward the result in this case at last brought to light the coins and diamond. Even Stoneham shuddered, however, on that eventful night, for, after he had explained the inscription to the chief of the tribe, the latter, support- ed by the others, threatened to take Stoneham's life unless he swore to go with two of them by the track of Zoo-zoo, to learn more about the 'plenty land' of their ancestors. He had brought it on himself, they said, by his persistent curiosity, and must take the consequences.

They had great faith in Stoneham, partly on account of his mysterious sailing craft, but mostly by reason of his great stature and reckless daring. They credited him with being able to accomplish any matter which he took seriously in hand, and from time immemorial their oldest and wisest men had talked in secret conclave about the mysterious path which lay somewhere toward the setting sun.

Stoneham meant, if possible, to satisfy both himself and them, and, after years of waiting, had at last pitched upon Sir Charles Dawson and Captain Buchanan as two men likely to serve his purpose on such an expedition, and the least likely to be missed if some untoward accident should overtake them before their return. It had been no part of his plan for Hartley to go with them. The two Englishmen, the two blacks, and himself (he had settled in his own mind) would be ample. Hartley's going upset everything.

Stoneham had arranged that night to meet Buchanan somewhere near the boat passage, and receive from him the gold coins and diamond, which were to be returned to the chief of the tribe, and also make final arrangements about meeting Sir Charles and Buchanan three weeks later somewhere on the Barcoo. He was in a bad temper, however, for it was that very day he had first heard that Hartley proposed to form one of the party; and there was something else wrong between himself and the captain.

It was nearly a mile by the windings of the creek from Smoke Island wharf to the bay. Nine o'clock had struck when the *Gadfly* cast off and moved slowly downstream. Stoneham was steering, and three of the girls, who formed the crew, were busy forward getting everything in readiness to make sail upon the boat when Stoneham gave the order. They wore woollen guernseys and short skirts, and trod with their bare, white, shapely feet noiselessly about the deck. They had dark oilskins and sou'-westers handy to put on when the thunderstorm, which was now growling ominously in the south-west, should break upon them. It was evidently going to be a rough night.

The craft, which was being skilfully navigated clear of rocks and sandbanks by Stoneham, was about eight or ten tons, and of rakish build. She was now propelled at half-speed by the electric engine, and moved almost noiselessly through the water. It was noticeable that everything about her was painted dark brown, except that she was white below the waterline; but, being fitted with water-ballast compartments, could be sunk on occasion, so that only the darker colours were visible. Her sails, too, were tanned brown, and as she moved down the creek not a patch of white was anywhere visible about her. At the distance of a few hundred yards on a dark night she might anywhere have passed unseen.

As they swept past a mangrove island and crossed over to the other side of the creek to escape a sandbank, the bay suddenly opened upon them.

'Haul down that jib,' said Stoneham. The sail came down immediately, without any flapping of canvas or the rattle of a ringbolt. It was evident that everything worked smoothly on the *Gadfly*.

Stoneham was going to lie to, at the mouth of the creek, under the shadow of the mangroves. He had caught the sound of a paddle-steamer going south, and had decided to let her pass before making sail. She had both masts stepped. He was seemingly taking unusual precautions.

It should be explained that the yacht was arranged to be sailed with either one mast or two, and only at night, when extra speed was wanted, was she fitted and rigged as at present. When carrying only one mast, as she ordinarily did when used by daylight, she would never have been taken for the same craft as that which had scaled half the night toilers about Moreton Bay.

Stoneham lit his pipe and sat down on the stern rail, while the girls sat or lay about the deck forward; they had each had a cup of strong coffee before starting, so there was nothing to do in the gallery, or elsewhere, and they sat and talked in whispers, and looked out into the night.

'What an awful big weird place the bay looks when it is dark,' said Alice to Dorna, just above her breath.

They spoke very quietly, for the least sound was heard on such a night for a very long distance. Between the muttering of the thunder down in the south-west, which was, however, rapidly drawing nearer, everything was as still as the grave – save for the beating of the stern paddle-wheel of the steamer. She was still a couple of miles away, but from the distinctness of the sound she might have been only a cable's length off.

Two white ghostly objects were noticed by the girls moving steadily up the creek, in perfect silence, under the mangroves on the other side. They were a couple of pelicans going up to a favourite fishing bank of theirs. Things were evidently very quiet for the birds to move along like that. Dorna put her hand on a double-barrelled breech-loader for a moment, and whispered her belief that she could bring them both down with one shot; but there was no sound save the lapping of the waters against the side of the *Gadfly*, and the sighing of the approaching tempest in the tops of the trees, and the beating paddle-wheel of the steamer, or the splash of an occasional fish as it leaped up and then fell back into the water.

There were a few lights visible on the mainland, and one or two on the islands far distant in the bay – bush fires probably, most of them.

For another quarter of an hour the silence was unbroken, for Stoneham rarely spoke to the girls except to give orders, and as usual sat wrapped in meditation and tobacco smoke. Soon, however, the steamer had passed south.

'Set the foresail and spanker.'

The yacht, as we have stated, carried two tall masts that night, but so rigged that the second could, if necessary, be easily unshipped. Both masts carried large square lugsails, and spankers with topsails. It was easy to see that the *Gadfly* had been built for speed. With the propeller at full power she could show her heels to any craft upon the bay; in fact, walk round and laugh at them. She was soon bowling along at a great rate, with the white foam heaped up in front of her bows, and an eddying wake behind, for it was nearly high water, and although Stoneham was keeping fairly inshore, he knew that there was plenty of water everywhere, and no risk of running aground; she was making at least fourteen knots. The moon was hanging low down in the west, but the stars were bright in front of them, and they could see that the bank of clouds, which was now rapidly sweeping up in their rear, formed a very curious spectacle.

The background of the sky was black as ink; but stretched right across, from horizon to horizon, was a great bridge or bow of white clouds.

The chain and forked lightning flashed brilliantly at the back of it, and reflected occasionally through it like the flashing of opals; but the white bridge of vapour showed no perceptible movement for several minutes, as though it was fixed across the sky. Then there came a brilliant flash which lit up the whole bay, and a peal of thunder quickly followed, and the fantastic creation melted before the pent-up fury of the storm.

'Lower away and furl the spanker.'

The girls stood by in readiness, expecting the order, and obeyed it with astonishing alacrity. They seemed as nimble as highly trained seamen, and had two reefs in each of the big lugsails before the storm struck them.

It seemed for a moment as though it would take the masts right out of her, although she was being driven by the propeller at full speed, and Stoneham put her dead in front of the wind. She shivered, and seemed to leap forward as the full force of the gale caught her; but it was only for a brief minute or two, when it rushed past howling and screeching like some band of mad furies convulsed with rage. It was just such a brief minute or two as has wrecked many a fine vessel upon the high seas.

Their course was altered after passing the lighthouse on Blue Nose Point, and they ran on for another half-hour; after which they furled the sails and cast anchor under the lea of an uninhabited island not far from the mouth of the Brisbane River.

'You can turn in for an hour,' said Stoneham to the girls; which they took to be his polite way of telling them that something was about to transpire which they had best know as little about as possible.

CHAPTER VI

STONEHAM'S GIRLS

I T MIGHT BE thought, from the little less than brutal way in which Stoneham habitually treated his family, that his wife and the girls would have been thoroughly cowed and their spirits broken. But this was far from being the case. Use is second nature, and, as Dorna put it, they were very much used to the old man's ways. And they were certainly very peculiar.

Before a man like Hartley, with whom he had reasons for keeping on good terms, he would be as smooth-spoken to the girls as though he were only a bit strict in his treatment of them. He would even tolerate, on rare occasions, visitors of the better class, like Captain Buchanan and Sir Charles Dawson, and would smoothly hint in a confidential sort of way that he would like to see some of the elder girls comfortably married; but he never tolerated anything which interfered with their work, and when nine o'clock came visitors' boats were always ready, and Stoneham would stalk gravely into the best parlour with a big hat stuck on the back of his head, and sit down stiffly upon a chair until the guests took the hint that it was time to leave.

A Presbyterian minister, who called at the island twice a year to see if there were any fresh girl babies to be baptized, was the only male, besides the aged schoolmaster previously referred to, who was ever allowed to sleep upon the island – that is, with Stoneham's knowledge.

If the old man was 'on the square', as the girls said, he posed before the minister as a true-blue son of the old Scotch Kirk, and boasted that the best Scotch Presbyterians hailed from the north of Ireland; but if he happened to be 'on the cross', he was only allowed time for a meal and a prayer, and had to find other lodgings on the mainland.

But the girls had a lot of their father's spirit, and as they grew up he found it wasn't exactly safe to knock them about much. They gave him to understand that he might possibly go too far, and there were, at any rate, four of them who were getting to be tall and fairly muscular women.

'You touch me if you dare!' said Marjory to him one day when he started to thrash her with his riding-whip for being absent from some farm work which he had given her to do.

'Curse you, you slut!' he called out in a towering rage, as, white with anger he was about to rush forward and strike her.

'Bess,' called out the girl to a younger sister, who stood trembling near them, 'go up and call mother.'

She had a loaded rifle in her hand, for she had been away to shoot an eaglehawk which had been after the young turkeys, and she stepped back as Stoneham drew near her.

Just before he hit her, he seemed for the first time to catch sight of the rifle. The muzzle of it pointed straight at his right leg, the girl's finger touched the trigger, and there was a very awkward look in her eyes. The man suddenly drew back, and called upon Bess, who by this time had scrambled straddle-legged upon Lucifer, and was cantering up toward the homestead for her mother. 'Come back, you fool!'

'Why did you send your sister up to the house for your mother?' he asked.

'So that she might help dress your broken leg,' said the girl, looking defiantly at him.

'Do you mean to say you would shoot your father?'

'You put that riding-whip across my shoulders, and you will see. I'm a woman now!'

He swore about it, and at his wife too, for the way in which she was bringing up the girls. But, if the truth was known, he rather liked her pluck, and boasted afterward to a settler on the mainland that his girls would as soon shoot a man as look at him, if he wasn't pleasant. But he only threatened Marjory once after that with his riding-whip, and that was the day she disappeared.

However, the girls were born and reared to it, and were cheerful enough when they got away from the presence of Stoneham.

They had made a tennis court for themselves, and were skilled in getting out of the old man's way for a bit of recreation. They even flirted with the old schoolmaster, to whom they said their lessons – and a good many other things – during the winter months. Then there was the mustering to do, and the girls' laughter as they raced madly after a mob of young bullocks, and the crack of their stockwhips, and the clatter of their horses' hoofs, when they came onto the bit of gravel at the yards, sounded decidedly healthy.

For one thing, they lived well. They could scarcely help it, for their mother sought to forget the disappointment of her marriage in good housewifery; and there was, besides plenty of fresh meat, fish in abundance, and an oyster bed on the rocks to the west of the creek, and milk, and butter, and fruit; in fact, a rough-and-ready abundance of all good things, and a healthy, wholesome appetite to enjoy them.

'If we only had a different father,' said Dorna one day to the girls and her mother, 'Smoke Island would not be so bad.'

'Mother,' she said, 'why ever didn't you marry a different kind of man?'

'Ah! You don't know what your father was like when he came courting. I could have married ever so many nice men, and well-to-do; but, you see, somehow I loved Aaron Stoneham.'

And then the kind-hearted woman would heave a sigh.

'Well, I am sure I wish you had married one of the other nice men,' said Alice. 'As it is, I don't know what's to become of us. Mr Stoneham has got to be the worst character of any man in the colony and his daughters are talked about everywhere as the "seven Smoke Island girls". I shall run away some night, and ask the first man I meet on the mainland to marry me, if it's only to be known by another name.'

But it would take many chapters to describe the family life of the Stonehams, and how the girls occasionally *did* like the old man, so we must come back to where we left the master of the *Gadfly* on board his craft, waiting for someone near the entrance to the Brisbane River.

It must have been fully two hours after they had cast anchor, when at last the dip of muffled oars was heard at hand. A boat with one man in it shortly after emerged from the darkness, and almost noiselessly glided up under the stern of the *Gadfly*.

Stoneham stood up, and without a word of greeting placed a longish parcel in the boat, and stepped into the stern sheets, as she slipped away again into the night.

'Did you see who it was?' whispered Alice to Dorna.

'Yes,' answered her sister, quietly and cautiously.

'Who was it, then?'

'Captain Buchanan.'

'Whatever can he want with the old man?' ejaculated Nettie, for all three of them were as wide awake as possible.

'Nothing, I fear, that's any good,' replied Dorna.

The girls peered into the darkness in the direction which the boat had taken; but the only sounds were those of the wind and water, or the occasional cry of a curlew, or other night bird.

'Do you think it would be safe for us to stand in nearer to the land?' said Alice.

'We should have to go dead slow, for fear of getting on a sandbank,' replied Dorna, who was captain in her father's absence. They had taken off their oilskins, for the rain had passed over some time before, and in their blue guernseys, short skirts, and sailor caps, were quite warm enough, for the night was still close, although the storm had somewhat cooled and cleared the atmosphere.

'Stand by to get up the anchor,' said Dorna to her sisters, as she switched the power on so as to move the *Gadfly* ahead.

The machinery of the yacht was so arranged that both engine and helm could be attended to if necessary by one person. So they soon had the anchor up, and were moving cautiously across in the direction of the river.

All at once they heard the sound of men quarrelling and exchanging blows in the distance. It seemed to be somewhere upon the bay, however.

'They are fighting in the boat,' said Alice.

'I don't think so,' said Nettie. 'Listen!'

The three girls listened, and distinctly heard the crunching as of shells beneath their feet.

'It's dead, low water,' whispered Dorna, 'and they're fighting on one of the sandbanks.'

She reversed the engine as she said this, and stopped the yacht. They were nearing a sandbank, and the three girls listened to the quarrel, and tried to make out exactly where it was going on. Just then the nose of the *Gadfly* grated against the side of one of the muddy, gravelly banks which are so common near the coastline of the bay at low water.

They almost immediately heard the sound of their father's voice, gruffly asking Buchanan if he was ready.

'I am ready anytime for you, you murderer,' was the answer which reached the ears of the startled girls.

Then followed the clash of steel. They were evidently fighting what seemed very much like a duel, on a sandbank some distance out from the land.

'Let them fight it out,' said Alice, bitterly.

'They are neither of them good for much, I fear. But they have chosen a most extraordinary spot for their encounter; fancy fighting a duel at midnight on a sandbank in Moreton Bay!'

'Do keep quiet,' said Nettie. 'One of them will be killed.'

'Well, I hope it may be the old man, then,' said Alice.

Just then the noise eased, and immediately afterwards they heard a cry, and a sound as of one of them falling upon the shingles.

Then came another long spell of quietness.

'I don't know which way to get round this bank in the dark,' said Dorna, 'or I would move the *Gadfly* nearer. You two keep her just here, and I will slip out and run along the bank and see if I can make out where they are; they may both of them be wounded.'

She went forward to get her boots, for the oyster, and other shells and shingles of these banks inflict most painful wounds when walked upon with bare feet; but she stopped and listened again, for they distinctly heard the sound of oars rolling along the thwarts of a boat. Then followed the noise which a heavily booted man will make getting into a boat; this was again followed by a splash in the water, as the boat was pushed off from the sandbank with an oar.

'Stoneham, you devil! You won't leave me here wounded, to drown, will you?'

There was no answer but the dip of the muffled oars as the boat was pulled slowly along the widening channel out toward the bay. It was necessary to row round for some distance before Stoneham could reach the yacht.

He saw at a glance that it had been moved from where he had left it at anchor.

'What did you move the yacht for?' he asked with an oath as he stepped on board.

The girls stood together, and waited for Dorna to answer him.

'Are you going to leave that wounded man to drown?' she said.

'Yes,' said Stoneham, with another oath.

'It will be murder!' replied the girl fearlessly.

The man paused a moment, as though he were going to say or do something, and then placed his hand upon the engine lever and switched on the power. As the propeller began to revolve, he put the helm over to turn the *Gadfly*'s bows in the direction of the bay; but as he did so Dorna sprang lightly from the side of the yacht upon the sandbank, and, running off, was almost immediately lost to view in the darkness. Her sisters screamed to her to come back.

'Hold your tongues, you fools!' said Stoneham. 'Do you want to bring any boats that may be about the bay down on us?'

He was, however, evidently ill at ease, and regretted the hardihood of Dorna in leaving the yacht; and he slowed down, and waited about listening several minutes. He even put the *Gadfly* up to the bank again, and stepped out and looked about, but presently returned.

'I won't wait about here,' he said. 'It will soon be morning, curse her! and there will be the devil to pay then! Run up the jib, and I'll give you a hand with the lugsail and the spanker.'

'But Dorna!' cried both the tearful girls in a breath.

'She's got to take her chance. Let her wade or swim ashore: I'm not going to stay here.'

'Dorna!'

'Stow that, or I'll pitch you overboard!' he called out roughly. 'Here, come and take the helm, Netta, while I get the sails up.'

Ten minutes afterward, with a fair strong land-wind filling the sails, and at full speed of the engines, the *Gadfly* was sweeping through the dark waters toward Smoke Island. How is it that fair winds so often fill the sails for brutal villainy? He would have to concoct a tale to account to his wife for the absence of Dorna. And he would have to frighten the girls, so as to somehow keep their tongues quiet.

After rounding a point, a stronger breeze caught the sails; she was running now at racing speed, and seemed to fly before the wind. She showed no lights. Stoneham stood erect at the tiller. Between two islands they dashed alongside and passed a fishing boat beating slowly up against the wind.

The men in her were Roman Catholics, and they crossed themselves in terror, and muttered a paternoster, as the dark, two-masted craft without lights, and seemingly without living occupants, rushed wildly on into the night.

Said one to the other in an awestruck whisper, as they watched her suddenly disappear, 'Them's The Fishers of Moreton Bay.'

CHAPTER VII

WHAT HAPPENED ON A SANDBANK

D ORNA HAD LEAPED from the yacht upon a sandbank, just as she was, in her bare feet. Fortunately there proved to be more sand than shingle upon it, and in her flight she only received a few scratches.

When Stoneham turned back to look for her, she had lain down almost flat upon the sand, for one very bright star cast a wonderful light upon the landscape. She kept still while the yacht was moving off, and heard the cry of her sisters to her; but she had determined to do what she could for the Englishman who had been wounded by the hand of her father, and left on this treacherous sandbank to drown.

She watched the *Gadfly* fade away in the distance under the starlight before she commenced her search for the wounded man. She had in the meantime been listening eagerly for any sound which might indicate his position. But the strange popping noise of the shellfish, and the creeping sound made by the claws of hundreds and thousands of small crabs, with an occasional weird cry of a bird or animal in the distant bush, or the splash of fishes in the water, were the only sounds audible. Dorna was as much at home with the bay and all its peculiar features and inhabitants as anyone well could be; but there is a peculiar loneliness when one is left, as it were, unexpectedly alone. Dorna thought that the bay had never before looked so strangely desolate, or the wild stretches of dark slimy sandbank so vast and uncanny, as they did that night. But she must go in search of Captain Buchanan. 'Supposing that he should be dead?'

Nothing could be more misleading than the miles of winding mud and sand which reveals itself at dead low water in the bay when seen by starlight only. By taking the bearings of two lights marking the entrance to the channel of the river, Dorna satisfied herself that she could again find the spot on which she landed; but half an hour's search assured her that Buchanan was not there. 'He must be on another bank,' she thought; and there seemed to be a fairly wide stretch of deep water lying between.

She had no fear of the water so long as sharks were not about, and she knew that at low tide they invariably make for deep water, so she determined to wade or swim across. It was now, she judged, past midnight, and somewhat chilly to undress for a bath; but there was nothing else for it, she thought, and turned to cross the bank again, when she suddenly remembered Captain Buchanan's boat. It had been cast adrift when Stoneham boarded the *Gadfly*. She wondered that she had not thought of this before, and at once looked anxiously around; but it was nowhere to be seen, so Dorna picked out a bit of the highest and driest ground, and slipping out of her scanty attire, stepped down into the water. It was deeper than she had expected, but she made no attempt to swim, not even when the water reached to her chin. It was perfectly calm, being protected from the wind by the sandbanks which wound in and out around it. The tide was on the turn.

Dorna believed that the boat was not far away, and she was hoping to catch its dark outline between her eye and the sky, or a star. After nearly half an hour's search she was successful, when she at once threw herself into a swimming posture, and a few minutes afterward, with a dozen or so vigorous strokes, had reached the boat and climbed on board. Dorna now felt immensely relieved; but, unfortunately, in wading about after the boat, she had lost the situation of the particular bank on which her clothes awaited her; and now that all danger to life was passed – for with the boat in her possession she feared nothing – it was specially aggravating that she should have to row about by the side of that sandbank – with a rising tide, too – looking for her clothes.

'Bother the clothes!' she said to herself impatiently. 'To think that I am in this fix after finding the boat – and that unfortunate man may be dying!'

Just then, however, she caught the Pile Light and another in line, and turning round to the bank and looking carefully, she soon found the missing garments. To attire herself in them, and start upon the search for Buchanan was the work of a very few minutes.

She now pulled slowly along the bank opposite to that on which she had landed from the yacht, carefully scanning the sandbank. She was glad that the tide was rising, for the boat occasionally stuck, and had to be pushed off again. Every few minutes she would rest upon her oars and listen. While doing this on one occasion she heard a moan.

'Thank God, he's alive, then!' she exclaimed; and picking up the anchor of the boat, she leaped lightly onto the bank, over which the rising tide was just beginning to creep.

The girl threw down the anchor to secure the boat, and ran to where a dark heap showed her that Buchanan lay.

'Are you much hurt?' she asked.

'I don't know. My leg and arm seem numbed or broken. I should probably soon have drowned if you had not come. But how on earth have you got here? Perhaps I am dreaming, or dying, and you are a good angel.'

'No, I am not,' said the girl. 'I am Dorna Stoneham; and I have got your boat here by the bank. Can you get up?'

'I'm greatly obliged to you, Miss Stoneham. There's some food and brandy in the boat.' And then he swooned away.

Dorna looked at him in the dim light once or twice. He was a young man, but a good length, and fairly heavy. And then the girl put her strong arms under him, and staggered with her unconscious burden across the sandbank, sinking down at every step until the sand and water came over her ankles. Finally, with an almost superhuman effort, she placed him carefully on the bottom of the boat.

Dorna found the brandy, and gave him some, and then put an overcoat she found under his head.

'Where am I?' he asked, as he came back to consciousness.

'In the bottom of a boat,' said Dorna, simply, and then set herself to row out of the winding sandbanks into the channel, and up to the Bungalow.

It was a stiff pull, but fortunately she had the tide with her.

'Captain Buchanan,' said Dorna to him as they neared their destination, 'don't you think we might somehow manage to keep it a secret about my father?'

'Certainly, if you wish,' said Buchanan, faintly.

'All right, then, I'll manage it; you will be too ill to say anything.'

There was more truth in Dorna's last words than she had imagined. Buchanan was ill, and there was no alternative but to send up a hasty messenger to town to bring down a doctor.

But Dorna, for a modest girl of nineteen, was in nearly as bad a plight as Buchanan; for she wore only a short skirt and woollen guernsey, and had neither stockings nor shoes, and had been necessitated at three o'clock in the morning, so attired, to rouse up Hartley and Sir Charles Dawson.

There was no prudery, however, about Dorna, and in the presence of danger to life – for Buchanan was more seriously wounded than he had seemed to be – she did not give a second thought to her bare feet and legs.

They carried Buchanan up to the house between them, and laid him on his own bed.

'Mr Hartley,' said Dorna, looking him straight in the face, 'I would send a man up to town for a doctor at once, if I were you; but I would not make any fuss by calling up the servants.'

'Why?' interrupted Sir Charles, impatiently.

'Because, I think, for Captain Buchanan's own sake, it had better be kept as quiet as possible – as well as on account of someone else.'

'Who wounded him?' said the baronet.

'You had better ask him that yourself when he is better,' said the girl, looking somewhat defiantly at Buchanan's friend.

'I suppose that I have saved his life, so far as it is saved; but that arm of his wants dressing, and I think that I can attend to it better than either of you gentlemen.'

'Miss Stoneham is right,' said Hartley, 'and we are only wasting time by talking.'

'That's right,' said Dorna, giving Hartley an approving smile. 'If you will get me a pair of scissors, or a sharp knife, I will rip his coat sleeve up and see whether his arm is broken, or whether it is merely a flesh wound he has received. He would have bled more if an artery had been cut.'

Hartley got the scissors immediately, and went into the kitchen, and finding the fire banked up with a huge log at the back of the fireplace, soon brought hot water. He was puzzling himself over what Dorna had said about Buchanan having received a flesh wound. 'He and Stoneham must have been fighting with swords; it's a most extraordinary affair. But how he came to be out, and we know nothing about it. And how comes it that this girl has brought him home in one of my boats, and claimed to have saved his life? It's no doubt a very queer affair.'

For a couple of hours, until Buchanan was safely in bed with his wounds carefully dressed, Dorna held command. Sir Charles Dawson and Hartley simply did what the girl told them to – not without some amazement.

It was quite light by this time, and Dorna went into the dining room, where Hartley had a cup of tea waiting for her. Sir Charles stopped with Buchanan.

'Do you think you could borrow me a riding habit anywhere, and some number five shoes, Mr Hartley, and then lend me a horse? I might lie down and have a sleep somewhere while you hunt them up.'

'Certainly I can, with pleasure; but you must be terribly tired after being up all night.'

'You need not trouble about that, Mr Hartley. I have been able to help your friend, and a few hours' sleep will set me right again. Women who go to balls think nothing of dancing until daylight; please don't make a fuss about a little thing. I am sorry that Captain Buchanan got hurt last night; I expect that it was a good deal his own fault. I found him on a sandbank in the bay, and I suppose that if I had not happened upon him he would have been drowned. Now you'll oblige me by not asking any more questions.'

Hartley looked at her in astonished admiration. He had been all his life used to society belles; but here was a girl of nineteen, after a night's adventure which would have taxed the strength and endurance of most ordinary men, looking as fresh as a rose, and seemingly utterly unconscious of her singular attire. Her blue wool-worked liberty cap, with its long silk tassel, was worn with a jaunty air. Her close-fitting guernsey set off her shapely figure, and her blue serge skirts, which reached only halfway from knee to ankle, set off her well-formed feet. Hartley had been in many a difficult situation before, but never had he felt himself to be so thoroughly bowled over as he was by this barefooted girl of Stoneham's.

He wanted to know a score of things, for, as has been said before, he was of an inquisitive turn of mind; but he would no more have thought of putting another question to Dorna, after what she had said, than he would if commanded to keep silence by the queen.

To understand the character of Dorna Stoneham, it must be remembered that she and her sisters had been brought up away from the conventionalisms of ordinary society, and had been treated by both parents not as girls are usually treated in a family, but as though they were boys and men.

Dorna never said no when she meant yes, or yes when she meant no. She had never been used to have other people wait upon her; had never habited herself to late breakfasts in bed; and knew nothing of the pleasures of being coddled for supposed delicate health. She had been used to obey her father, and in turn be obeyed by her sisters; and, except from fatigue or overwork, had scarcely known an ache or pain in her life. Nor had she any particular respect or regard for the opposite sex – the only man she had known with any intimacy was her father, and him she neither respected nor loved. And she classed all men more or less in the same category. 'They are a set of tyrants, the whole lot of them,' she would sometimes say to her sisters; 'and I am glad that I have been brought up like a man. I'm as strong as many of them, and can do what they do better than most.'

And yet she was a winsome woman, as she stood up to be conducted by Hartley to her room. There was grace in every line of her supple and well-knit frame; she stood gracefully, and walked gracefully; her oval face was well set upon a graceful neck and well-formed shoulders; her features were Grecian in their classic regularity, and the soul in her violet eyes told of an unawakened womanhood, which might yet hear a voice that would arouse the deeper nature for weal or woe.

Hartley looked at her, and knew as by instinct that the deeper springs of Dorna's life had never yet been moved to action. Love would come, he thought, some day, and its first kiss would touch the marble, and arouse the girl's whole being to a higher form of life.

'But would it come?' thought Hartley, for it had long been his belief that thousands of the race pass through life with its richest treasures unrevealed. That is, with love unawakened; because the voice of the true heart-mate was never heard.

It was a strange thought, perhaps, to flash across his mind as he, Bright Hartley, bachelor, led barefooted Dorna Stoneham to her chamber, with all the deference he might have paid a queen. But it was this: 'What if he, fully twice her age, should be able to learn the secret which might awaken this girl's love?'

It's strange how young some men's hearts keep, and how natural it seems for them, after they have learnt and tasted of all life's sweets and bitters, to wish to associate themselves with women, who, like their own hearts, are yet young and fresh. Possibly it's a blind instinct of the soul yearning for immortality, which is ever young.

CHAPTER VIII

MORE ABOUT DORNA STONEHAM

WHEREVER HARTLEY GOT them from, Dorna found a handsome riding habit of dark cloth, and a pair of number five shoes, and also stockings, on a chair just within her room when she awoke. Gloves and a handkerchief were also there; and Hartley's thoughtfulness was shown in an assortment of cuffs and collars, and other knick-knacks for ladies' attire.

Someone was evidently listening for her footsteps, for she was no sooner up than a female servant tapped at the door and asked if there was anything further she could bring her. Dinner, she said, would be served in half an hour.

'No, thank you,' said Dorna. 'I shall do very well.' She had slept for nearly twelve hours.

Dorna had made full use of Hartley's thoughtfulness. The riding habit fitted her very well, and with neat collar and cuffs, and her hair gracefully arranged, she would scarcely have been known for the same, except for her voice and bearing.

On meeting Hartley, Dorna inquired after Buchanan, but not with any marked anxiety. She had done her duty, and he was safe, and there, so far as she was concerned, was an end of it.

Hartley told her that the captain might be a week or two getting round, but that the doctor said he was, thanks to the skilful hands of his first nurse, in no danger.

'Would you like to see him?' said Hartley, as they went into dinner.

'No, thank you, Mr Hartley; he wants to be kept quiet.'

'But I think that he would like to thank you.'

'That can easily be left for another time,' said Dorna.

Sir Charles had heard a good bit about the Stoneham girls from Hartley during the day, and had anticipated the meeting at dinner with some curiosity. He had seen enough of the girl in the morning, however, to know that it was useless anticipating either her manner or conversation.

The change which her altered dress made, certainly took him by surprise; while Dorna had such an utter contempt for mankind generally that she did not feel the least confused when Hartley placed her at his right hand, and she found that she was to dine in his company, with Sir Charles Dawson as a *vis-à-vis*.

Sir Charles had made one or two remarks about Dorna and the Stonehams to Hartley of a by no means complimentary character, and the latter had made up his mind that the representative of Smoke Island should, at any rate, have every opportunity of appearing to best advantage. He was certainly pleased with her improved appearance. Some women look their best in a close-fitting, well-cut riding habit – possibly Dorna was one of them. She had certainly scored a point for a start.

Hartley commenced to talk about the bay and yachting, as he ladled out the soup. He knew Dorna could talk about that, and had no other thought but to furnish a common topic for interesting conversation.

But Dorna imagined that she scented danger. They would be twisting it around to the previous night's adventure, so she partook of her soup in cautious silence, simply responding Yes or No.

'The girl can't talk,' thought Sir Charles; but what could be expected?

Hartley, however, guessed the cause of her reticence, and saw he had made a false start. He was annoyed with Sir Charles, too, who was condescendingly polite to Dorna. While she was thinking to herself 'what stupid creatures men are.' And yet she seemed to know that Hartley was beseeching her to save the credit of Smoke Island and the rumoured cleverness of the Stoneham girls.

Dorna looked at Sir Charles after the first course, and mentally concluded that being an English baronet had not done any great things for him.

'He puts on airs,' she thought. 'I'd like to see him on a flighty horse, or in a stiff gale of wind on board the *Gadfly*.' And then all at once Dorna determined to put her best foot forward for the honour of Smoke Island.

One of Dorna's strong points was botany. She guessed, by certain plants she had noticed about the house, that it was a subject which Hartley was not wholly unfamiliar with. So after a rather awkward pause (for Hartley was losing heart at his want of success) she asked Dawson what he thought of the Australian bush flowers.

'Not a great deal, Miss Stoneham; they are really so few and scentless that they don't call for much thought.'

It was not a polite answer, and Hartley felt inclined to kick him beneath the table, but there was no necessity, he had met his match.

'Ah! You must have seen them when they were asleep,' said Dorna, quietly. 'In the morning, when they are wide awake and fresh from a bath of dew, they perfectly fill the bush with perfume. I think there is nothing more fragrant in the world than the Australian bush an hour before sunrise on a summer's morning. Now, do not you agree with me, Mr Hartley?'

Hartley hastened to do so most emphatically, for he was delighted to find Dorna coming out of her shell.

'You see, you have not been here in our springtime, when the wattles are in bloom, and the bush everywhere rich with beauty and fragrance. You know, your wild flowers in England are all more or less unintentionally cultivated. England is such a little place, you cannot help it; but here you see Nature left entirely to herself. Now I think, Sir Charles, that I am the best judge of the beauty and fragrance of our Australian flowers, because I love them, and they only tell their secrets to their friends.'

Sir Charles was dumbfounded at such talk as this from a Stoneham girl, and replied, cautiously, 'I think that you have the best of the argument.'

'Thank you,' she replied, smiling. 'Now let me ask you, have you seen a good collection of our Australian orchids?'

Sir Charles acknowledged that he had not.

'Ah, I thought not. You know, your European orchids are of the earth, earthy – terrestrial plants; but ours are epiphytes – they lift themselves above our heads and flutter in masses of snow-white beauty in the air, and rain down fragrance. But then, you know,' she continued, with an arch smile, 'they only do it for women, because they love flowers and nature, while men—— '

'Don't stop, Miss Stoneham,' said Dawson, who almost gasped for breath.

'Well, if I must finish, men regard such things as unworthy of a thought.' Dorna said this with a mischievous twinkle in her eye.

At the witty reference to the baronet's unhappy speech, Hartley laughed until he almost choked.

By the time dinner was over the Englishman, to Hartley's great delight, addressed Dorna with far more deference, while that lady pinned him down to botany, and led him on and argued with him in a bantering tone, which, alas! bordered very closely upon polite contempt.

'Were you able to get a horse up for me, Mr Hartley?' asked Dorna, after dinner.

'It is impossible for you to go home tonight,' exclaimed Hartley.

'You will really be doing me such a favour,' pleaded Dorna.

'But it's dark,' said Sir Charles.

'No, it is a clear, starlit night,' retorted Dorna; 'and I really wish to go home,' she said, turning around again to Hartley.

'But it's a ride of at least twenty miles to your mainland paddock, and then there is the three-mile row across to Smoke Island; and whatever would your friends say at your returning so late?' said her host.

'What time is it now, please?'

'Eight o'clock,' said Hartley.

'Then, if you can lend me a good horse, I can be safely home before midnight.'

'But you cannot surely ride home alone by wild bush roads at this hour?' ejaculated Sir Charles, as he looked at the determined girl in amazement.

Dorna faced round to the baronet as though thoroughly amused.

'Did you look at me when I arrived here with your friend this morning?' she asked.

'Y—es,' he stammered out; 'that is, I observed you, of course.'

'Of course you did, for I came here without shoes or stockings, or gloves, and with untidy hair, after carrying your friend ankle-deep in mud and slime off of a sand-bank in Moreton Bay. Now, did I look like a girl that would be afraid of the night, or the bush, or the bay, or anybody, or anything?'

'Certainly not,' said Sir Charles, smiling as he recalled her appearance.

'Well, then, although Mr Hartley has lent me this riding habit, I'm just the same Dorna Stoneham, and I really wish to ride home tonight.'

Hartley laughed heartily at this, and said, 'We are no match for you, Miss Stoneham, you will evidently have your own way. But I must confess to what is troubling me. I have two ladies' saddles, but they are both up in town.'

'Oh, that doesn't matter,' said Dorna. 'You can spare a man's saddle, I suppose?'

Sir Charles looked at the tall, graceful, animated girl before him – for they were standing together in the drawing room – astounded.

'You don't ride – h'm!' he stammered, and then stopped abruptly.

'No, I don't!' she said, with a tinge of amused annoyance in the tone of her voice. 'Have you never heard,' she continued, 'that all the best Australian girl riders learn to ride sideways on men's saddles?'

'Don't say another word to him,' said Hartley, laughing. 'You see, he is quite a new chum. I will come with you myself, and then I can bring the horse back with me. I have the horses in the stable, and by the time you are ready the man will have brought them round, and we will be off.'

'That's a most extraordinary girl,' said Dawson to Hartley, when Dorna had gone to her room.

'Yes, she is a bit out of the common,' said Hartley, dryly. 'Only that you must stay with Buchanan, I'd like you to come with us for a few miles, and see how an Australian girl can ride a mettlesome horse on a man's saddle. I'm going to put her on Beauty, and ride Sultan myself, for I would hardly care to ride the mare tonight; but she'll manage her, I'll bet.'

By this time the horses were fidgeting about restlessly in front of the house in charge of a groom, Beauty snorting at the gleams of light which flashed into the garden from the drawing room. The mare was not really vicious, but she had not been ridden for several days, and was high-spirited and nervous. Both horses had strong double-rein bridles and men's saddles complete.

Dorna had borrowed a saddle-strap, and came out upon the verandah, where the gentlemen were waiting, with a small parcel in her hand.

'I am afraid the mare will be a bit fidgety,' said Hartley. 'It is six months since she had a lady on her back.'

'She will be all right,' said Dorna. 'What is her name?'

'Beauty.'

'Just detach the offside stirrup, please,' she said to Hartley, 'and I will fasten this bit of a parcel upon the pommel, and put the stirrup to my length.'

The mare snorted as Dorna stepped toward her, and suddenly sprang back, pulling the groom round with her.

'Give me the reins,' said Dorna.

There's a soothing effect in the very way some people touch a horse; and by the time Hartley had unfastened the stirrup, Beauty had become better acquainted with Dorna, and stood still while she strapped the parcel on in such a way that it would make a comfortable leg-rest for her when in the saddle.

Beauty had unintentionally in wheeling about backed right up to a bit of rising ground, of which Dorna quickly took advantage, and sprang into the saddle without assistance.

She was barely seated, however, when Beauty noticed the skirt hanging by her side, and made a little kick at it, and then tried to shy off from it, and reared. Both Hartley and Sir Charles watched the animal's performance in some alarm. But Dorna's hands were down with a firm but gentle pressure on the bit, and her confident, calm voice was soothing the nervous animal.

'Jump, Mr Hartley,' she cried; 'you see she won't wait.' As this was said, Beauty reared again, so Dorna slackened the tightness of her rein, and touched her with her heel. The mare immediately sprang forward at a canter.

'Run!' cried Hartley to the man, who still held his horse for him to mount; 'the drive gate is not open.'

But Beauty reached the gate almost before the man had started to run, and Dorna, feeling that it was useless to attempt to pull her up, put her to it, and cleared it with a bound.

Sir Charles Dawson's last glimpse that night of Dorna Stoneham was as she cleared that gate, and he stood for several minutes afterwards, overwhelmed with astonishment, looking away into the darkness, and listening to the sharp clatter of the horses' feet upon the hard roadway.

Hartley knew too much to race closely after her. He was sure that in a quarter of an hour, or less, if no accident occurred, Dorna would have the mare well in hand. But it was much faster riding than he was accustomed to, and he was a bit suspicious that the girl was not over anxious to pull the mare in.

'That girl is something like the horse she is riding,' he said to himself, as he heard her racing across a wooden bridge fully half a mile ahead of him.

But Sir Charles Dawson was saying much stronger things about her to Buchanan. 'If she's a specimen of Australian bush girls, they're simply wonders. Why, she came in without shoes or stockings, talked botany like a member of the Linnean Society,[6] and went out over the summit of a five-barrel gate. I shall certainly have to put her into my book.'

But Sir Charles Dawson was mistaken, for Dorna was in most things above the average of Australian bush girls.

Her bringing-up had made her a specialty; and even Bright Hartley thought that in Dorna Stoneham he had made the acquaintance of something entirely new in the way of girls.

They had covered nearly five miles before Hartley caught up with her.

6 The Linnean Society took its name from the Swedish naturalist Carl Linnaeus (1707–1778) and was concerned with developing the biological sciences. The Linnean Society of London was founded in 1788; the Linnean Society of NSW was founded in Sydney in 1874.

'I hope that you were not frightened, Miss Stoneham?'

'Indeed I was, Mr Hartley. I was afraid that your horse might attempt to jump that gate.'

'Could you not pull up before?' said Hartley, somewhat rebuffed, but ignoring Dorna's insinuation.

'I really don't know,' said Dorna; 'but I thought it safest not to try, it spoils a horse's mouth, you know, to saw on it; and, besides, you only waste your strength, which, when a horse is running away, ought to be kept for more serious extremities. I suppose your friend, the baronet, almost went into hysterics when I jumped that gate?'

'I really had not time to wait and see,' said Hartley, laughing.

'Now, which is the best way?' said Dorna, pulling up her horse at the junction of two roads.

'They both lead your way; but one is longer than the other,' replied her companion.

'By all means let us take the shortest, then,' said Dorna.

'That's the one, then, to the right; but it's rough.'

'Oh, that does not matter,' said Dorna. 'You should see some of the cattle tracks we girls gallop over on Smoke Island.'

Hartley was by no means deficient in pluck, and, for a fairly stout man, was a good rider. The night was clear and the stars shone brightly, and he felt inclined to show this wilful Stoneham girl that he was not the milksop she seemed to take him for. He knew a road across the bush which might save them a good two miles, or rather, it should be said, he knew it partially, and believed that Sultan knew it well, so he suggested that they should take it. Dorna agreed at once, and a few minutes afterward they were riding single file along a narrow track upon the turf, Hartley in front.

'Now, Mr Hartley, you may go as fast as you like, only don't get lost.'

Sultan snorted when Hartley, thus encouraged, gave him his head, and touched him lightly with his spur; and then, reckless of fallen timber or water-washed gullies, and the darkness caused by the foliage of the trees, he bounded off, with Dorna, riding Beauty well in hand, close behind him.

The mettlesome horses soon grew excited, and it became a gallop – two up and two down; but Sultan was familiar with the track, and kept to it, and all went well, until suddenly they came upon a mob of cattle camped near the path, and one lazy bullock, lying in the way, unfortunately rose upon his feet just as Hartley's horse was in midair leaping over him. The rest may be imagined.

Dorna just saved herself, and Hartley had rather a bad spill.

They rode along after this more soberly, and Bright Hartley was a sadder, and, perhaps, wiser man; do what he would, the Smoke Island girl always seemed to have the advantage of him. All the night he had been trying to make a good impression, but seemingly without the slightest success. And now, to wind up, he thought, he had actually been thrown off his horse.

It was but little after ten o'clock when the heated horses reached the shores of the bay, and in the distance there loomed before them the dark outline of Smoke Island.

'Do you see those two lights?' said Dorna. 'They're candles in two windows of the girls' rooms. That means that the old man is away at Stradbroke Island. We can turn the horses into the paddock, and bring the saddles across with us in the boat, lest someone should steal them.

I'll row you over; you'll want something to eat and a few hours' rest before you ride back again to the Bungalow; and then, too, you can take this riding habit back, which it was really very good of you to lend me.'

Hartley thought it his duty to see Dorna safely home; and Stoneham being away, he willingly consented to the proposal. He wanted to see more of Dorna, too; he was fairly fascinated with the girl – and all the more so because he could not make her out.

CHAPTER IX

HARTLEY HAS THE WORST OF IT

THE LANDING PLACE at Stoneham's paddock was a freak of nature. Two sheer rocks, about eighteen feet high, arose perpendicularly from deep water, and attached themselves roughly, like the capital letter C, to the land, forming within, a basin of about half an acre of perfectly still water, with an entrance between the rocks fully twenty feet across. A more secure or convenient place for embarkation it would be difficult to imagine.

The only drawback was the descent; but this was not nearly so precipitous as might have been expected, the path having been made more accessible by a few rough steps cut in places out of the rock.

Here, under a Moreton Bay fig tree, a boat was sometimes to be found, with oars and sails placed ready for the use of some member of the Stoneham family who might have business upon the mainland.

Down this pathway Dorna and Hartley, each carrying their saddles, made their way to where a boat was in waiting, the former going forward to unfasten it.

'Here's luck, now,' called out Dorna, as she jumped into the boat, and pushing it toward the steps, fastened the painter to a handy tree. 'Some of the girls have been across with supper – and actually there is enough for two. I am certainly hungry, and I am sure that you must be after that very awkward tumble you had.'

'Bother that tumble!' thought Hartley. He sat down in the boat opposite to Dorna, at her invitation, with a fair-sized basket between them. Enclosed in a snow-white cloth were sandwiches and sweet, buttered scones, and also a basin of cream and fruit, and a jug of new milk.

'It is a supper,' said Hartley, 'fit for an epicure.'

'They must have known that you were coming,' said Dorna, looking at him and laughing mischievously; 'they would know that I could not possibly eat all this, unless, perhaps they thought I would have been fasting since last night.'

Hartley praised everything, and ate with great relish. He had ridden nearly twenty miles. 'It is the most romantic picnic I have ever had the good fortune to attend,' he said.

'A riding habit is a very awkward thing in a boat,' said Dorna, presently, kicking at her skirt the while with her number five boots, until they peeped out from beneath the obnoxious garment.

'But you are dying to have a smoke,' she continued, 'so I will go up and get a parcel from the stables, and then we can start.'

To Hartley's amazement, Dorna presently returned barefooted, and attired exactly as on the previous night, when she took rank as first officer of the *Gadfly*.

He gazed at her in the semi-darkness in astonishment, while Dorna busied herself about the boat, but said nothing.

'How long will it take to pull over?' asked Hartley, as she completed her arrangements. 'I'll take the oars, you know.'

'Oh! there's a good wind,' said Dorna. 'I'm going to sail across. If it keeps blowing as fresh as now, we ought to run over to the beach in twenty-five minutes. You can swim, I suppose, if we should happen to get capsized?'

'What the dickens is she going to be up to now?' thought Hartley. 'I've a great mind not to go across at all.' But Dorna was pushing off by this time, and he was so fascinated with the girl that he would have gone anywhere almost, and almost have run any risk, to have continued in her company. He was speculating, too, as to whether he was not a great deal too shy and deferential to take her fancy.

'I dare say,' he thought to himself, 'she'd think a lot more of me if I put my arm round her waist, and gave her a kiss.'

He offered to help step the mast, but Dorna thanked him, and said she preferred to do it herself. She had the sail up in no time, and as they caught the breeze, held the halyard in one hand, while she steered with the other. They were soon bowling along at a great pace toward the island, with a wake of phosphorescent light behind them. Dorna managed the boat as easily as a smart coachman would a carriage and pair.

'You're very quiet, Mr Hartley,' said Dorna, at length. 'I hope that tumble off your horse has not hurt you.'

'Shall I tell you what I was thinking of?' said Hartley, ignoring the sarcastic reference to his unfortunate mishap.

'Yes, if you like.'

'Well, I was thinking what a splendid girl you are, and how clever, and how much I should like to kiss you.'

Both Dorna's hands were, of course, occupied, so as she said nothing Hartley took her silence for consent, and slipped his arm around her waist, and was about to steal the coveted kiss. But at that moment Dorna took her hand off the tiller, and suddenly pulled hard upon the sail, the effect of which was that the boat swung round and heeled over on Hartley's side, and was in a fair way to capsize. Dorna, being prepared, braced herself with her feet; but Hartley, who was quite unprepared, rolled over, at which Dorna gave him a vigorous little push, at the same time letting go the halyard, when she had the satisfaction of seeing Hartley tumble into the bay, and the boat, relieved of the pressure of the sail and Hartley's weight, right itself. As Dorna brought the boat round again, and heard Hartley puffing away like a porpoise in the distance, and occasionally calling to her, she laughed until she almost cried.

'He's too fat to sink,' she said to herself; 'and it will teach him to keep his hands off Smoke Island girls in the future. But fancy, how wet he'll be; we shall have to rig him out in some of the old man's clothes!'

As Hartley scrambled on board, sopping wet, and with all the lover's ardour washed out of him, Dorna was full of apologies.

'You see, it was your own fault!' she exclaimed reprovingly. 'If I had not been very quick, the boat would have capsized; you should never try to kiss anyone in a boat without getting permission. Supposing that we had both of us been drowned!'

Hartley naturally felt a little sulky after this; but his respect and admiration for Dorna were increased rather than otherwise. She never lost her temper, and was even kinder to him, he thought, than before. He was completely puzzled; but when afterward, rigged out in some of Aaron Stoneham's things, which were about twice too long for him, Dorna gravely gave an account to her mother and sisters of how kind Hartley had been, and how he unfortunately had a spill from his horse, and then tumbled out of the boat into the bay, he looked at her with a comical expression, which, if caught, would have made the fortune of a humorous artist; while the girls, who had hurriedly attired themselves to receive the late but welcome visitors, looked at Dorna from the corner of their eyes, and wondered whatever she had been up to.

Dorna, however, made no reference to the events of the previous night, except to casually remark that she had been accidentally left ashore near Mr Hartley's house early that morning, and was much indebted to him for lending her a horse and seeing her home – and the family were too wise to ask any questions.

Next morning Dorna was awakened soon after it was light by one of her sisters.

'Dorna! Dorna!'

'Oh, bother the cows!' exclaimed Dorna, half-awake. 'Get Mr Hartley to go down and milk for me; he knows how to do most things; and he will no doubt strip them dry, and then capsize the bucket and spill the milk.'

'Dorna, wake up! The old man's back.'

'You don't say so!' cried Dorna, at once arousing herself. 'Where is he?'

'That's what we can't find out; but the *Gadfly* is at the wharf, so he is somewhere about.'

'All right, I'll come; but mind, you may look out for squalls.'

With strong shoes on, and neat print dress, Dorna was soon with her sisters at the yards. The saddle horses had been run in as usual, and the cows were in the bails, the dairy fire alight, and everything well forward.

'Molly, put the bridle on Brownie, and I'll have a ride round and see how things are,' said Dorna.

A few minutes afterwards she was cantering through the long grass, saturated with morning dew, down toward the wharf. It wanted fully a quarter-to-six, so Hartley was not likely to be about for another hour or more. She was anxious to see her father, and have it out with him before he could meet their visitor.

There was no sign of anyone about the wharf, however, so she rode on to the black fellows' humpy, to see if Tom or Jackey had returned; but her call awakened no response, so she turned and rode more slowly back to the wharf again, and dismounting, threw the bridle rein over the broken bough of a bush tree.

'He may be asleep in the sheds, or on board,' she said as she cautiously looked around; but finding no sign of anyone about the wharf or sheds, she stepped onto the *Gadfly*. Everything there was in fair order; the deck wanted washing down, but the tarpaulin covers were on the brass-work and other fittings. On looking into the 'tween decks, Dorna started, however, for stretched upon the bottom the yacht was a tall aboriginal, with a gash across his forehead; stiff and dead.

The yacht was fully decked with sliding hatches to the hold and cabin. These Dorna hurriedly closed, and then hastily mounted her horse and cantered across to the shingled cove, where she and Hartley had landed on the previous night. To do this she had to pass the house and yards, but no one took any particular notice of her – she might have been going after a stray cow, or some of the calves. One boat only was kept here – that in which Dorna had brought Hartley on the previous night over from the mainland. As she got out of sight of the house she urged her horse along at a gallop, and in a few minutes was at the wooden jetty which run out into the sheltered water of the bay.

The boat was gone!

'We must get that boat back somehow before Mr Hartley is about,' said Dorna to herself. 'The old man is evidently off, and something dreadful has happened. I must get mother to keep Mr Hartley without his clothes until we are ready for him; and Nettie and Alice will have to go across with me for the boat.'

Dorna rode hurriedly back, and sent Alice and Nettie down to get the boat ready at the wharf, while she went up to speak to her mother. A few minutes after, she was sitting in the stern sheets of the boat steering, while her sisters, each pulling a pair of sculls, sent the light craft rapidly through the water. There is no need to describe the trip across; they were back again before Hartley got his clothes. Mrs Stoneham apologized; she had asked the servant to press them for him, she said, so he could not well complain of having been kept an extra half-hour in his room. By the time he had had his breakfast the girls were away at their work, except Alice and Nettie, who were ready to take him across to the mainland.

He saw no more of Dorna, and before ten o'clock was on his way back to the Bungalow, riding one horse and leading another, and, if the truth must be told, by no means satisfied either with himself or his adventures.

'What a girl she is though!' he exclaimed to himself. 'I shall have to keep quiet about that spill, and capsize into the bay. Dawson and Buchanan would plague the life out of me. I don't think Dorna is a girl to talk much, and 'pon my honour, with all her tricks, I believe she likes me. Pity they have such a brute of a father; he leads them a dog's life, I know. But what does it matter to me; to think that at my age, and with my position, I should take on in this way over a bit of a barefooted girl like that; but she is a wonderful creature, when you come to think of it. I wonder what there is that she cannot do?'

If Hartley could have seen Dorna Stoneham at that moment he would have been still more surprised, and perhaps horrified. She was removing, as well as she could, single-handed, the evidences of a crime. That the black had been killed by her father she was certain, and in her own mind she had decided that the best thing was to bury the body and say nothing about it.

She determined that she would tell no one, not even her mother, and had, for this purpose, sent both her sisters across to the mainland, the two others she had set to work husking maize at the barn, and with a single steady old draught mare she was down alone at the *Gadfly*.

'When shall we be done with the trouble that this man brings upon his family?' she said. 'Crime upon crime! Crime upon crime!' she repeated to herself. 'He seems to have settled upon this island in order that he may indulge his evil passions without let or hindrance, and we are compelled to screen him. What wretched mystery, I wonder, is there at the back of the death of this native? Then, too, he has taken four horses and the buggy from the mainland paddock. It's evident that he has not gone alone. Probably he has Tom and Jackey with him; but where has he gone, and why has he killed this black?' The girl was evidently greatly agitated, but she nevertheless proceeded with her self-imposed task. She had fastened the body up in a piece of sail-cloth, and dragged it on shore, and then hitched a spare chain, used for hauling logs, around the corpse, and hooked the other end to the swingletree, and with a spade on her shoulder, led the mare, pulling the body behind her, toward a piece of marshy ground a short distance away, among some ti-trees near the bank of the creek.

Here, in the soft soil, after cutting the turf off in sods, she dug a shallow grave and buried the body, and replaced the turf, flattening it down with the spade. Only the crows, which cawed upon a neighbouring tree, witnessed the weird and ghastly funeral. By the time her sisters had returned, the mare had been turned loose in the paddock, and Dorna had gone up to the house.

'I shall lie down for a bit, Mother,' she said. 'I feel tired and upset.'

'Very good,' said Mrs Stoneham, utterly unconscious of anything very unusual having happened.

'I wonder when he will be back?' said Dorna to herself. 'I cannot meet him again after this. I must leave this miserable island! Marjory will be glad enough to have me. I'll go at once, before the old man comes back, or anything more comes out about these latest troubles. Heaven only knows what will be the end of it; but it is no use telling Mother or the girls, it would do no good that I can see. If he was not my father I would go and give information to the police. I am sure that he has committed crimes enough to be hung.'

Hartley, like other people, may have guessed that Stoneham's life was a long way from being law-abiding, but he little dreamt of the dark deeds which some of the

Stoneham girls were acquainted with, or what they had borne and suffered in their efforts to shield him from the law – not for his own sake, but for the sake of the family pride.

CHAPTER X

THE BUNGALOW STUCK UP

IT WAS AFTERNOON before Hartley reached the Bungalow. One of the horses cast a shoe on the road, and there was no blacksmith's forge nearer than Broadmeadow, which was four miles off the road.

'Hang it all,' grumbled Hartley, 'my luck seems to have deserted me. This comes of having a special liking for a woman. I first narrowly escaped a broken neck, then drowning, and now Beauty must cast a shoe; and yet somehow I feel as though I could chance a lot of bad luck for the sake of Dorna Stoneham. I can't think how it is the girl attracts me so. I wonder when I shall see her again? But there's the family, and the father. My goodness! it would be the devil's own luck to have to call Aaron Stoneham "father-in-law". I wouldn't do it for the brightest eyes, or sweetest lips, or daintiest foot, or warmest heart that ever was. No, sir, there's no necessity; the mere mention of the father would settle the matter. I could not think of it. I might if he were dead.'

He rode along for some time after this in silence, keeping a sharp eye upon cattle, and fences, and undergrowth, and other matters which seemed to have special interest for him. 'Great fools, these people,' he said. 'Old Humphrey gave twenty pounds an acre for that land, and I wouldn't give him twenty shillings for it; and then, too, instead of making something out of it for himself in rental, there it lies, and he lets these clever ones run their cattle over it. I wonder how many thousand acres of high-priced land in this district are now lying open, with half the fences down? Bushfires, of course, are blamed for it; they are extremely convenient for those who own big herds of cattle, but no land. And what cattle they are, too!' he exclaimed, as he came upon a mob of young heifers with a big ugly crossbred bull among them. 'It would be a benefit to the colony if every one of these scrub bulls were shot, and left to feed the crows. Just look at those heifers, with their coarse heads and horns, and thick tails and long legs.' And Hartley looked as though he could wish for nothing better than to put a bullet between the eyes of the whole herd of them.

It was a hard, gritty, 'made' road that Hartley was travelling upon, and he trotted quietly along so as not to distress the mare. He was generous to a fault to both his servants and his animals.

As soon as he got off the highway, however, and struck a cross-country blacksoil road, he urged the horses into a canter. They wanted little urging, and Hartley found that Beauty led well at any pace. Walking, trotting, cantering, or galloping, she never hung back, but kept head to head with her companion. 'These would make a splendid pair for that trip of ours to the path of Zoo-zoo,' he thought. 'They're worth a hundred sovs, though – rather too valuable for the far west – and, besides, one of them is a mare. I'll send a wire through to Martin to get half-a-dozen staunch horses handled a bit by the time we reach the Barcoo. I wonder, by the way, what Stoneham's up to?'

It was after two o'clock when he threw the reins to his groom, and went into the house. He thought the man had a queer look about his face, but Hartley went past without speaking to him, except to say 'Good day, Jim,' and in the front room was met by Sir Charles Dawson.

'I am glad that you are back again, Hartley,' he said excitedly; 'we have had a queer thing happen last night after you left. The house has been stuck up.'

'Stuck up! Nonsense! What do you mean?' queried Hartley, in a breath.

'Just what I say,' replied Sir Charles. 'About two o'clock this morning a couple of men appear to have walked through the French lights. I was sleeping in the same room with Buchanan, as he seemed restless, and wanted me to do so. When I awoke two men were in the room; one, a tall fellow with a bullseye lantern, had covered me with a revolver, and his companion seemed to be doing the same for Buchanan.

"'Don't move or speak," said a muffled voice – it was like a man talking with a stone in his mouth, and was doubtless done so that his speech should not be recognized. "I'd shoot either of you just as I would a dog, and there are enough outside to take care of your menservants."

"'So you escaped me, then, you cursed dingo!" he continued, addressing Buchanan. "Only for the trouble it would make, I'd put a bullet through your carcase, just where you lie – and I will, too, if I catch you out west." He said this,' said Sir Charles, 'accompanied by some of the foulest oaths I ever listened to. Buchanan lay still and said nothing, and I have not been able to get anything out of him since. In fact, he is not fit to be worried; and the shock of this adventure was only likely to prove bad, in his wounded condition.'

Hartley, on hearing the story, strongly advised Sir Charles to say nothing further at present to his friend. 'Let him get better first,' he said, 'then we will question him; there is evidently something more at the back of all this which he can explain, if he will.'

Hartley knew well enough, however, who the tall man was, and he guessed who the others were that he had with him. 'Out west,' he repeated to himself as he sat alone at his lunch; 'is he going out west by himself? There's something very strange about his connection with this captain; but I am going west myself now, whatever may be the consequences.'

Having business to attend to, Hartley drove up to town that evening, and stayed the night. 'You won't have another visit,' he said to his friends; 'they don't do that sort of thing two nights running.'

He questioned his man, however, closely, as to anything he had heard or seen, and found that he had got out of his room and hidden by a hedge in the garden. There were three men, he said, with a buggy and pair, and two saddle horses.

The two men he saw on foot were both unusually tall, the third remained with the horses.

'Did they steal anything?' asked the man.

'No,' said Hartley, shortly.

'A very strange thing, sir, begging your pardon; it's not often that armed bushrangers stick a place up, to pass the time of day!'

'That's very true,' said Hartley; 'but there's no use you talking about it, or me either. Those chaps were no bush-rangers or common thieves, and, between ourselves, I would sooner that you kept your tongue quiet about it up in Brisbane.'

'Very good, sir,' said the man, who from this knew perfectly that his master had some reason for wishing nothing more to be said about the matter.

It annoyed both Sir Charles and Hartley, however, to find that, as Buchanan slowly recovered, he remained thoroughly reticent as to the cause of his accident, and the personality of the midnight housebreaker who had threatened to do for him if he caught him out west.

'Let us go through with our understanding,' said Buchanan, grimly, 'and when the right time comes, I will tell you all that you will care to know.'

So it was settled that they should start as soon as Buchanan was strong enough, and in the meantime Hartley had made a trip to Sydney, and was evidently putting his house in order before he adventured upon what he felt convinced was a very risky enterprise.

It was curious to note the temperament of these three men in prospect of the expedition. Hartley had possessed himself of the documents, and might have been seen in his library poring over maps, and reading somewhat dreary narratives of early explorations in the interior. He was smitten with a malady only known in new lands – the desire to exploit a new and unknown territory, and, if possible, discover undreamt-of sources of wealth. The legend of the path of Zoo-zoo had laid a spell upon him, and he pondered over the possibilities suggested by the mysterious inscription of the boomerang by day, and dreamt about it by night. The thirst for adventure and treasure, and the desire to know, had come back upon him as strongly as in the days of his first colonial experience, and he prepared his equipment, and forecast the probable wants of his party, even to the enumeration of a spade, in case Buchanan or Dawson should die on the road, and therefore need to be buried.

When he, with some little hesitation, explained to his friends why a spade was to be taken, they laughed somewhat uncomfortably.

'Hang it, Hartley! You should have let us down more gently than that; you might have said it was to dig for treasure with. It's enough to make a man sick, to think that a spade forms part of his equipment in case he may die.'

'Ah!' said Hartley, 'You don't know how awkward it is to have a man die on your hands in the bush, and be without proper tools to make a decent grave for him. I was once in that fix, and had to leave an acquaintance to be worried out of all recognition by the crows.'

'Oh, take your spade, then, by all means,' said Buchanan; 'but it's my opinion, before you have gone two hundred miles, you will have to drop half the things you propose taking by the roadside.'

Hartley was no doubt methodical and cautious, too much so in regard to the matter they had in hand; but he did not want to lose a chance. He felt persuaded that there was treasure at the end of the path of Zoo-zoo, and commercial instincts were just then abnormal with him; he was going there to stay until he had found something worth taking up. He even arranged a code so that he might be able to telegraph his instructions secretly to an agent in South Australia about making application for land. He was not called Bright Hartley for nothing.

As for Buchanan, he was going under the impulses of a still more powerful incentive. He was going westward, hoping for revenge.

Sir Charles Dawson went, Englishman-like, because just then he had nothing better to do, and the others were going.

It's astonishing how far Englishmen have travelled, and astounding to know what they have gone through, simply because they were at a loose end, and the other fellow was going. A Scotchman, an American, an Australian, or a Jew, would want to know whether there was money in it. A Frenchman would look for honour and glory; but an Englishman will go through the whole racket of a hazardous adventure on the strength of some other fellow going, and his having nothing else in particular on hand.

So, at the set time – several weeks later than was at first intended – the three adventurers, impelled by their respective motives, started westward to explore the path of Zoo-zoo, first heard of in 1770 by that heroic navigator and enthusiastic explorer, Captain Cook.

CHAPTER XI

Dorna's Account of her Adventures

~

THE FOLLOWING ARE extracts from a voluminous package of letters which reached Smoke Island some short time after the incidents referred to in the previous chapter. They were written from a place called Western Plains, and were indited by Dorna to Alice; but they became to be regarded as family property – so much so that Alice thought it wise not to make any personal claim in regard to them.

~

After telling Marjory and her good man the story of my remarkable adventures, they insist that, for the sake of the family, and especially of my mother, I should write them down in full. I objected to this, not being very much of a letter-writer; but John, who I suppose you know is Marjory's husband, has just fixed me up a seat and table under a shady willow tree, which grows at the margin of the great lake that flows for miles and miles on these lonely western plains in the direction of the White Mountains, so I must, of course, do my best.

I used to think Smoke Island and the bay grand and wonderful; but oh, girls, if you could only see this place! It is most wonderful, marvellous! I don't think that there can be such another spot in the world. They say it's over a thousand miles from the eastern coast; and a vile, wearying road it is to travel by, but it's a perfect Beulah Land when you get here.

However, I must begin my story at the beginning.

The old mare Blossom is the only creature that knows why I left Smoke Island so suddenly, and until she tells you, I don't think anyone else will. I may say, however, that on the morning upon which Mr Stoneham brought back the *Gadfly*, and then took his very sudden departure, I was made aware of a matter which decided me to go at once. With the help of Blossom, for all our sakes, I removed the tokens of what seemed to me to be another crime; but I made a big vow that it should, God helping me, be the last time.

You know where the money lies buried in the mainland paddock, in case any of us should have to run away to Marjory. I found more there than I expected. Nettie makes a good treasurer. You will have found out by this time that I took fifty pounds – I thought it would spare that.

I did not hurry after I had crossed over in the boat to the mainland, for it was quite dark, and I guessed that the old man would not return for a day or two. I sat on the rocks looking over to the old island feeling sorry, and yet glad, as I waited for the dawn. It looks a sweet place from the mainland, does the island, and I tried to forget everything, and carry away only the vision which I saw when the dawn light at last came streaming across the farther islands from the eastern sea.

I could hear the cocks crowing, and some of the dogs barking, and I knew that you would all be getting up. Smoke Island, with its red cliffs and white beaches and green, cool foliage, made me think of the 'Summer Isles of Eden,'[7] that that daft old schoolmaster of ours – him with the wig – used to grow so sentimental about.

Well, I was glad that we had agreed that if any of us did run away there should be no goodbyes. It's a bit rough on a girl, when it comes to the pinch, to turn her back on the home of her childhood, no matter how cranky a father she may have; so I choked down a lump in my throat, and whisked a tear out of my eye, and turned round and whistled for Popsey. He came trotting up to me like a collie, and rubbed his nose against my arm, and followed me down to the stable for a feed of corn. I did not understand it at first, and it seemed quite a providence, for the grass would have wet me up to the knees with the heavy dew upon it if I had had to run Popsey in; but I remembered he was alone, for the old man had taken the other four horses.

As I was about to feed Popsey I had another surprise; you know I brought my brown riding skirt with me, and my dark felt hat, and my own saddle. What should I find on the top of the corn bin, but the parcel with the riding habit and all the rest of the things which I told you Mr Hartley had lent me. I felt certain that he had left them on purpose, intending that I should find them, so I just took him at his wish and put them on. The boots fitted me most comfortably, and when I looked at myself in that old bit of glass which Nettie nailed up in the buggy shed, I really felt

<hr>

7 From Alfred, Lord Tennyson, 'Locksley Hall' (1842): 'Summer isles of Eden lying in dark-purple spheres of sea'.

quite flattered with my appearance. I made up a fair-sized parcel with the things I wanted to take, and wrapped them up in the brown skirt, and strapped it well to the saddle. Popsey was a bit fresh and fidgety, but I had not very much trouble to mount.

On getting outside the paddock, I wheeled him round to take a last look at you all and the island. You know that wattle which grows near the gate, where the magpie's nest is: I pulled a bough of it down and kissed it (it's the bottom branch but one on the right-hand side), and told it to pass it onto the first Smoke Island girl that came to hand; then I pulled a sprig off and stuck it into the bosom of my habit, and gave Popsey his head, and we were gone.

I always loved a canter along that bit of turfy track by the paddock. You see, too, it was troublesome to think; and one of those cheeky magpies followed me along, and snapped his beak close by my ear, as much as to say, 'Dorna, are you going off without one word of goodbye?' I believe I should have cried, only that I just then noticed that a big blue gum tree had fallen right across the track, and that I must either pull up and scramble through the top branches or jump it near the roots. Of course I did the latter, and as we landed on the other side Steve Molesberry made his appearance, which immediately stopped any tendency I may have had to tears.

'Good morning, miss,' said he; 'that's a purty horse you are riding, and it's an early start you have. Are you for town?'

'Good morning, Steve,' I said, for I thought it best under the circumstances to speak him fair. But he looked so artfully at me, as much as to say, 'there's something up,' that I thought I'd give him one, so I said, 'Only to the crossroads for a constable, to show him a couple of faked heifers of ours which we have found on the mainland.' I looked him in the eyes, and rode on, and he never said another word. I'd keep my eyes on those Molesberrys if I were you; they don't keep that big punt at the mouth of Wynyard Creek for picnic parties.

Having started, I wanted to get right away as quickly as possible, so I took the top road until I crossed the big creek, and then turned in by the near track for Ipswich. You see, I intended to avoid Brisbane. I knew that I could buy all I wanted at the 'Modern Athens', as Mr Hartley styled the picturesque little town which I afterwards found nestling amid the hills at the 'head of navigation'.

After the first fifteen miles I pulled Popsey in a bit, and inquired the way to Peachey's orchard, and stopped there for some lunch. The old fellow made quite a fuss, and wanted me to tell him the whole history of the Stoneham family since he sold Mother that pair of prize Aylesbury ducks; but you may guess that it was not very much he learnt from me.

I got into Ipswich as the clocks were striking four. Popsey had hardly turned a hair, and no one would have dreamt that we had come forty miles. I rode straight up to the best hotel and ordered a room and dinner, and then sauntered round to the stable to tip the groom and see that he fed Popsey well. He was not a bad sort of a boy, but like most Queensland youths, a bit too familiar to a girl without an escort. But perhaps it was excusable, he had had no experience with Smoke Island girls.

However, after enjoying a good dinner, I went into a big shop where they seemed to sell almost everything, and laid out fifteen shillings on the heaviest ladies' riding whip they had in stock. The shopman stared at me after I had rejected several as not being heavy enough. I expect he thought I must have been stuck up coming into town by some obstinate mule of a horse with no go in him; but you may guess I did not want the whip for Popsey. Then I picked out one of the latest improved hammerless revolvers, and bought half-a-hundred cartridges and a small silver watch. That shopman stared at me as though I were one of the New Women that people are talking about, when all at once I heard a voice at my elbow—

'How do you do, Miss Dorna?'

I was that startled, I almost dropped on the floor, and, turning round, who should confront me but old Weston, the schoolmaster. You remember him; he was the one that the old man sent to the rightabout for being too sweet with ——, you know who. I felt that mad at being discovered in this free and easy fashion that I felt as though I would have liked to have broken in my new riding-whip a bit across his shoulders. But his next observation was a staggerer.

'I suppose,' said he, 'you have come to Ipswich with your pa?'

'What the goodness do you mean, Weston?' I ejaculated, catching hold of him by the wrist. 'Is my father in Ipswich?'

He looked at me very funnily for a minute, just as he used to in the old days when the old man was on the cross, and said:

'I'm married, Miss Dorna, and live in Ipswich. I saw your father with Tom and Jackey about half an hour ago in the main street, near the post office. Come out by this side door; we live across the river. Let me have the pleasure of introducing you to my wife.'

I smacked my skirt with my riding-whip, and said, with a shake in my voice, 'I thank you, Mr Weston, I think I will.'

I would not let the old chap see it, but I may say it was the biggest knockdown blow I ever had in my life. I felt worse than when the old man thrashed me that time in the big stockyard.

All the way over to Weston's cottage I am confident that I did not speak half-a-dozen words.

I should say that Weston has reformed from the drink, and has a school. His wife proved to be a bonnie, motherly little body and has a couple of nice children, so I made up my mind at first sight to take them into my confidence, for I would not for all I possessed just then have met with the old man. I was very kindly invited to stay for a day or two with Westons, until the coast was clear; and I set the schoolmaster to find out as much as he could about the old man. Mrs Weston seemed to be horrified with the little she heard about the state of affairs; but her husband said 'Ah! my dear, you don't understand the remarkable character of Aaron Stoneham.'

Well, my adventures began that very evening, for, of course, I had to go down to the hotel and bring over Popsey – you know Weston was always a frightful coward about a horse.

'I'll shadow you down Miss Dorna,' said he, 'if you prefer to go for the horse after dark.'

I told him I thought that I'd as soon go alone, but he persisted, so when it was quite dark we went together, and he waited at the corner while I went in for the horse. There was some delay in paying up the score, and saddling up, and so on, and just as I was about to get on Popsey, who should I see at the gate, staring at me as I stood full in the light of the big yard-lamp, but Jackey.

The groom had gone into the stable for something, so I whipped the revolver out of my pocket – it wasn't loaded – and walked straight up to him; he was grinning like a ring-tailed monkey – I never liked the wretch.

'Miss Dorna,' he began. I aimed that revolver straight between his eyes, and just said, 'One word more, Jackey, and I'll shoot.' I saw that the revolver had put the fear of death into him, so I hissed rather than spoke, 'Jackey, turn round and walk slowly up to the corner; if you run, or if you stop, or if you cry out, I'll shoot.'

I did not know what on earth I was going to do, but it gave me a minute to think. I kept close up to him, and at the corner gave the reins of the horse to Weston, and said, 'Lead him home, and then come for me to the railway station.' I had formed a plan, as I thought, to get rid of Jackey without his meeting my father.

The position of the railway station, I should say, had caught my attention in the afternoon, and I guessed that Jackey knew where it was too, so I muttered in great excitement, 'Walk to the railway station, Jackey; if you stop, or call out, I'll shoot, if I'm hung for it.'

'Miss Dorna, don't shoot Jackey,' said he, evidently in mortal terror. Well, I followed the wretch onto the platform, took a second-class ticket for him to Brisbane, and then watched him for twenty minutes, until the train came in. I saw him into a carriage, and watched the train off, and then walked down to Weston's cottage, thinking what a stupid I was to take so much trouble. Jackey would, of course, get out at the first stopping place, and in an hour or so would be back in Ipswich. This I learnt afterwards was actually the case, for by the morning train Aaron Stoneham, with four saddle-horses and swags, and two blacks, were booked for D——. I was both puzzled and alarmed when Weston told me of this. It was the very direction I had to travel in myself. 'Whatever could they be after out west?' I thought; anyhow, I determined to give them a fair start, so I stayed for a couple of days longer, partaking of the hospitality of the Westons.

CHAPTER XII

DORNA'S ADVENTURES CONTINUED

WHEN I KNEW that the party in front would leave the train in D——, I determined, on the advice of the schoolmaster, to go on south to the end of the railway line, and then take the coach as far as I could west. I cannot explain to you the dread I had of again meeting with the old man. I felt somehow that he was bound on a journey which might upset all my plans. What he was travelling westward for I then had no idea, except that I thought it might be convenient for him to get out of reach of law and civilization for a time; but I was puzzled as to why he had the blacks with him. However, I felt sure that he would not dream of my going beyond Ipswich, so two days after he had left I determined to continue my journey.

Weston wanted to accompany me a bit of the way, but, of course, I would not hear of it.

I could not obtain exactly the information I wanted, but I hoped to be able to coach it for at least two hundred and fifty miles after leaving W——, then I should have to trust to my wits.

Well, I determined to travel in my riding habit, and take my bridle and saddle with me, and packed up my belongings in a pair of saddlebags. I said farewell to my good friends – kissed Mrs Weston and the bairns, and squeezed old Weston's hand, and told him he had a splendid little wife, which seemed to please him greatly, and so I started.

It was, of course, the first time I had been in a train, and I was a bit puzzled about things; but I tried not to betray a sign that anything was strange, although I got a bit of a shock at the first tunnel. There were three other people in the carriage, and on the opposite seat was a young squatter, who evidently thought me very innocent, for he caught hold of my hand in another tunnel further on; but I drew it back, and then pushed it rapidly forward again so that it knocked against something.

When we got into the light there were tears in his eyes, through a spark or something having got into one of them from the engine – at least, that was his explanation of the matter; but he did not feel about for my hand in any more tunnels. I talked a little to them all, and made myself generally agreeable. One was a rough-looking old chap, who, they said, owned half one of the towns somewhere, and several big stations. He was very civil – and so was the young squatter, after the spark from the engine got into his eye.

Presently I got tired of looking out at the interminable bush scenery, and shut my eyes and commenced to think, and what with the motion and rumbling noise of the wheels, I found the train a great place to think in. I thought over everything that had happened to Captain Buchanan that night, and of other things you don't know about; and then I began to think about my father, and Jackey, and Tom; and the more I thought of them the more puzzled I was, until the desire to know what those three were up to at D—— became irresistible, and I there and then determined that, whatever might be the consequences, somehow or other I would find out.

I went in with the rest of them and had some lunch at a railway station, and after that the train slowly climbed up the magnificent range of mountains to the tableland. I cannot tell you how I gazed across that wonderful landscape as we darted in and out through innumerable little tunnels. They told me that as the crow flies it was only sixty miles to the sea; but it was the thought that Smoke Island was just across there that affected me most.

I went straight on that night to D——, and slept at a big wooden hotel in the centre of a small, dried-up sort of a little town, which had sprung up mushroom-like in the middle of a big blacksoil plain. The young squatter had left; but the old one was most pleasant and attentive, and I had a real good time with him, although I little guessed what was coming.

We were off at half past five the next morning – Mr Jeremiah Crumbs, the squatter, and myself on the box seat, and three Chinamen inside. I suppose I looked really nice, for Mr Crumbs had got me some flowers from somewhere, and Jim, the driver (a long individual, who told no end of unconscionable yarns for my special benefit), looked quite smart. We had not a bad team, and he made them travel, for we did eighteen miles before breakfast.

I found Mr Crumbs to be held in great respect; and the attention which they paid me all along the road was simply overwhelming. I could not make it out; the landlady would be waiting at the elbow of her husband as the coach dashed up to the end of a stage – for Jim always made a point of shaking up his horses, and going in at a swinging trot.

I said very innocently to Jim on the second day, 'You have wonderfully nice clean hotels along this mail route; and the landlord and landlady are so smart and tidy, and the servants so clean. And we have had roast turkey twice, as well as lovely joints.' At this Jim smiled and winked and shook his head in a most extraordinary fashion, and said it was the best road to travel he had ever worked.

'Yes,' chimed in Mr Crumbs, 'it has occurred to me, Jim, as being very fortunate that everything should be so pleasant. Someone must have told them that we had a strange young lady with us, on whom we wished to make a favourable impression. I never saw Mrs Blakewell so clean and well-dressed in my life before, and certainly never ate such a dinner in the house. It was very creditable; and as for old Blakewell, he looked to me a bit screwed – a most extraordinary thing – and he congratulated me on my company, and wished me luck!'

I found out the next day that that horrid driver had passed the word along by two stockmen, who were in front of us, that Mr Crumbs had been married in Brisbane, and that I was his wife. He did it, of course, for a joke; but that day Mr Crumbs must have heard some whisper of it, for he became uncommonly attentive, and seemed to have made up his mind to turn the joke into a fact. I felt a bit uncomfortable, but we had a very startling incident which determined me to take temporary advantage of Mr Crumbs' evident admiration.

His buggy, it seems, was waiting for him at the next township, which place, in the ordinary course of events, we should reach at four o'clock that evening; so I suppose he thought there was no time to lose. I had been very pleasant with him all the previous day, for he really was very nice to me; and the way in which I allowed him to assist me on and off the coach must have led him to think that he had a chance – as though I would marry any of the vain, selfish creatures!

Anyhow, at breakfast, I found that he had persuaded Jim to ride inside with the Chinamen, who, he said, he was afraid were drinking too much, and he would 'tool' the team along the next stage. So he and I were alone on the box. He certainly drove in great style, probably he was showing off a bit; but I feel sure they did something to the team we started with after breakfast. The men would not hitch on the outside traces of the leaders until Mr Crumbs had the reins gathered up for a start and everything was right, and the moment those traces were hitched on, the man holding the leaders jumped clear away, as though there was going to be an earthquake, and the whole team made a jump which you would have expected to jerk the body of the coach straight off the wheels. The two front horses, it transpired, belonged to a doctor, who was having them quietened in the coach.

There was a creek about two hundred yards in front of us, and the mad things went down and through it at a gallop. I thought once or twice that we should have struck a tree or stump, the coach swayed about so; but Mr Crumbs coolly smoked a cigar all the time, and kept the horses well in hand. I knew Jim was a bit scared, for I saw his face peering out from the couch quite whitish, as he saw one of the leaders kick up, and put his head down and ears back, as though he meant mischief. Jeremiah

Crumbs, however caught him a flick with the whip just at the moment, which let him know that the man holding the reins was his master. We raced up a hill, and he then pulled them up, and we swung along splendidly for half an hour, only occasionally breaking into a canter.

A few minutes afterwards we mounted a ridge, and saw a long downhill in front of us, with a bridge crossing a gully, and beyond that a long rise, and to my horror, halfway up the rise, I saw three horsemen jogging along at a regular bushman's pace, and one of them leading a packhorse.

I knew the whole crowd of them at once: it was the old man, with Tom and Jackey! And at that very minute Mr Crumbs began to talk quite confidentially, and I felt sure, from the tone of his voice and the general look of him, that he was about to propose to me.

I shall never forget the events which followed, as long as I live. 'Miss Stoneham,' said Mr Crumbs, clearing his throat, 'have you noticed how well horses run in double harness? Those two leaders are really proud to be together, and they pull splendidly, although they were so skittish at starting; but this offside horse is the younger of the two by several years, and yet they are a perfect match.'

We were trotting along very steadily downhill with the brake on, and I kept my eye on the party in front, who I reckoned in a few minutes would disappear over the crest of the hill.

'Whatever shall I do?' I thought.

'Do you know, Miss Stoneham,' continued Mr Crumbs, 'we seem to get along really well together – pull in harness, you know. I wish,' he said, 'we were hitched together for life; I'd love you and take care of you, as I am sure a younger man never would. You know I've plenty of money, and you are just the woman I have been dreaming about all my life.'

We were now nearing the end of the hill, and I looked up into his glowing old face, and felt quite ashamed at deceiving him; but there was no help for it, so I said, 'Are you quite sure that those two horses pull well together, Mr Crumbs?'

'Yes,' he said; 'but if you would marry me, I would not ask you to pull a bit – I would do all the pulling.'

He was terribly in earnest. But I wanted to get hold of those reins, so I said, 'It's your splendid driving, Mr Crumbs; let me drive them up the hill myself, and then I shall be better able to tell whether they are really a well-matched pair.' He seemed to hesitate, so I smiled, and reached out my hand to take the reins.

'Wait until we are over the bridge,' he said.

After we crossed he handed me the reins. 'But,' I said, 'I must sit on the driver's seat, or I cannot drive properly,' and I gave him another smile. I believe that he would have given me my own way after that if he had known that I was going to wreck the coach right away, and kill the three Chinamen, and I quite melted towards him.

He leaned forward for me to pass him without another word, and as I dropped down in the driver's seat I grasped the reins firmly, and then lifted the whip out of the socket and dropped it back again – I wanted to be sure that everything was clear. We were on a bit of sideling, so I got the horses well in hand, and put them on the lower side of the road. I saw him gather confidence as he watched me handle the ribbons; he little guessed that I had helped break in more than one four-in-hand on Smoke Island, with only rope reins.

'You know how to handle a four-in-hand, Miss Stoneham,' he remarked.

I chirruped the horses into a smart trot, and then said, 'They go splendidly, Mr Crumbs; now you must let me drive them for half an hour.'

'But, Miss Stoneham!'

'Now do,' I said.

'Perhaps I'll let you call me Dorna,' I gasped, for I was desperate. 'If you don't, I think I'll hardly ever speak to you again.'

He at once, without a word, moved right over to the other side of the seat so as to have his foot handy for the brake on his side, and then said, 'Dorna, you shall drive just as far as you please.' It was delicious to hear how he said 'Dorna'. I knew that I was safe then.

'All right,' I said, 'that's a bargain,' and with that we came to the top of the hill, and there in front of us was the party of three.

My heart beat wildly; but I shortened my grip of the reins, and chirruped again to the horses. It was level ground, and we went along at a swinging pace, and were quickly overtaking them. I put both feet down on the splashboard, and cracked the whip, and the horses broke into a canter.

'Steady! Miss Stoneham,' exclaimed Mr Crumbs, and with that he called out 'Cooee' to the men in front.

The old man and the two blacks turned their heads around, and pulled their horses off the road to make way for the coach.

'My golly!' I heard Jackey exclaim; 'no gammon, that's Miss Dorna!'

When the old man saw me he turned perfectly livid. I just caught a glimpse of his face, and then, terrified lest he should call out to me, I lifted the whip and brought it straight down across the backs of the leaders, then caught up the lash, and put the thong end smartly onto the pole horses.

The whole four of them leaped into a gallop, and I saw my admirer reach across to grab the reins.

'Don't you touch!' I screamed. 'Do you hear those men galloping after us? They are three bushrangers.'

At that very moment there was the report of a revolver, and a bullet whizzed above our heads. The old man had evidently gone mad!

I shook the horses up again, for we were on a splendid bit of blacksoil level country. My word, how they did travel! But we could hear the party of three shouting behind us, as they galloped madly after the coach.

'Haven't you any firearms?' I said.

'No,' said he.

'Here,' I said, 'is a revolver,' and I pulled out the one I had bought at Ipswich from my pocket, with my left hand. He took it and fired three shots behind him without looking, and then said, 'They're pulling up, I think; I must have hit one of them.'

'It would not carry so far,' I said; 'and you had better save the other shots, if we are leaving them behind.'

It never occurred to me before that there should be so much difference between four horses galloping because they are whipped, and the same horses galloping in fright. They were corn-fed, and every vein in their beautifully sleek bodies swelled out, and every nerve seemed intensely strained. They were that scared that they snorted at the very pebbles on the road; but the old coach rattled along after them like a whirlwind, and as Mr Crumbs said afterwards (very poetically, I thought), 'I sat on the box seat driving like a queen of the storm.'

I had my foot on the brake on my side for a while, but not hard down, for I was afraid of the machine catching fire; and I guessed that by the time that we were clear of that party of three, we might want all the leather on it in some awkward pinch or other. There were no fences just here, and Jim had made a bit of a track for the coach here and there off the main road to clear a hole or something. I took every one of these without a moment's hesitation. I had noticed that the old man behind was riding a colt of Lucifer's – almost as good as his sire – and I guessed that with no wheels, and mad Stoneham on his back, he'd take a lot of shaking off.

We were perfectly flying now, and the undergrowth on each side of the road swept past us like a long piece of green ribbon.

All at once I called out, 'Don't put the brake down too hard, Mr Crumbs,' and with that I showed them that trick with the whip I taught Alice in Smoke Island stockyard. The old man must have heard it (for it cracked like a pistol shot), and probably saw it too, and knew that under the circumstances it spelled 'Defiance!' in big capitals.

Really, I can't think what possessed me to do it, but I felt as though I had the strength of three men for the time being, and that those mad horses were like kittens under my hands. I took my foot right off my side of the brake, and just said to Mr Crumbs, 'You steady her a bit on your side over the ruts,' and then, just to show off a bit, as the off-leader's rein had got twisted, I straightened it, and did so as deliberately as though we were waiting to start. You should have seen the look Mr Crumbs gave me!

But without doubt it was the grandest, maddest coach ride I ever had, or heard of, or ever hope to have again; and the only thing I regretted was that I hadn't Bright Hartley sitting alongside of Jeremiah Crumbs on the box seat.

But it took some driving, though, for I had to steer that mad team clear of holes and ruts, and also keep as far out as possible from overhanging boughs, and avoid jerking the harness; this, however, was thoroughly strong – what there was of it; the pole horses were running without breeching – just bridles, collars, hames, and traces. These coaches, which carry her Majesty's mails out west, are, however, enormous affairs, hung on great leather springs, with very powerful brakes – so you may imagine, with four spirited horses running away with the affair, it was something like driving an avalanche.

All this time there was fearful shouting from inside the coach. The Chinamen were frantic with terror, and Big Jim had to hold one of them in.

After the shooting he called out, 'What's the matter? What's the matter?' and then started to climb out through the window.

'Jim,' I said, leaning over to him, 'for heaven's sake stay where you are, or there'll be bones broken. Some of those Chinamen may jump out. We are all right. That was a bit of a brush we have just had with bushrangers.'

You should have seen his face. I heard him swear to the Chinamen that there were no burning bushrangers within five hundred miles.

All this had happened in a few minutes, and the horses were still tearing along at a mad gallop and we were just on the brow of a long hill. Mr Crumbs leaned forward again to take the reins.

'Put the brake hard down on your side,' I said. 'We cannot change seats now, and I can drive them just as well as you, or Jim either.' It was astonishing how cool I kept.

It was lucky that we did not meet with a team or anything on that hill, for it was half a mile long, with a wide shallow creek at the foot of it. There were several pretty sharp curves, too, but the coach swung round without capsizing, although I more than once felt that we turned corners on two wheels, but the other two came down again all right, or I probably would not be writing this.

As we neared the creek, however, my hair began to fairly rise on my scalp. Some fools had fallen a tree that morning fair across the roadway!

I saw Mr Crumbs turn as white as a sheet, and he gave me a look as much as to say 'Goodbye, sweetheart, we shall soon be at the end of our journey.' But I ejaculated, 'Keep your foot on that brake!'

Then I put mine hard down, and pulled those horses in with both hands, and, just before we reached the tree, turned them straight in among the undergrowth. They never flinched one bit, and the saplings went down before the weight of the coach with a swishing noise, some of them breaking off like cabbage stalks, but most of them springing up behind the coach again half-broken and bent.

On we flew downhill, crashing into a lot of young pine saplings like a mad bull into a maize paddock. We barked several trees with the wheels, but, of course, where the horses and swingle-bars could pass the coach followed, and we luckily escaped hitting any heavy timber or old stumps. In a few minutes, after jolts and bumps which nearly sent Mr Crumbs and myself flying off the box, and which battered the heads of the frantic inside passengers against the roof of the coach, we landed bodily into the creek, on the top of a lot of loose shingles.

As they splashed into the water, the horses at once commenced to pull up.

'Put the whip onto them,' shouted Mr Crumbs, 'and head them for the bank.'

In a few minutes the coach was on the road again, and by the time we were fifty yards up the hill those horses had had enough of it, and at the top I pulled them up and handed over the reins to Jim, who climbed onto the box looking as solemn as a gravedigger.

'I reckon, Miss Stoneham,' said he, 'you have quietened these here horses a bit during the last quarter of an hour. But what the Jerusalem (only that was not exactly the word he said) do you mean by all this shooting?'

No one answered him. Mr Crumbs looked at me with a wonderfully mixed expression on his face. I was no doubt a bit red and ruffled, and I had split both my gloves.

'Miss Stoneham,' he said, 'wherever did you learn to drive? My word, Jim, I'll stand champagne and a dinner all round when we get into Cattle Creek township! Miss Stoneham, you're a daisy!'

'But how in thunder did that black fellow come to know that your name was Dorna Stoneham?' queried Jim.

'Perhaps your two friends, the stockmen, told him,' I said.

Jim was regularly bowled over, for he did not want Mr Crumbs to know any further particulars of that little incident, so he gathered up his reins and drove on without another word.

'What's that?' said Mr Crumbs.

CHAPTER XIII

FROM JEST TO EARNEST

I SAW THAT Jim was a bit afraid of the squatter, for he was a little god in the district we were approaching; and if I had shown myself displeased on account of the foolish practical joke that Jim had started, Mr Crumbs was so infatuated with me that it might have caused him to lose his billet. So I smoothed things over as well as I could, and as there was not a strap broken, and no one hurt, not much more was said, and we drove up to the next stage just as usual, only about three-quarters of an hour before the regulation time. I wanted to caution them not to say anything about the bushrangers, but I felt too nervous, so decided to let things take their chance.

'You're early, Jim!' said the hotel-keeper, as we pulled up. 'Horses been running away?'

'Noo—o,' drawled out the driver; 'it's these horses of the doctor's that knowed a nearer road through the bush.'

'None of your gammon, Jim.'

'Beg pardon, mam,' he continued, looking the while across from me to Mr Crumbs. 'Fine day, Mr Crumbs.'

Jim was pulling sundry parcels out of the boot of the coach during these remarks, so Mr Crumbs helped me down the while, and I was shown into a beautifully clean bedroom by the robust lady of the house, who informed me very respectfully that dinner would be served in half an hour.

The champagne was there all right at dinner, for Mr Crumbs decided not to wait until we reached the township, so Jim was invited in to eat with us. No doubt the expensive wine helped to deepen the general impression that Mr Crumbs was no longer a bachelor. I inquired of the girl, who I noticed scanning my fingers – no doubt for a wedding ring – whether any stockmen had passed the previous day. She answered in the affirmative, which quite explained everything to me.

'Dorna,' commenced Mr Crumbs, as we stood alone near the coach just before they brought the fresh horses up.

'Mr Crumbs, I only allowed you to call me by my Christian name while I was driving.'

He looked greatly ashamed, and corrected himself. 'I beg your pardon, Miss Stoneham, but you said neither Yes nor No.'

It was a critical moment. I dared not fall out with him, so I said, 'Mr Crumbs, you are very kind, and I really have a good deal to thank you for; but I must have time to think, and we have twenty-five more miles to ride together before we come to Cattle Creek township; you may ask me again then.'

The old chap became quite radiant at this, and, as the champagne had gone all round the coach, we started off again the best of friends. I was only troubled at the recollection of the length of Jim's conversation with Mr Bruce, the landlord; there were some ominous gesticulations, and I overheard the word 'bushrangers'. However, Mr Crumbs told Jim to keep his horses moving, and we did more than the regulation six miles an hour. We drove down the main street of Cattle Creek township shortly before four o'clock.

The whole town was decked out with green bushes, and here and there a bit of bunting was flying.

'Bless me!' said Mr Crumbs, 'these good people must have entirely lost their reckoning, and think that it's Christmas Day!'

Jim looked mighty solemn, and I heard him swear under his breath that those benighted stockmen had carried the joke too far. I gave him one look, at which he hung his head in pretended repentance, but I could hear him half choking with suppressed laughter.

As we drove up to the principal hotel, we saw that they had big gum bushes tied to each of the verandah posts, and a little crowd, in which I afterwards heard were the police magistrate, and clerk of petty sessions, the telegraph master, and poundkeeper, and other officials, raised quite a little cheer.

Mr Crumbs handed me off the coach, looking quite confused, and called the landlady forward to take charge of me, and then led the way into the bar to shout for the general public. It was a dreadful sell!

The landlady, who was decked out most gorgeously, showed me into the best parlour, which was simply smothered in antimacassars, and asked me to take a seat while the girl took some water and my luggage up into my room.

'You'll not think of going out to the station tonight, marm, of course,' said she; 'we have the big bedroom specially done up for you. Mr Crumbs does not usually care for it – says it's too big; but excuse me a minute, that chambermaid takes a lot of looking after,' and with that, before I could get out a word, she had bustled out of the room.

It was a dreadful position to be in, and I began to positively hate old Mr Crumbs!

Just then who should come in, as red as a turkey cock, but the gentleman himself. I at once rose, full of offended dignity, feeling that I did not care twopence if I walked all the rest of the way to the Western Plains. I'd stop this farce. And yet I knew that Mr Crumbs was just as much the victim of this horrid practical joke as myself, although from my standpoint I felt that I had a perfect right to blame him for it all.

'Miss Stoneham,' he said, in evident distress, 'these people have made such a great mistake that I am almost ashamed to look at you. A report has somehow preceded us that we are married, and the news is all over the district, and there's a congratulatory address being prepared for us down at the courthouse by the C.P.S., to be signed by the leading townspeople.'

'But of course you have told them that it is all a foolish mistake,' I said, almost crying in my indignation.

'No, I couldn't bring myself to do it,' he said, almost crying himself in his nervous excitement and perplexity, and alternate hope and fear.

'You see, Dorna,' he continued, hurriedly, 'the parson just happens to be visiting the township, and you told me that I might ask you again when we reached here; and, my dear Dorna, you might marry me at once, and I'll love you, and by jingo! my dear, I'll prove it, for I'll have old Blake, the lawyer, up before we're married, and I'll settle fifty thousand pounds upon you, and Marraroo Plains station into the bargain, and you'll be the richest and happiest little woman in the whole district.'

This really splendid offer completely took my breath away, and I was that puzzled I did not know what to say.

'Dorna,' he pleaded, as I was silent, 'say it's a bargain, and I'll send round for the lawyer and parson straight away.'

'Mr Crumbs——' I commenced.

'Don't call me that,' he said; 'say Jeremiah – that's what Bella always calls me.'

'Who is Bella?' I asked, partly out of curiosity and partly to gain time.

'My sister. But, Dorna, don't you trouble about her, or anyone else. Now, what do you say, my dear sweet lass, shall I send for lawyer and parson, and have the job fixed up tonight?'

You know I never was much of a fool, and I wasn't going to throw away a chance like this without carefully weighing it, so I said:

'Jeremiah, I feel flattered and honoured by your very generous proposal, but it would not be fair to either of us for me to take advantage of it tonight. You are excited through the singular events of today's journey, and by the absurd practical joke which has been played upon us. If I consented to marry you in haste, you might repent at leisure all the rest of your lifetime – you know so little about me——'

'I know that you're a perfect jewel,' he protested, stopping me; 'you're the grandest, bravest, sweetest girl that was ever born! I couldn't repent it, and if anyone else objected they would have to go. You would be my wife.

'Good gracious, Dorna! call me Jeremiah once again,' he exclaimed; 'I feel as though I am half-crazy with joy,' and at that the foolish old chap picked up the soft felt hat he had been wearing, whirled it round his head, and threw it with a loud thump up against the ceiling.

'Jeremiah,' I said, 'have you been drinking any more champagne?'

He quietened down in a moment, and became as calm and placid as a judge.

'No,' he said, 'it wasn't champagne, it was feelings.'

'Sit down,' I said.

He did as he was told, and waited patiently for me to speak. It did seem ridiculous, and I thought what fools men make of themselves when they first take a fancy for a woman. Here was this rich squatter throwing his hat against the ceiling, and dancing around half-cracked, because a bit of a girl like me had called him Jeremiah, while all the time there probably wasn't another person in the whole of Cattle Creek township who would have dared to call him anything less nor more than Mr Crumbs. However, I did not love him a bit, and for the time being, at any rate, I had no intention of marrying him, for I had set my heart on going out to Marjory at Western Plains; besides, I did think once about Mr Hartley; he certainly had taken a fancy to me, or he would not have stood so much of my nonsense. But there! I did not want to think, or know, or say, or do anything, except get out of Cattle Creek township as quickly as possible.

'Jeremiah,' I said, 'how far is it to your station?'

'Fourteen and a half miles.'

'Is your sister at home?'

'Yes.'

'Then you drive me out there at once, and don't say anything at all to these people; and you might tell the parson you'll be pleased to see him out at your station to conduct divine service some day early next week.'

'May I kiss you, Dorna?' said he, with a beaming face.

'No,' I said, 'certainly not. I have not promised to marry you yet.'

'But you'll call me Jeremiah, and let me call you Dorna?' he pleaded.

'By the way, there is a dinner laid for us in the big room,' he continued; 'and I see the police magistrate and a few others hanging round, waiting to be asked in.'

'Tell them that we are going on to Clifton Plains tonight, and that I prefer for us to dine alone. And hurry them around with that buggy.'

A handsome single-seated buggy, with a manservant on horseback, waited for us after dinner, and hats were lifted and curtseys dropped and smiles given us as the pair of grand blood horses rattled our buggy out of the township. I bore my blushing honours, I should say, with becoming modesty, knowing that a hundred women in that township would have leaped at the chance of signing themselves 'Mrs Jeremiah Crumbs'; but I said very little on the journey, for I felt tired, and also uncomfortable at this most awkward fix in which I found myself. I was really only about three hundred miles west of D——, and I had at least another five hundred to travel to get to Marjory, and my only friend in all the district was this wealthy squatter. It was a funny fix to be in – even for a Stoneham girl; and I wondered whether Jeremiah would prove as ardent towards me in his sister's presence, and in his own house, as upon a coach. Men are queer creatures, and often take sudden changes. 'Bella Crumbs! Bella Crumbs!' I kept saying to myself.

'Sisters are apt to boss their brothers,' I thought, and I wondered how Jeremiah got along with Bella. I knew from the first that she was bound to hate and despise me – it was in the natural order of things.

The stars were shining brightly overhead as we crossed a stony ridge, and then drove through a pair of heavy gallows gates which the man had opened for us, and rattled up to the white front entrance gates of Clifton Plains head station.

CHAPTER XIV

MISS BELLA CRUMBS

YOU WILL BE getting terribly tired of reading this long letter, but the strangeness of my story must be my apology for its length. I want you to know it all, and somehow, although it seems to me an astonishing amount of writing, probably it will appear less to you. I would sit up all night to read about your goings on at Smoke Island since I left you, although I expect you have got on all right enough without me; and as for the old man – but there, I must try and tell my story without anticipating.

I don't think anything can be more exasperating than having to wait by yourself, as I had to do, in a strange house. But you know men have not a bit of thought!

Mr Crumbs, on our arrival, called out for his sister, and showed me into a sort of best parlour off the hall, and then went back to the buggery, and that was the last of him I saw for the night.

Now, fancy that, for a man who had just before thrown his hat up against the ceiling, and urged me to marry him that very night! I sat there expecting every moment that

Miss Bella Crumbs would bustle in to greet and welcome me, if only in deference to her brother. But I saw no Miss Bella Crumbs!

I must have sat alone for nearly half an hour, when an ancient, sour-looking, middle-aged woman came in.

'Tea is ready, marm,' she said.

'May I go to my room and take off my hat first?' I said.

'Yes, marm, certainly. Miss Crumbs is away visiting a sick woman, the wife of a stockman, across the creek,' – (there is always some place across the creek about a station). 'Mr Crumbs has gone over to Woolshed Paddock to see a valuable horse that has been taken ill,' she continued.

You may guess how glad I felt that I still retained the appellation of Dorna Stoneham. It would have been just the same if I had been Mrs Jeremiah Crumbs! He would have gone off after that wretched horse and left me.

However, I told Betty, the servant, that I was tired and would not wait, so I hurried with my tea. It was a good, plain meal laid in a bachelor and spinster sort of room, with stiff, straight-backed chairs covered in haircloth. I sat up as proper as you please, and the aforesaid elderly individual told me to please make myself at home, and ring if I wanted anything. 'Miss Crumbs,' she said, 'may be in at any moment.'

I heartily wished that Miss Crumbs and Mr Crumbs might both delay their coming until I had finished with the steak and tomatoes and apple pie. I got Betty to take my things to my room, and I finished my tea and announced that I should retire for the night.

It was not a bad room they had given me – indeed, it was both comfortably furnished and commodious. There was a kind of bay window, in addition to a square one, and big cupboards. I found in the morning that the bay window looked on to a flower and fruit garden, which sloped down to the creek. There was no key to lock the door, however, so I propped a chair up against it, and was soon asleep.

When I awoke in the morning there was a pleasant-faced woman of about five and thirty standing smiling at the foot of the bed, with a cup of tea in her hand.

'I'm Bella,' she said with a smile, 'and I've brought you a cup of tea. I am so sorry that you had such an unfortunate reception last night. Jeremiah has been up these two hours, worrying around, and he would have me come right in with the tea, to apologize the very moment you woke up.'

It was nice tea, with sweet, rich cream, and lovely thin bread and butter, and I found Bella Crumbs almost as nice as the tea, so we were soon good friends. Jeremiah had told her, she said, that he was going to marry me, and, looking at me with an approving smile, Bella said that she liked me at first sight, and was very glad. And really, when I heard from her the story of their early life, I was not so much surprised that she wanted Jeremiah married.

However, I made a great fuss, for I wished to continue my journey at once; but they would not hear of it, and, to induce me to stay for a few days, Mr Crumbs promised that, as I would not have him to accompany me, Bella should go with me several days' journey, and that we should have two trustworthy stockmen to travel with us, and see after the horses, etc. They would ride and drive spare horses in front of them, while Bella and myself drove together in a buggy.

I should like to tell you all about the house and gardens and station, but it will never do to begin, for I don't know where it would end. I learnt from Bella that their father, Thomas Crumbs, had been 'sent out' as a boy for some ridiculous thing. He was a baker's lad, and went home to his master fourpence short in his cash one night, so an enlightened English judge of those strange days had him deported with others to Botany Bay. Well, when their mother died, she left Thomas Crumbs with two boys, Jeremiah and Ezekiel, and one girl, Bella, and money and property to the value of over a quarter of a million. There were four stations well stocked, and a heap of money invested and in the bank; but her father swore that if one of them attempted to get married during his lifeline he would not leave them a cent.

They all three of them had any quantity of opportunities of marriage; but they worked on and waited, hoping that their father would change his mind, or, as Ezekiel said, 'do some other thing.' But they worked and saved and grew richer and richer in vain, the old man keeping everything under his thumb, and would neither change his mind nor die. So at last Ezekiel, who had been in love with a girl for nearly ten years, told him he was not going to wait any longer, and one day marched out with only a five-pound note in his pocket, and got married, and forfeited his share; but Jeremiah, who was the eldest, and Bella, the next, went on in the old round, day by day, and year by year, until the old man at last died, when they found out that Jeremiah had been left two-thirds and Bella one-third of the property, but on condition that not a penny of it was given to Ezekiel.

'You marry Jeremiah, dear,' said Bella. 'I don't want him to marry any of the womenfolk in the neighbourhood. He is wonderfully struck with you, and he has been a good son and a good brother; and although he is a little old, he is not as old as he looks, and I am sure he will make a pattern husband.'

She was only a little woman, but really I found her that good and kind that I almost said 'Yes' to her brother so as to please her; but almost was not quite; and I couldn't properly forgive him for leaving me by myself that first evening. I told him that it would have been just the same if I had been his wife, and that if he wanted to marry me he would have to fetch me from the Western Plains.

'All right, Dorna,' he said, 'you shall go, and I will be at Western Plains with a parson within a month after you arrive there.' So it was settled, and after three weeks' travelling, and a lot of hairbreadth escapes and wonderful adventures, here I am at last at Western Plains, writing about my travels, and in the daily expectation of finding myself face to face with Jeremiah Crumbs.

What I shall say to him when he comes – which I am afraid he will – I cannot tell. I am sure that I don't want to marry him – nor anyone else. It's my belief that one-half the married women have been bothered into it by the men.

I ought to tell you that the last hundred odd miles I travelled by myself. I expected that Marjory's husband would be waiting for me at Yarrabong station, so I sent Ralph and Jansen, the two stockmen, back when we reached the supposed borderline between South and West Australia – no one here knows exactly where they are. I travelled on to Yarrabong alone. You see, it was a great plain country, and when they left me in return, Yarrabong was actually in sight, so that it seemed all right enough. But it is very difficult in gauge distances correctly on these plains. It looked about five miles, but proved to be nearer five and twenty.

However, I must not let myself run on with any details of what I saw that hot afternoon on those great far-reaching prairies, where the grass was on an average five-foot high, for I have to tell you of my next two days' adventures, which will bring my story to a close for the present.

I scared the people at Yarrabong, as well as myself, however, that afternoon over a mirage I saw, which I took for a fearful grass fire, and rode up to the station at a gallop to let them know about it.

I found Yarrabong a queer place. The people are named Twining, and they are the nearest neighbours but one to Marjory and John. They don't rent or own the place, but just squat on the land, and scarcely see a visitor from one year's end to another. There are three brothers of the Twinings, all bachelors, and really not nearly as rough as you might expect. Their father was a shepherd, and the boys managed to save a hundred pounds or so shearing, and bought a hundred head of cattle, and pushed out into the Never Never country. They have an arrangement by which they get mail once a quarter; but they owe allegiance to no Government, and pay no rent. For years they carried their lives in their hands with hostile natives.

John's run is just the same, and is divided from the Twinings' by a strip of desert; but the few sheep they have are shepherded by blacks, and the cattle look after themselves. There is, of course, nothing in the shape of overstocking out here, so the absence of boundaries and fences makes no difference.

I found, on making myself known, that my telegram, which was supposed to have caught their quarterly mail, had not passed through, so John was not there to meet me. It was seventy miles on from there to Western Plains, and I intended to ride that distance by myself. I could, of course, have waited at Yarrabong. Two of the Twinings were at home, and when they knew I was Marjory's sister, and that my brother-in-law, John Holdfast, of Western Plains, was to have met me, they pressed me, in their rough way, to stop for a day or two, and then one of them would ride over with me; but as I learnt that I could have a fresh horse, I persisted on going on the next day, for I had a spell at another place that week.

There was another thing, too. Although the Twinings were kind, and all that, I found out that they had no white women about the place, and I could not feel at home there. The station homestead was just a number of rough slab shanties, with covered ways between them.

I guessed, too, that I had turned the elder of the two brothers out of his sleeping quarters; and although they were hospitality itself, and, in a rough way, did every possible thing to make me feel at home, I could not bear the place.

After an hour or so a black gin,[8] who could talk English very well, was brought in to wait upon me; she had shoes and stockings on, and a neat print gown, and a coloured handkerchief fantastically twined around her woolly head. But the simple creature, in her vanity at being so dressed, let it out at once that she was got up for the occasion, and soon made me know that she thought herself so fine a lady that she could not be expected to do any work. I stumbled over her on one of the verandahs afterward, smoking a

8 A derogatory colonial term for an Aboriginal woman.

short pipe and playing cards with three other blacks. It is a wild, rough life on these interior stations, I can tell you, although I believe the Twinings are better than most.

I determined, therefore, to go on, especially as I learnt that a couple of teams had been through the previous month, and that there had been no rains to destroy their tracks. You see, there are no proper roads out here – just bridle paths from place to place, and these are so little used, and so cut up by cattle and other tracks, that travelling is done by the sun, and compass, and watercourses, and the lay of the country, as much as anything else. Wild horses (brumbies) and wild cattle are occasionally met with, and, when you camp out, it is wise to keep a lookout for dingoes, so you may imagine that the Twinings regarded me as a very daring and extraordinary sort of woman; but I gave them to understand that I was a regular bush girl, and had not had an ordinary bringing-up.

You will wonder, perhaps, how I managed to get along from station to station in this wild country after parting with Bella Crumbs; but you must remember that I had the two stockmen with me until now, and we got introductions from one owner or manager to another, and the sight of a young girl on horseback out in these wild parts put them all in a flutter, so that we had no trouble to borrow horses, or anything we wanted. Then, too, both Mr Crumbs and John Holdfast were known by name; and it is wonderful how hospitable and neighbourly these far western squatters are.

Jim, the elder of the three Twinings, said at last, with great gravity, that he would not think of my going all the way alone, and announced at supper that he should ride with me the next morning as far as his outstation, which was thirty miles on the road, and then he would get his man to put me well upon the road the next day, unless I would prefer for him to come on with me. He said that he had not seen John Holdfast for several months, and would not at all mind the ride over.

So it was arranged, and we left Yarrabong soon after sunrise the next morning, riding regular wiry bush horses. Mr Twining's was a brumby they had broken in, and the horse would look round at me every now and then for the first few miles, and snort at me like a wild thing. I suppose I was the first woman he had ever seen on horseback. Mr Twining had put me upon a splendid blood horse, which he said had won several races, but was as quiet as a lamb, except when ridden fast in company with other horses.

I don't know why that morning ride was so specially impressed upon me, unless that I now, for the first time, began to feel that I was nearing my long and weary journey's end. There was a heavy dew on everything as we passed out of the sliprails of the station paddock by the side of a stockyard, and were at once upon the wild, trackless, fenceless bush.

We rode through a belt of she-oaks, and there was neither road nor track, for the teams previously referred to had left by another set of sliprails. We picked them up later on, and then kept to a bit of a track, for I found that the people here do their best to keep a track marked for general convenience; but I soon saw that I could never have found my way here alone.

'I would like to reach the Rock Wells, if possible, by about eight o'clock,' said Twining; 'but we must not knock the horses up at the start, if you are to get into Western Plains fairly early tomorrow. There is some good sweet grass at the wells, and there is water still there, so we can give the horses a feed and drink, and have some tea and damper for ourselves.'

He talked away, and gave me all sorts of information as to what to do if I was lost, and how to distinguish between cattle tracks which led to and away from water. The outstation we were going to was known as Salt Bush Hollow, where he had a German superintendent and his wife stopping, with a couple of black boys as stockmen. It was a bit of country by a small lagoon – a sort of oasis in a desert – and he had two or three hundred head of cattle there. He said that the chief work of his people was to see that none of the stock was speared by the blacks; there was no fear of their leaving the outstation, as there was always plenty of water and grass.

The country we were now riding over was mostly black and chocolate soil; but there was no water, except in floods; and then, he said, the whole place in a few hours was turned into a great sea.

'How do people escape them?' I asked.

'I will show you,' he said. 'Just on the other side of this flat I was caught in a flood-storm once, and had to camp for three days before the water went down; and the old camp is still there.'

It proved to be a sort of platform about three-foot high, made by pulling logs together and piling them up in a square, and on top of the other, and then putting boughs over them for a support.

'I was for nearly three days,' he said, 'camped on the top of that affair, with my horse tied to a tree, standing in about two feet of water. As soon as it began to fall I started, and had to swim in several of the hollows; and I rode then miles by the sun, without once seeing the colour of the ground until I reached the station fence. That was the worst flood I have known.'

The flies were very bad here and for an hour or so after we had camped at the Rock Wells, where we found good water, and had something to eat. The flies are little black wretches such as are unknown on the coast, and they are terribly troublesome, especially in well-grassed country. All the men wear veils. When we got on to the desert, with nothing but a few spinifex bushes about, they entirely left us; but they came back again when we reached the grass country, which for many square miles surrounds Salt Bush Hollow outstation. They are specially bad for about two or three months during the hot weather – and then look out for sandy blight!

However, we rode into the outstation about midday, and found not a creature at home except a couple of dogs. It was just a rough shanty made of strips of bark, with a lean-to; three rooms in all. The woman was down at the lagoon with her two children, as Mr Twining guessed, doing the family washing, and he rode down to bring her up. The poor creature kissed my hands and cried when she saw me; she hadn't seen a white woman for over eighteen months.

Imagine the sort of lives these people must live out here; and yet it was a pretty situation, for the house was erected upon a rise overlooking a great grassy hollow plain, with the lagoon, which seemed to run itself out into a big swamp at one end, sparkling in the clear atmosphere under the summer sun.

CHAPTER XV

THE WESTERN PLAINS

THE SUPERINTENDENT'S WIFE had me to herself that afternoon, for Mr Twining and her husband went off looking up some cattle. The good woman really made one wonderfully at home and comfortable, and told me all about her past life. She had been a German servant-girl, and had moved from one station to another farther and farther westward, until meeting with a countryman of her own, she fell in love, and rode sixty miles to be married, and then came straight out to this terribly lonely place.

She told me that they had once been for five months without flour in the house; but this was one of the least of her troubles. She was so pleased to have one of her own sex to talk to again that she did not know how to do enough for me.

The next morning Mr Twining accompanied me with the intention of riding through to Western Plains. He explained that there was some rough hilly country, with stony barren ridges, and a strip of yellow sandy clay desert for about five and twenty miles, through which we should have to pass; and that afterwards it was a pretty smart descent to Western Plains.

'Jack Holdfast has a wonderful bit of country out there,' he said, 'and the grandest waterhole in the interior – a regular big lake.'

Somehow that morning I could not help thinking about the old man and Tom and Jackey, and I wondered whether by this time they would have returned to Smoke Island.

A little before midday we came upon a mob of wild horses. The stallion with them snorted and pranced towards us with his long waving tail and great flowing mane and splendid paces; he looked a really grand creature. But Mr Twining unslung his rifle, and looked suspiciously around.

'Those horses ought not to be so far up on the ranges as this,' he said; 'they must have been disturbed by someone; there are likely enough some blacks about.'

'Are the blacks here dangerous?' I asked.

'No, I don't think so,' he replied. 'We always treat them fairly, and they are learning that it is best policy to leave us and our cattle alone; but wait for a minute, there's a track here, I see, which is fresh.'

He jumped off his horse, and examined the ground carefully.

'Why,' he said at last, 'there's someone on in front of us leading a packhorse; a most extraordinary thing that he should have passed the station unknown to anyone. But he cannot be alone.'

After a long and patient examination of the bush in several directions he came back to me and said:

'I have found the tracks of at least two more horsemen. They must have been camped somewhere near the lagoon at Salt Bush Hollow last night, for there is no water within six miles, unless they have come from the Wild Horse Lagoon; but it's queer that they did not call at the outstation. Looking out, I suppose, for land. Confound it! we shall soon get such a population out here that one of these wretched Governments will be sending us a notice to pay them rent.'

'Why do you think there is a packhorse?' I asked.

'Oh, that's easily seen by the tracks,' he answered; 'no two riders would keep together as two of these tracks do. One must be a led horse. We'll push on, however, and find out about them from themselves. It is most extraordinary! unless, like you, they should be making for Western Plains. I generally credit myself with knowing all about anyone travelling in these parts; but I am puzzled, I confess. Two of them are riding shod horses, too.'

We were now riding over thickly treed ranges, and there was no chance of seeing any distance ahead.

My companion was seemingly travelling almost entirely by the sun and the lay of the country.

'If these people are strangers, how is it that they can make their way so confidently through such wild and trackless bush as this?' I asked.

'They have a black with them,' replied my companion, 'and he is evidently a good tracker. They are now following the tracks of the teams; we have only just struck them again, and on these stony ridges it is not so easy to make them out, as they are getting fairly old; but we shall be on to the plains soon, and then you will see them distinctly. Here is a bit of good road, suppose we canter for a while, and see if we cannot catch them up.'

Just as he spoke we heard two reports of a repeating rifle, quickly following each other.

The sound seemed to come from our right, and yet it was evidently some distance ahead.

'They're shooting scrub turkeys for supper, or they would scarcely have fired twice like that; they might have saved themselves the trouble, however, for there are plenty of them and other game near the water which they seem to be making tracks for. They are leaving the Western Plains to the left, and are now riding towards the Blind Stockman's Waterholes on the margin of the Big Desert; but what they want there is a puzzler!'

'Yes, it's a queer name for the waterholes,' he said, in reply to a remark of mine. 'There's a story slung on to it; but let's ride along this spur, and I'll perhaps get some information about these people, and, if I am not mistaken, show you a pretty bit of landscape into the bargain.'

After a quarter of an hour's rough riding we turned around a big projecting rock and came on to the brow of a precipice. A tiny rock platform, which seemed to project right out from the side of the mountainous range into space, afforded just room enough for the horses to stand.

We were above the tops of the highest trees which grew upon the steep hillside below us, and far as the eye could reach there stretched an immense area of rolling downs, almost treeless, and in the far distance, right upon the horizon, at least thirty miles away, was what seemed to me the ocean.

I was so overwhelmed with astonishment that for a few minutes I could not say a word. You may laugh, but you cannot possibly imagine the sensation.

To look down upon that wonderful panorama, after having been boxed up, as it were, among monotonous honeysuckles and gum trees, with dry, hot winds and a limited horizon for nearly a month, was as though the mind had been suddenly released from a sort of prison, and was once more permitted to look out upon the world. I suppose the fact was I missed the bay and the ocean!

Twining was not looking at the landscape, however, but carefully scanned the bush at the base of the range, where he evidently saw something which interested him.

'It will take nearly an hour for me to overtake them,' he said at last; 'but I must find out who they are. I will put you on a spur which you can follow right on to the plain, and then you can easily pick up the teamsters' tracks and jog along, and I will overtake you before you have gone half-a-dozen miles.

'Call the dogs,' he said, referring to two fine animals which he had brought with him, 'and I will tell them that they must go with you until I come.

'Here, Hector! Castor!' and as he called their names he made a gesture to them in my direction, which they evidently perfectly understood, and in a moment he had touched his horse with the spur, and I heard him cantering off through the trees.

I called the dogs, and they came trotting after me as though I was a mob of young cattle they had been left in charge of. They were a queer-looking couple – a sort of cross between a kangaroo and cattle dog – but they were wonderfully intelligent – invaluable for working cattle in wild country.

I have explained that Mr Twining was making a short cut through the bush instead of tracking the party in front of him. He no doubt knew just where he would pick them up. But I was on their tracks, and through a most remarkable incident I found out just where they had turned off to the right, and who they were.

I was walking my horse along, talking to the dogs, when I happened to notice a freshly broken branch to the right of me, and near to it there lay something white – it appeared to be a piece of paper, and I was riding up to see, when one of the dogs leaped forward and brought it to me in his mouth.

It was evidently something which the travellers in front of us had accidentally dropped, for you don't find pieces of paper lying about promiscuously in the bush at this distance from civilization. I slid out of the saddle and took it from the dog.

It was an envelope, and I may say that Robinson Crusoe's astonishment was a very trifling thing, when he saw the footprints in the sand, compared with mine.

It was an empty envelope addressed to 'Aaron Stoneham, Esq., Smoke Island, Moreton Bay'.

I almost fainted at the thought of the narrow escape I had had. The party which Mr Twining had ridden after was none other than the old man, Long Tom, and Jackey.

You may imagine my feelings! I was that upset that it was with the utmost difficulty I mounted my horse again.

To know that those three were within a mile or two of me was terrible. For the time being I was downright sorry that I had not married Mr Crumbs!

I seemed to lose sight of all other considerations in my desire to get as far away from them as possible. Mr Twining never crossed my mind. I determined to push on to Marjory at any risk. Following the spur, the timber became less dense, and opened out as we struck the slope leading on to the plain. Then I zigzagged to and fro until I hit the team tracks. They were quite distinct, and I urged my horse into a smart canter in the direction which they took.

I soon had to pull up, however, for the grass grew in big tussocks, and my nag was several times very near falling, so I pushed on as fast as I dared, turning now and then an anxious glance behind me, expecting every minute to find myself followed by Mr Twining and the party of three.

'What on earth,' I ejaculated, 'do they want out here? Why have they turned off in the direction of the Blind Stockman's Waterholes?' I rode on hour after hour in a state of feverish excitement, followed closely by the two faithful dogs, until the mountainous range behind me seemed to drop nearer to the plain, and the trees in front grew more distinguishable.

I was getting terribly tired, and my horse flinched a bit under the saddle, telling me very plainly that the side-saddle was chafing him. How thankful I was that the teamsters' tracks continued to be fairly well marked. They were like company in that lonely place.

I watched the sun sinking, seemingly more rapidly, toward the horizon, and wondered when I should see the waters on the lake burning beneath its rays. Trees now began to be sprinkled here and there around me, and shut out the distant view; but far as I could see behind me, there was no sign of horsemen, and my nag seemed to pick up a bit, and the tired dogs would now and then run on for a few yards in front, sniffing the air. Although I could see nothing, I knew by the increasing number of the trees and the subdued excitement of the weary animals, that we were nearing our journey's end.

And then I experienced a queer sensation. I believe that for a little while I fell asleep, and rode on in a state of semi-consciousness. I seemed to see endless processions of parties of three passing on each side of me. They made no sound, and spoke no word, but just rode past, gazing at me in mute astonishment, I thought. Then all at once I heard a dog bark, and woke up. On each side of me was the everlasting, park-like, bush scenery, and, underneath, the blacksoil plain; but, instead of the flat, there was a rise in front of us – only a very gentle slope but sufficient to make the westering sun dip for the time being below the horizon. On a level bit of the road we came to a gate. How the sight of it set my heart a-beating! The horse was splendidly broken in – fortunately for me – and pushed his body up close beside for me to unfasten and open it without getting off his back; and when we passed through he pushed his neck against it to close it, and stood there quietly until I had fastened it, and turned his head away.

I don't know what I should have done if he had not done this, for I was so exhausted that I could never have remounted if I had once got off his back.

After riding for another half-hour, a second gate presented itself. And then I do not know how to find words to describe what I felt and saw.

Before me, almost as far as the eye could reach, was a great sheer of clear, rippling water, upon which, within a stone's throw of the shore, a small yacht rose at anchor, with a Union Jack at the masthead, and a dinghy towing behind; and nearer the shore another boat; and to my left a tiny lawn, with a flagstaff, and a garden, and fruit trees and a house – *and Marjory*!

That was the last I remembered, for something happened then, and I woke up to consciousness the next day in bed, after having given Marjory and her husband a great fright, and a night of anxious watching and nursing.

All this, however, occurred more than a week ago, and I am finishing this letter in a dear little room of my own, which has a glass window – you must know that glass is a luxury out here – facing upon the lake. And dear old Marjory is just the same as ever; and she has a splendid husband, and a boy baby, who tyrannizes over the whole homestead, including the aforesaid splendid husband.

Mr Twining turned up next day, and – goodness knows why – has stopped here ever since; but he is returning today, and will take this letter with him, and send it on at the first opportunity.

He overtook the party of three, but could not make anything of them. He said there was a white man and two blacks; and that the first-mentioned told him he was out there on private business, and made it a rule to camp out in preference to calling at stations, where probably they would want to know more about other people's business than he would be inclined to tell. Twining said that he was a sourish customer, but a great fool, or he would not go out there, where, ten chances to one, he would either die of thirst or hunger, or be speared by the blacks.

I have, however, left the most startling piece of news for the postscript. Early this morning three travellers hove in sight; they were none other than Bright Hartley, Sir Charles Dawson, and Captain Buchanan. You should have seen them!

What brings them out here I cannot imagine. The whole thing is the most extraordinary and romantic incident that was ever known. They cannot have come after me, for they were perfectly thunderstruck when they saw me. And the old man out here too, and Long Tom and Jackey, I am expecting every day to see them call up at the station.

All we want now is Jeremiah Crumbs. But I am afraid the poor old chap must have got lost, or been unable to secure a parson, or have been thrown from his horse and died in the bush.

But just imagine now, that we are all of us here in the centre of Australia; I positively can't believe it! But I expect that I shall soon, for Marjory says that, with such a lot of men to feed, she's afraid of the flour running short, and the nearest store is distant about three hundred and sixty miles! However, there's fish, and game, and beef, and mutton in plenty, so we shan't starve. Kindly understand, however, that there is not room for any more Stoneham girls at present out here at Western Plains.

Your affectionate sister,
DORNA.

CHAPTER XVI

BEULAH LAND[9]

THE SINGULAR EFFECT which the sight of a great expanse of water has upon the mind of anyone who has long dwelt or travelled in the hot interior of Australia has been suggested in Dorna's letter, recorded in the previous chapter.

Hartley had experienced it before; for a hundred miles outside of fences, gates, and sliprails, is a very fair example of all the other hundreds of miles until civilization is once more reached on the shores of the great Indian Ocean; but to Sir Charles Dawson and Captain Buchanan it was a new, and, after the first few days, not altogether pleasant experience.

The awesome *silence* of the Australian bush is one of the first things to impress the observant traveller. Animated nature near at hand is, of course, quiet; but there are no distant sounds, as in African and Indian jungles. The warm, dry air, fragrant with the peculiar odour of

---

9 See John Bunyan's *Pilgrim's Progress* (1678): 'by this time the pilgrims were got over the Enchanted Ground, and entering into the country of Beulah, whose air was very sweet and pleasant . . .'

myriads of gum and other eucalyptus trees, is perfectly voiceless; in fact, the silence is remarkable, for, except near a watercourse, where a current of air is always moving, there is no 'sound of a going' in the topmost branches of the trees. The perfect stillness is deathlike; as though nature stood around compassionating your hardihood in having penetrated into those vast monotonous solitudes, where so many thousands have died raving mad of thirst and hunger.

The monotony of the landscape also assists, in the first instance, to make Australian interior travelling positively gruesome to the inexperienced. There is the same bush track, or no track at all; the same species of trees, the same hot sun, the same dried-up water-courses, the same general characteristics of the country; no extended view of landscape; but, like the mill horse, plodding around and around in a monotonous track, the traveller feels as though the whole world had been turned into an interminable series of flats and ridges, planted with the same blue and white and red gums, and stunted undergrowth.

For the sake of brevity, we pass over the incidents of the long journey of Hartley and his friends from the Barcoo station, where they left their buggy. For the first week afterward they had a stockman with them in charge of the packhorses; but, for sundry reasons, they then sent him back, and drove the three spare horses with packsaddles themselves. The horses, however, jogged along without trouble; more often than not in single file.

It said something for Hartley's bushmanship that, with comparatively no loss or disaster, they had reached the Western Plains.

'Did you ever see anything like this in your life?' said he to his friends, pointing to the lake, on the day following their arrival.

They were strolling around for a smoke and confidential yarn, and stood together on a rocky eminence which overlooked the lake. A fresh wind was blowing toward them, and they could hear the dash of the waves below them, like the roar of breakers on the beach of a miniature sea.

'It's simply grand,' exclaimed Sir Charles, 'after the frightful monotony of that dry bush journey. I am not surprised now, Hartley, that you brought a spade. I wonder whether we shall ever get safely back again to the seaboard?'

Buchanan was silent; but Hartley replied, with animation, 'Look here, my dear sir, what we have gone through is not a circumstance compared with what we have before us; but we are in luck – far more so than I ever expected. To come through without the loss of a horse, or being bushed for a single day, is wonderful; but to find a place like this – practically ready-made – as a base of operations, is luck that I never expected.'

'My own opinion,' said Buchanan, 'is that we ought to remain here for a week, and thoroughly recruit. If what Hartley says is correct, we have an adventure before us which must involve great physical strain and no little hardship, and we ought to thoroughly explore the lake, and get to understand as much as possible of the blacks, and of our general surroundings, before we push out into the desert.'

'A spell will certainly do the horses no harm,' said Hartley.

'But I doubt whether we can take them,' said Buchanan. 'Holdfast has been telling me that to the north-west there are hundreds of miles of desert, and there will be absolutely nothing for them to eat.'

'We may be able to skip the desert,' said Hartley, 'or find edible trees or shrubs, sufficient, at any rate, to keep them alive. We will certainly take them as far as we can – you can buy fresh horses, but you cannot buy fresh legs. A bushman, you know, never spares his horse when it is a question between the horse and himself. We had a fellow lost off my Barcoo station for a week, and I'm blest if he didn't cut a steak out of his horse's flank and eat it, and then plastered the wound up with clay, and rode the horse twenty-five miles into the station. It was a desperate thing to do, but the fellow saved his own life, and the horse seemed very little the worse for it.'

'I am afraid that we shall be trespassing upon the hospitality of these good people,' said Sir Charles.

'Don't trouble yourself about that,' remarked Hartley. 'To entertain strangers without murmuring is one of the unwritten laws of the Australian bush; besides, we can keep them well-supplied with fish and game while we are here, which will help to pay for our board. Then, too, that team of mine should be through in a fortnight or three weeks with ample supplies to make up for the cost of our living.'

They had heard Dorna's story, and the knowledge that Stoneham was somewhere in the neighbourhood, accompanied by two blacks, all of whom might be regarded as unfriendly, was the principal source of apprehension.

'Confound it!' exclaimed Hartley, looking far more serious than he had done before, 'I don't half-like Stoneham's being out here with those blacks. They may be connected with others, and we shall probably find ourselves surrounded by a whole tribe of hostile natives some evening just about sundown, and with Stoneham acting as guide, philosopher, and friend to them, we would have a rough time. John Holdfast must know all about the country and the blacks; now, I propose that we take him into our confidence, and ask him to make one of the party. We might, if necessary, offer him a lump sum as compensation for lost time, and a share in anything we may discover.'

'Do you think he knows that his father-in-law is in this part of the country?' asked Buchanan.

'By George! these are remarkable girls,' exclaimed Hartley, voicing the thought which had arisen in his mind, rather than attempting to answer the question. 'They can be as quiet as the grave about anything, if necessary; but I fancy that both Holdfast and his wife know just as much as does Miss Dorna Stoneham.'

'But would Holdfast be willing to leave his womenfolk here without protection, in case of the place being attacked by blacks?' suggested Sir Charles.

'I think he would go,' replied Hartley, thoughtfully. 'They have a married couple and a boy, besides the regular station blacks, some of whom are occasionally hired on wages; and now Dorna has come, she is as good as another man.'

'It's a puzzle to me how people can live out here,' said the baronet. 'It's a bit of wonderful country, I own, and with that broad breezy lake in front you almost forget that you are in the interior of a continent; but think of the weary journey to get here, and the isolated life.'

'Use is second nature,' replied Hartley. 'Station people generally get so attached to the life that, even when they do visit a town, they soon get homesick for the bush again; and, really, when you are in the bush, a few hundred miles further west does not make much difference. Especially if it brings you to such a place as this.

'I can scarcely believe myself that we are where we know ourselves to be. But we'll have to explore this lake before we make another start. Holdfast says the blacks are ugly and awkward on the other side, and that he has never penetrated to the northern extremity, but he believes that it runs up north for about forty miles. We might make a trip in that direction tomorrow. A wind like this would take us up grandly.'

'Do you think Holdfast is altogether friendly?' said Buchanan.

'He will be more so, I think, if we tell him what we are after,' replied Hartley.

'Why?' asked Sir Charles, puffing away vigorously at his pipe.

'Do you see how comfortable all the surroundings of this place are?' said Hartley, replying to the question by asking another.

His two companions nodded.

'Well, you don't think that it is wool, and fat stock, and hides, and tallow that does it?'

'What else can it be?' said Buchanan.

'I'll tell you,' said Hartley. 'It's the same kind of stuff that we have come out here looking after – it's diamonds and gold dust; and he gets them from the blacks. That yacht is part of his commercial equipment. I found it out this morning by accident. And I think the sooner we take him thoroughly into our confidence the better; and we must give him to perfectly understand that we won't interfere with his affairs, nor let on that we know anything. He is the very fellow to make one for the trip to the path of Zoo-zoo.

'That reminds me,' he said, and with the words he drew a field glass from his pocket, and carefully scanned the north-western horizon.

'Look!' he exclaimed excitedly, 'we can't very well go wrong. With the glass you can just catch the cloud-like summit of the White Mountains. They are in the direction of "*the setting sun of winter*"; and I'd swear that the great desert which they talk about is under water in a wet season. You remember what the legend of the boomerang said about "*Beware of the great waters!*"'

The three men sat down on the short herbage, and smoked for a long time after this in silence, looking away across the broad expanse of water in the direction of their quest. Hartley's thoughts occasionally, however, wandered off from the details of their adventures to Dorna, and he mused in astonishment upon her marvellous ride. He had heard something, too, about the kindness of Jeremiah Crumbs, and he had seen for himself the sheepish looks of Jim Twining; but he was eminently practical, and decided to chance the risk of anyone else winning her, and defer any further attempts at love-making until his return from their adventure; but Cupid has ever been wilful, and it was a dangerous risk for Hartley to remain for a whole week under the same roof with Dorna. 'I don't believe it would be safe for me to fall further in love with her yet,' he said to himself; 'it might change my luck!'

Sir Charles Dawson was also thinking – but not of Australian eyes, nor lips, nor dimples, but of home. Somehow he was sorry now that he had allowed himself to be persuaded into this adventure, for he had a presentiment of approaching ill. The sight of that cool inland sea, after the long journey through the bush, had awakened memories of the old land – of a mountain lake near to his ancestral mansion, where the solemn shadows of great mountains stretched themselves upon the waters at early morn and dewy eve. In that quiet lake district there was an English girl who was no horsewoman, but who was delicate in health, and timid as a fawn; and yet she was very dear to him, and there was nothing in the beauty of Australian women or Australian scenery, by bush, or lake, or sea, which pleased his fancy as did that mental picture of the home and love beyond the sea. 'I'll write my book,' he said to himself, 'if I ever get back from this immensity of bush and desert alive; but it will be my first and last book upon Australia.'

Buchanan's thoughts were the darkest of the three; and alas! well they might be, for Stoneham was his uncle, and the murderer of his mother, and the despoiler of his own happiness and estate; and he had sworn, in an hour of not unnatural bitterness, to force him to make reparation for the many wrongs he had done to himself and his family, even at the peril of his life. But this was not yet known to his companions. He had stumbled upon Stoneham by accident in Moreton Bay, and very singularly he had disclosed what he knew about the path of Zoo-zoo before either was aware of the other's identity; but since the encounter on the sandbank, Buchanan had brooded darkly upon revenge, and his thoughts were continually with Stoneham and his black attendants. He was in no hurry, however; he could afford to wait his time, for Stoneham was bound for the same place as themselves, and they were certain to meet somewhere upon the path, or near the ancient dwelling place of Zoo-zoo.

'I believe Dorna Stoneham has named this bit of country "Beulah Land",' said Hartley, breaking the long silence. 'It is no doubt a wonderful place – a regular oasis in a desert; but who knows what there is beyond those White Mountains. If the whiteness is caused by snow, there must be rivulets and rivers and fertility on the other side. I should not be surprised, now, to find that a river is feeding this lake at the northern end.'

'But if there was, Holdfast would have heard about it from the blacks; and he says that there is nothing in that direction but a desert,' said Sir Charles.

'That's true,' replied Hartley; 'but my opinion is that there is a good bit to be found out yet about this lake. A great sheet of water such as this is bound to have feeders. Now, here's an idea,' continued Hartley, addressing himself to Sir Charles, 'that you might put into your book. This continent contains all the natural conditions necessary for the formation of a great and productive country; but they need to be manipulated artificially by the intelligence and industry of man. You have splendid land, but in many parts no water, except by boring for it. Things generally are dumped down grotesquely; but all the ingredients of success are present, and money, brains, and industry will bring them together, and yet transform the interior of this country. It is my belief that, like the United States of America, every portion of it will one day be settled and cultivated.'

'Very likely,' said Buchanan; 'but we shall none of us be here to see it. But let us go and find out if lunch is ready,' he said, getting upon his feet, 'and we can then have a chat with Jack Holdfast.'

CHAPTER XVII

A Mysterious Track

THE DINING ROOM in which the family and visitors gathered for lunch was the principal apartment of the station premises. Sitting within, one could scarcely have imagined that the materials of which the house was constructed were so primitive. It was papered with ordinary wallpaper, the ceiling being covered with a very light marble, the whole being pasted upon canvas. A fair-sized door opened upon a wide verandah, and windows without glass, but with strong swing shutters, and reed blinds on the inside, gave ample light.

The dwelling was constructed of roughly split timber and saplings, made weather-tight on roof and walls with large sheets of stringy bark. There was very little sawn timber anywhere about it, and what there was had been cut by hand; but Jack Holdfast had at this time been squatting at Western Plains for over seven years, and for three of them had been married. The whole place and its surroundings surprised everyone who saw it, for Marjory was as tasteful in arranging her somewhat primitive household furniture as her husband was handy with his tools. Compared with Twining's place, and other residences within two or three hundred miles, this Western Plains station, although the farthest of any from civilization, was a luxurious mansion.

Things generally would have been far rougher, but since Marjory's arrival the gold dust and diamond trade with the blacks had assumed considerable proportions, and, unknown to any of his neighbours, Holdfast was a wealthy man. Money for such pleasures or comforts or luxuries as they wanted was really no object. He had brought two shipwrights up with materials, at an extravagant cost, to help build his yacht and boats; and latterly he had two bullock teams continually upon the road, when travelling was possible, to fetch supplies for the use of the station. He would have bought the freehold of his homestead, but it seemed so unlikely that he should be disturbed; and then he was far from being sure as to exactly which of the Australian colonies he was resident in. The advent of Dorna and our three travellers was the first serious intimation he had that he might find himself necessitated to protect himself against possible intruders.

The lunch was a light, pleasant repast, to be followed by the regular dinner at sundown; and the men walked down to the stockyard afterward to look at the horses, which had just been run up.

As they went Hartley gave Holdfast a fair idea of the business which had brought them to Western Plains.

John Holdfast was a tall, thin individual, an expert bushman, and ideal pioneer squatter. Tough, wiry, and dexterous, he had pushed farther and farther west, until at eight and thirty years of age he was known as one of the smartest of the adventurous band who, reckless of danger, had made homes for themselves in the very heart of the continent. He could track like a native, was a dead shot, and a fearless rider; in fact, he possessed a remarkable combination of that knowledge, skill, and experience, which alone had enabled him to hold his own with the varied aspects of wild nature in that far-off spot.

'There's a mob of brumbies, I hear, camped about eight miles out. I want to clear them off; they become troublesome when they get too near the homestead,' said Holdfast.

Saddles and bridles were soon forthcoming, and the party rode off from the yards by a track along the lake, and passed out of the paddocks into the bush. After a while the track entirely disappeared, and they rode along through the lightly timbered country.

'This is a very remarkable thing you have told me,' said Holdfast, when they had passed out of the paddocks, 'and I may say at once that I am willing to go with you, and take a share of what may be found at the end of the path of Zoo-zoo. It will, likely enough, mean at least a month away; but it's my off season, so that will not matter much. I have often wondered what there is at the end of the Big Desert, and it will be far safer for a fair-sized party to go together. Besides, what you have told me seems to partly explain something which has often puzzled me – and others too. There's a mystery out here which has been the topic of many a conversation on the yacht and by camp-fires, and I think that if we make up a sufficiently strong party we may fathom it.'

'What's that?' inquired Hartley.

'Hist!' said Holdfast.

His experienced eye had caught signs of the tracks of the mob of wild horses he was in search of.

They now fell into single file behind him as he tracked the brumbies through the bush.

Lifting his hand presently, he turned his mare, and told them to follow quietly, and they might see some sport. Fifty yards nearer, the mob, which comprised a stallion and half-a-dozen mares, could be seen quietly feeding. The mare Holdfast was riding was evidently interested, for she pricked up her ears and trembled slightly. They had just reached an unusually large tree, which had been partially burnt in a bushfire.

Dismounting, Holdfast unfastened the girth and crupper, and took off both saddle and bridle, and let the mare go. She walked leisurely in the direction of the mob, and, after a few minutes, whinnied, and then commenced to bite at the grass.

The party were now sheltered behind cover. Holdfast, down on one knee, with a repeating rifle ready to raise to his shoulder, watched the brumbies as they lifted their heads curiously and looked toward the new arrival.

Susan – for that was the name of Holdfast's mare – had been broken into the business, and, instead of trotting across to them, stood still.

'Whoa, lass!' said Holdfast; and at the familiar voice she put her head down and began to feed.

The stallion immediately trotted over to her, and the rifle was raised to Holdfast's shoulder; but the mare was between him and the stallion.

A few seconds of anxious waiting, and the mare put back her ears to bite at him, and he wheeled round. Instantly a report rang through the bush sharp and clear, immediately followed by another, and the fine animal dropped to the ground, with the bone shattered in the fore and hind legs. The horses were at least a hundred yards distant.

The stallion gave a sharp cry as Holdfast's second shot hit him; but, having dropped with his legs under him, still kept his head erect, as though more confused than hurt by what had happened.

The mares scampered off at the noise of the gun, but only for a few yards, when they wheeled round again. Holdfast's mare stood quietly all this time by the side of the wounded stallion, and the mares came cautiously back, and one by one were ultimately shot down by Holdfast's deadly weapon. He then gave a peculiar call, at which Susan returned to her master.

'You're a wonderful shot!' said Sir Charles, as they gathered round the dead brumbies; 'and that's a marvellous mare you have.'

'You can teach any intelligent animal anything if you can have it entirely alone,' he answered. 'I was for months here, and this mare heard only my voice – was fed and watched and groomed by myself, and made a friend of. You know, a bit of sweet corn, kindness, and firmness will go a long way with most animals. No one ever rides her except myself; in fact, I don't believe she would let any other man remain long on her back.'

'Why, she's as quiet as a sheep!' exclaimed Hartley, laughing.

'I'll bet you a five-pound note,' said Holdfast, 'that you cannot keep for three minutes on her back!'

'Done!' cried Hartley.

'Don't be a fool, Hartley!' said Buchanan. 'Don't you see the thing is as full of tricks as a bagful of monkeys?'

'No; she has no tricks,' said Holdfast. 'But any horse long accustomed to be ridden by only one man will kick up if a stranger gets into the saddle.'

'There's five pounds on it, however,' cried Hartley. 'So here goes!'

Taking the reins in his left hand, he placed it on the mare's mane, and swung himself into the saddle. He at once sat well down, and gripped the pads firmly with his knees.

For a moment Susan stood perfectly still, as though overcome by the suddenness of the thing; and Hartley shook the reins to suggest that she should move on.

At that, however, Susan laid her ears back, until they seemed to be a part of her head; then down it went with a vicious jerk, and all four of her legs seemed to leave the ground at once.

Hartley was by no means a bad rider, and for a few moments he pluckily kept his seat, until a combined rear, kick, and jump seemed to throw him clear of the saddle right into the air, spread-eagle fashion, after which he alighted across the carcase of a dead brumby.

He immediately picked himself up, very little hurt, amid the laughter of his companions, while Susan once more stood demurely by, as though the last scene had only been a portion of a frequently rehearsed performance.

When Holdfast saw that Hartley was not hurt, he flung the reins on the mare's neck, and put his foot into the stirrup.

'She'll fling you next, old man,' laughed Buchanan.

'No fear,' said Holdfast. 'That's a trick which almost any animal will do if allowed to become used to one rider. But let us get along, and I will show you the mystery of the Western Plains.'

The grass was now waving around them in luxuriant greenness.

'It's like a wheatfield,' said Holdfast; 'but I have seen it as bare as a board in a drought. And yet there never need be a drought in this country.'

'Why?' asked Sir Charles.

'Because the water of the lake is above the level of this part of the plain, and by simple gravitation thousands of acres might be irrigated.'

'How do you account for that?' asked Hartley, who had recovered again, and seemed struck with the possibilities suggested by Holdfast's words.

'I cannot account for it,' he answered. 'The lake is too large to be the crater of an extinct volcano, or anything of that sort; but there's the fact, for I have roughly taken the levels. The water in the lake never varies in height, winter or summer, and is at least a foot higher than hundreds of square miles of this country.'

'Does it ever rain here?' asked Buchanan.

'You bet!' was Holdfast's laconic answer.

They now came to a sudden depression, with a gradual fall in the surface of the plain of two or three feet, and were immediately confronted with a vast stretch of yellow loamy sand, upon which there grew a few sage bushes; but further away to the north-west even these disappeared, and the hot afternoon sun shone sweltering down upon a vast spreading landscape of desolation. The mountains which had been made out with Hartley's field glass from the eminence near the lake were not visible.

The trees which lined the banks could be followed for some distance to the left; but due north it was a desert, the first sight of which had much the same effect upon the minds of the three travellers as does the first sight of the ocean. The same melancholy, the same mystery, and, to some extent, the same majesty; but it was a desert – treeless, houseless, fenceless, a veritable sea of solitude and death.

'How far is it across?' asked Hartley, breaking the silence.

'No one knows,' replied Holdfast. 'If anyone ever explored it they have not returned again to tell.

'But,' said he, 'let us ride along the border of the desert, and I will show you something.'

It was most remarkable how the clearly defined line of demarcation was continued for miles between the grassland and the barren sandy loam. The arid, lifeless condition was probably caused by its being strongly impregnated with some mineral; but it was as though a line had actually been drawn east and west, upon one side of which there was luxuriant fertility, and upon the other only barrenness.

Suddenly Holdfast drew in his mare, and backing her upon the grass, pointed with his hand to the ground just in front of him, and then due north.

There was a plainly defined track, some three feet wide, reaching away into the wilderness. It was hollowed out, as though the feet of countless multitudes had passed in sad procession along it into the desolation, and by some strange peculiarity the eye was enabled to follow it almost as far as anything could be distinguished.

'That bush track has puzzled every one of us,' said Holdfast. 'Who made it, where it leads to, and how it is that dust storms or rain have not obliterated it, no one knows. I discovered it five years ago, and it has been the same ever since; but that's the direction we shall have to take next week, if you are still determined to continue your journey. I have been thinking it over all the afternoon, and it strikes me that that is none other than "The path of Zoo-zoo".

CHAPTER XVIII

An Adventurous Cruise

AFTER DINNER THAT night there was a council of war, in which both Marjory and Dorna participated. It was held in the bright moonlight, which, in front of the house, glittered upon the still waters of the lake (for there was very little wind blowing), and cast long shadows over the garden walks and lawns, and among the outbuildings and trees. The yacht and boats moored near the jetty, and every feature of the landscape was brightly illuminated.

'The worst of moonlight,' said Hartley, 'is that it casts such deep shadows; one hardly knows whether it is a fallen tree or shadow in front of you when you are riding fast.'

'You should leave that to your horse,' said Holdfast.

'Ah, but suppose there's a buggy at the back of your horse, how then?' exclaimed Hartley.

'Yes,' drawled Holdfast, 'it's awkward then, I allow; but there is not such a thing as a buggy within three hundred miles of us, so we won't bother about that. I would not mind doing sixty or eighty miles, however, on a good horse a night like this.'

'On Susan, for instance,' suggested Buchanan.

'No, not on Susan,' laughed Holdfast. 'She's good as gold for her proper work, and she can put in a good long day too, with an easygoing amble that would astonish you; but I have a horse here, with a bit of Arab blood in him, we call Fleetfoot, and I've done seventy miles on him in six hours and a half; but that's a yarn I must tell you another day. If I don't mistake the look of the weather, we shall have plenty of wind before morning, and I would suggest that, after we have a good all-round talk about the trip to the White Mountains, we get the yacht provisioned for the run to the northern end of the lake tomorrow, so as to start as early as possible in the morning. It's all unknown country, and you cannot tell what adventures may be met with.'

'How is it that you have never explored that portion of the lake?' asked Sir Charles.

'Well, you see, I generally take a couple of black boys with me to help to navigate the yacht, and about ten miles up there is a curious rock, which rises up from the lake, and beyond that it is all "taboo" to them. Besides, with only five people on the place, and two of them women, I did not care to run unnecessary risks; there may be other rocks, although I don't think so, for the lake is very deep at that end, and the water is singularly cold, even in the height of summer, and there is a perceptible current. But let us leave that now, and begin from the beginning. If Mrs Holdfast and her sister are to be left to take care of the station while we are away, they have a right to know all about our plans, and have some voice in the matter too.'

Jack Holdfast was always thoroughly loyal to his wife.

The whole story of the inscribed boomerang was told by Hartley amid an almost breathless silence, for Dorna and Marjory now heard it for the first time. Hartley kept nothing back, even referring to the enmity which so evidently existed between Stoneham and Buchanan, and hinted that this part of the business Captain Buchanan might feel inclined to throw some light on.

'Anyhow, it is clear,' said Hartley, 'that Aaron Stoneham and his black boys are out here on the same lay as ourselves, and that if he meets with us he won't be exactly friendly.'

'So that is what has brought him here?' said Dorna, with a sigh.

'He must be dead,' ejaculated Sir Charles. 'He would never make his way across that scorching wilderness.'

'I don't know so much about that,' said Holdfast. 'Those blacks are devils in a dry country; they are up to dodges and expedients to save their skins which few white men would think of. My opinion is that we shall do well to keep our eyes open and our powder dry, when we go ashore at the north end of the lake tomorrow.'

At last Marjory spoke. She was willing for John to go if he was satisfied with the project after he had been on the north-shore end of the lake; but there was an undertone in her speech which plainly said, 'John, don't go.' However, they sat and talked until nearly midnight, and then the men decided to carry down some further stores, and arrange for the boy Jim to sleep on board, and call them an hour before daylight.

'We all know how to handle the yacht,' said Holdfast, 'so if we want more sleep we can take a watch below while running up the lake. I shall keep well out in deep water.'

The first streak of dawn was in the east when Marjory poured out the coffee for them, and Holdfast reported that everything was ready for a start.

'Marjory and myself are going with you,' said Dorna to Hartley.

'I am sure that I am delighted,' said that gentleman, somewhat taken aback, however.

'I have no doubt you are,' said Dorna; 'but my sister is going to bring the baby.'

'Splendid!' exclaimed Sir Charles.

'Don't you believe her!' said Marjory, laughing. 'His infant highness will remain in the custody of Mrs Bennett, who is a good nurse, and can manage him well. We shall not give you any trouble, and we shall both bring rifles, so we shall be quite a formidable party.'

The wind came, just as Holdfast said it would be, a regularly strong south-westerly, and the yacht, *Marjory Holdfast* – for that's what was neatly painted on the prow and stern – made good headway, with a free wind on the quarter.

'We shall have to sail her close-hauled coming back,' said Holdfast.

'If we get back,' said Buchanan; 'the shoreline seems to run north-easterly from here, and we may have it right in our teeth.'

'Oh, there's no fear of being stuck so long as some wind is blowing,' said Holdfast. 'We have room enough surely to work our way back again, however the wind may be.'

They were now nearer to the western shore of the lake, and the view was becoming increasingly picturesque. A ridge seemed to have been broken off abruptly, and its huge fragments literally tumbled one over the other in gigantic masses of rock into the water. A quick imagination might have conjured up towers and castles and ruins from amid the singular scenery, which at irregular distances was covered with stunted trees.

'We are now in the taboo country,' said Holdfast. 'Debble debble lives up here, according to the black boys. I was sailing in this direction one day, and the two boys I had with me threatened to jump overboard and swim ashore if I did not put back. I should not at all wonder if there is not some natural phenomenon farther on, which gives this place an ill look to them. I think we might as well slacken sail and take soundings.'

'What is the length of your line?' said Hartley.

'Fifty fathoms,' replied Holdfast.

'Then you'll get no soundings,' said Hartley.

This actually proved to be the case. They had now run some five and twenty miles, and the stretch of water had suddenly narrowed to a kind of strait not more than a mile and a half across. Precipitous peaks rose on each side of them, great bluff rocks running up in places sheer out of the water. The whole scene was most wild and picturesque, especially as they proceeded, when a number of small islands gradually hove in sight. Navigation, of course, became more difficult, but the water continued to be of great depth and of astonishing coldness. Dorna averred that there could be no fish in it, or they would take a fatal chill.

'How can a cold-blooded thing like a fish take cold, Miss Stoneham?' asked Hartley.

'Now, Mr Hartley, don't please pretend to know anything about the fish in this lake. They must have been here from the beginning of the world, and are, doubtless, different to every other kind of fish you ever met with.'

Just then a glistening monster leaped up in front of the yacht.

'I beg your pardon, Miss Stoneham. I don't profess to understand them; but the one that just jumped out to get a breath of fresh air evidently had not caught cold.'

'Ah, but you saw the size of him,' retorted Dorna. 'That must be the sole survivor – the exception which proves the rule.'

'He'll catch cold yet,' said Buchanan, leaning over and splashing his hand in the water. 'It is, no doubt, remarkably cold, and decidedly damp.'

They were now sailing close in to the eastern shore, which was covered with dense undergrowth, when suddenly the crack of a rifle was heard, and a bullet struck the water only a few feet from the yacht.

The astonishment of the party was complete, as shot followed shot, one or two whizzing unpleasantly near to them. As by instinct, they all of them dropped down into the cushioned well of the yacht, except Holdfast, who sheltered himself behind the mast, and keenly watched the shore.

Hartley, who was steering, at once turned her bows away from the land.

'It's Stoneham!' ejaculated Buchanan, and he grasped a rifle which lay near him, and was about to lift it and aim; but a glance at the two sisters was sufficient to deter him, and he dropped the muzzle.

'That was pesky close,' said Holdfast. 'We'll have to give that shore a wide berth coming back. It's a good twelve miles from here, I should think, to the northern extremity, where we propose to land, so there is no likelihood of our having a second edition of the episode.'

'There were two rifles fired,' said Buchanan.

'It's the old man,' said Dorna to Marjory. 'There will be bloodshed before this miserable affair is done with.'

'But if they are following the path of Zoo-zoo, what brings them here?' replied Marjory.

'No good,' said Dorna, the old look which so often had darkened her face at Smoke Island showing itself.

'Marjory,' she said, 'I would sooner die than shoot the old man; but I would put a bullet through those miserable blacks he has with him as soon as I would look at them. There will be trouble before this is over.'

The four men were now in close conference. Holdfast assured them that there was not a breech-loading or repeating rifle (if any rifle at all) in the hands of the blacks in the district. It could be no one else but Stoneham.

'If we were alone,' said Buchanan, significantly, 'it would have been better to have landed, and have it out at once. We are bound to meet them before this is over.'

They were all agreed on this, and were thoroughly perplexed as to what had kept Stoneham so long hanging about.

'Do you think that he has been there, and come back again?' suggested Sir Charles.

'Not possible,' said Holdfast.

The wind was blowing fresh, and the yacht made good sailing, so they had no further fear of dangerous missiles from the shore; and as they expected to land in another hour, Dorna and her sister prepared an early lunch.

The skilful contrivances of the yacht were now shown to advantage, for a fair-sized table was rigged, and as they had the wind almost abaft, and were sailing on an even keel, it could be laid without any need for 'fiddles', or danger of broken crockery. They were soon enjoying a savoury meal, for the keen morning air had sharpened their appetites.

Hartley had secured a seat near to Dorna; but it was noticeable that Buchanan seemed also inclined to be attentive to that young lady. She, no doubt, appeared to advantage in a coquettish liberty cap and semi-sailor costume. The morning was delightfully fine, and the fresh breeze tempered the hot sun. There was an exhilarating sense of novelty, for the scenery of the lake on both shores had become decidedly romantic, and, notwithstanding the recent *contretemps*, the party was an animated one, for the presence of Stoneham and his antipathy was no secret to any of them.

'How do you think those three on shore are managing for provisions?' asked Hartley of Holdfast.

'There's plenty of game around the lake,' said the latter; 'and they must have brought flour and sugar and tea with them on the packhorse. But they will soon be running short, unless they are careful; and it's a risky thing for them to attempt to cross that desert unless they are well-provisioned. They are no doubt making their way slowly to the head of the lake, and then intend to strike across the desert from there to the White Mountains. Not a bad idea either!'

'How far should you imagine it to be?' asked Sir Charles.

'About two hundred miles,' replied Holdfast. 'If there was water anywhere on the road, one could ride that distance without grass, with a bit of corn; but the water settles it. I think, however, that I have hit upon a plan; but we shall have to cross the desert on foot – that is, after the first day.'

Dorna and Marjory had become unusually quiet. The presence of their father, and his determined attempt to commit a cold-blooded murder – for they felt it to be nothing else – was an unpleasant subject for thought. But the scenery around them absorbed their attention, for it was every minute becoming more singular and fantastic. The shorelines were rapidly closing together, and it seemed as though the lake terminated in the distance in a kind of narrow bay or creek. The foliage was diminishing, too, upon the shore; and through openings in the trees it could be seen that the country around this end of the lake was barren and desolate.

'What a remarkable formation!' cried Hartley, a quarter of an hour afterward.

They were sailing into a gorge with low, precipitous cliffs, seemingly of trap or limestone, on each side of them, which narrowed in until they were not more than three hundred yards apart. The water was evidently very deep, and as they glided along the silence was startling. They were the first explorers who had ever sailed into that remarkable natural port.

'You might imagine that it was a long succession of wharves,' said Sir Charles.

'Yes,' said Holdfast. 'One can scarcely believe that those square sides and surfaces were fashioned like that by nature.'

'This explains why the blacks avoid the place,' said Hartley. 'It looks as though giants had been at work piling up these huge square causeways.'

The head of the gorge presently appeared, but the cliffs then vanished, and the appearance was that of an artificial landing stage hewn out of the solid rock. It was not three feet above the surface of the water, and formed a natural wharf of square blocks of perfectly smooth stone.

'It reminds me of the natural pavement at Port Arthur, down in Tasmania,' said Sir Charles.

They were but a few yards from shore when the sails were dropped, and there should have been plenty of way on the boat to have carried her right up to the landing place, but in a few minutes they found themselves at a standstill.

'There must be a remarkable current here!' cried Holdfast, in astonishment.

The big oars were got out, and it took some vigorous pulling to bring them to the shore.

'What is your explanation of it, Holdfast?' said Hartley, as the individual addressed ran out the sounding line fathom after fathom without getting bottom.

'It's plain enough, I think; the weight and line are being carried out by a strong bottom current. There must be a great underground river, which at this point runs into the lake.'

The whole surroundings of the spot on which they had landed were certainly most fantastic and remarkable. In front of them, and as far as the eye could reach, was the great sandy desert, and for miles on each side of the gorge were the square-shaped rocks.

'I don't wonder that the blacks have tabooed this place,' said Holdfast. 'The water is the only redeeming feature about it. I'm hanged if I should care to have to camp here alone. It's the most weird, uncanny-looking bit of scenery I have ever put eyes on in Australia.'

'And yet you are willing to go yonder with us,' said Buchanan, pointing across the hot desert.

'I shall have to think that over again,' said Holdfast; 'but men will go into queer spots, won't they, when there's the prospect of adventure and *gold*?'

CHAPTER XIX

A Party of Four

I T MAY BE said by the more youthful readers of this story that, so far, there has been but little love in it. The statement is doubtless true, but at the same time the picture of life presented in this narrative is a correct one.

Love, such as poets sing of, and with which painters seek to glorify the features of their ideals, and which all true men and women at some time of their lives long for, is a rare exotic, a flower of peerless beauty, which, like the aloe, blossoms only at rare intervals. Happy is that woman who is desired by a true heart-mate with a supreme desire. Who finds one absolutely meet to unfold and enjoy her womanhood, as she his manhood. Heart-mates who delight each in each after the rapture of passion is over, and when the keen eye of knowledge and experience discerns the naked soul. But few are gifted with the genius of love, although there are thousands and millions who walk together with mutual and wholesome satisfaction in the paths of wedded life. Happy, indeed, are they who find each in each, forever, the other's one all-satisfying supreme desire.

Certainly, so far, Dorna had not found her heart-mate. Hartley admired her, and in some degree, no doubt, loved her, but he was a man of the world, versed in the tricks of trade and the diplomacy of finance and the intrigues of life. He knew well what the average woman was, and had gauged her shallowness and measured the little circumference of her life. Not that he blamed her for it, for he knew that she was mostly what custom and society had made her; but in Dorna he saw a woman of nature, who had communed with that great teacher of the soul in its many wonderfully varied forms.

For Dorna possessed, in a large degree, the strength and the weakness of that great environment of night and day and land and sea which she had been familiar with from childhood. In some moods she was rude and rough and reckless, but in others as gentle as the summer light and evening dews. And Hartley knew it, and was attracted by the very novelty, and tried to imagine himself capable of awakening the girl's love; and yet he asked himself whether, if he did so, she would satisfy him as a wife, or he satisfy her as a husband.

It will be seen that Bright Hartley, in matters of the heart, as well as in money-making, was not a fool.

But the *Marjory Holdfast* was now sweeping homeward again in the afternoon sunshine. The wind had gone round more to the west, and being fair on the beam, enabled her to show her sailing powers, and also to show off her occupants, for as they sat together well on the weather side of the yacht, they formed a pleasant picture.

Dorna was steering, and Marjory, engaged in an animated conversation with Buchanan, had one hand lightly resting upon her husband's shoulder.

Buchanan thought them a well-matched pair, and conscious of the relationship which existed between himself and the sisters, as yet unknown to them, regarded them with interest. He had found out that Holdfast's history was a singular one, although by no means uncommon in Australia. To find men who can read Latin and Greek, and whose rank in life is hidden beneath such nomenclature as Brown or Smith, shepherding, stockkeeping, or mining, is a more common thing in the wilds of Australia than in any other region in the world. And although Holdfast had picked up the current slang, and to some extent, manners of the bush, there was something behind it all which betokened the gentleman. He was reticent of speaking of his early life, but things cropped out by accident which told of a superior education in his youth, which long years of roughing it in the bush had not entirely obliterated.

That Marjory and he were well-wedded was seen upon the surface – to the extent of their capacity they loved, and the passing years in that isolated spot had bound them the closer to each other.

Buchanan had noticed this, and appreciated it all the more because Marjory was his cousin. In fact, as he looked at them, he felt inclined to dissuade Holdfast from joining in their hazardous enterprise. 'Why,' he thought, 'should another man, and he married, risk his life when there is really no occasion?' He did not realize, however, the passion for exploration and adventure which becomes second nature to hardy pioneers in the vast interior of any great continent. It is like the passion which dwellers on the coast have for the sea.

Holdfast had been thoroughly smitten with the infection by the sight of the gorge and natural pavement that afternoon, and nothing but Marjory's 'Don't go, John,' would now stop him.

But Marjory read her husband's face, and would certainly place no obstacle in the way of his going. She felt that without him the risk to the party would be much greater. And she had been accustomed to have him away sometimes for days together; but, notwithstanding hostile natives, and the everyday dangers of the bush and lake, he had always returned near to the appointed time. He should go to the White Mountains if he wished – and he would come back again.

They decided eventually to start on the third day, and ride the first fifty miles of desert, and then turn the horses adrift, except one for a packhorse.

'Won't that mean the loss of the horses?' said Sir Charles.

'I don't think so,' said Holdfast. 'You see, we will ride to the end of the grass, and then give them a good day to fill themselves and rest, and start by moonlight on the path of Zoo-zoo – for, I suppose, that's the best name we can give to this mysterious bush track of ours. Of course, there is just a chance that the path may lead to a bit of an oasis with water; if so, we can take the horses on, but if not, we will turn them back after riding fifty miles, and plant the saddles and other things somewhere until we have a chance of getting them again.'

'Could you not take a dray, with provisions and all you want on it, across?' said Hartley.

'It would never do,' said Holdfast; 'there's too much sand. If there is an oasis there, we shall be able to push through with the horses, but if not, it will be best to take one packhorse on with us, and do the second fifty miles on foot. We might take a second packhorse to carry water, but the animals would pretty well drink all the extra water carried; a horse can do without food, but it's astonishing how soon they lose heart if they cannot get a drink. I would sooner be without the extra horses; after the first day we can manage all right.'

'Pity you have no camels here,' said Buchanan.

'Yes, they would be just the thing for an expedition such as this, but I would rather be without them. If we had camels, we should have drivers and traffic; and the country is being developed quite fast enough to suit me.'

There were no further adventures to disturb the trip back to the homestead, and Dorna asserted that she would be able to sail the *Marjory Holdfast*, with the aid of her sister, anywhere about the lake. 'She is just big enough for two to manage comfortably,' she said.

'You're a great sailor, Dorna,' said her brother-in-law; 'But you'll find it easier if you take a couple of the boys with you, as well as Marjory, supposing you go out sailing while we are away.'

The next two days everyone was busy. Holdfast had to leave things straight for the working of the station, and there was much to see in the way of preparation. Hartley wanted to wait for his teams, and would ride out twice a day to the verge of the plains in hope of seeing them approaching through the long grass in the distance. In that singularly clear air things could be made out with the naked eye for very long distances, and with a glass the teams might have been discerned a day's journey away. However, Holdfast urged Hartley to abide by their arrangements, and not wait; the wet season might be coming on in about three months, and he hoped to go and return before then.

'Do you have a wet season each year?' asked Sir Charles.

'No,' said Holdfast; 'I have only seen one regular wet season since settling here; and although I was not out in the direction of the desert at the time, the blacks say it was covered with water. It is now two years since we had any rain to cause floods, so it is all the more likely that we may have such a season this year or next. Anyhow, all that we want is at your service on the station; and your stores, when they arrive, will make up for what we take with us, so there is no excuse whatever for our deferring the start.'

It was on Saturday, July 24th, 18—, that the little band of adventurers waved their hands on top of the rise to Dorna and Marjory, and passed out of sight. Both of them wanted to ride with the party for the first ten miles or so, but the vote went against them.

'We've got the packhorses to look after,' said Holdfast, 'and the sooner we get into regular marching order the better. Besides, I would sooner go off knowing that you were safe at the station. I should imagine all sorts of things if we left you to ride back alone through the bush.'

The real reason why he set his face against their going, however, was that they had agreed to thoroughly examine the shore of the lake for Stoneham and his blacks before proceeding.

Buchanan was of the opinion that Stoneham had found out all about the occupants of Western Plains, and expecting their party would comprise only himself, Hartley, and Sir Charles, would be found somewhere in ambush waiting for them. So, after consultation, they had decided to make straight for the spot from which the shots were fired, half-hoping to find Stoneham's party still camped there.

'Won't you travel a bit faster?' asked Hartley of Holdfast.

They were walking their horses; but Holdfast said, 'No, we are all in good time; these horses are soft, and, with our heavy swags, pretty well-loaded. You will have to get into the bushman's jog, with a very occasional canter when the road is exceptionally good. It is half the battle, on such a trip, to handle your horse well.'

'All right,' said Hartley; 'you are to be captain this trip, and I don't think we could have had a better one, so we will follow instructions, only that Susan of yours has a most uncomfortable pace for other horses.'

There was a general laugh at this, for they were all mounted on station horses, and Hartley had evidently got hold of one that was a bit rough.

'Now, don't grumble, Hartley,' said Buchanan. 'Don't you see these horses will all camp quietly at night with Susan; and I suppose she will do exactly what Holdfast tells her to.'

'You've just hit it, Captain,' said Holdfast. 'The horses will all keep together, and Susan won't let them stray far.'

They were jogging along at five miles an hour – not a bad pace for bush travelling, but one which a good horse, on grass only, will keep up pretty well all day, and cover a lot of country.

'We shall hit Stoneham's camp about three o'clock,' said Holdfast; 'and my idea is, if he has gone, to track him for another ten miles or so, and then camp for the night somewhere near the lake.'

'Are there any other blacks about here?' asked Hartley.

'No; this is taboo country to the lake blacks; and it is very evident that those with Stoneham are strangers, or they would never travel, much less camp, about here.'

It was after three o'clock when Holdfast called the attention of the party to some recent tracks. Hartley professed to be able to read them; but Buchanan and Dawson could make nothing of them.

'How do you know that those marks have not been made by a large bird, a turkey, or by a kangaroo?' said Buchanan.

Holdfast smiled at this, and kept his face to the ground as he rode quickly on in a straight line through the trees and undergrowth.

'Here's the camp,' he said at last, turning round in the saddle; 'but it has been empty at least two days.'

Before them were the remains of a gunyah, and also the ashes of a fire.

'There are three of them, and they have four horses with them,' said Holdfast. 'They are not bad bushmen either,' he continued, glancing around.

'I suppose it's too early to camp, or I would suggest that we stopped here for the night,' said Hartley.

'No, it's not a bad camp; but we shall do better to push on a bit,' said Holdfast.

'I would like to know how you can arrive at conclusions so rapidly?' said Sir Charles. 'You come into this camp, and at a glance make positive statements about its late occupants as though you had previous information about their doings.'

'Oh, it's very plain,' said Holdfast, as they rode on. 'Now, you see this bit of a flat? That's where they camped their horses; and it bears out what I said about their being good bushmen. You see, a good bushman never turns his horses out at his own camp, where the fire is, and he intends to sleep. He takes his horses down and waters them, and then puts them on a bit of good grass in a certain direction from his camp. Horses will rarely if ever cross a camp in the night, but will usually feed away from it; so in the morning the traveller knows in which direction to go to look for his horses, and, if he goes early, he will have no difficulty in tracking them through the dewy grass. I saw by the grass under the gunyahs how many had been sleeping there, and by the marks of the horses' feet how many had been hung up after they were saddled for a start. Then, the arrangement of the camp showed good bush-craft. No; these men we are after are no fools, and we shall need to keep our eyes open.'

There was evidently no endeavour on the part of Stoneham and those with him to blind the trail, and they rode on for another two hours, when Holdfast called a halt, and the horses were unsaddled and hobbled out in a bit of a glen within view of the lake. This was after Holdfast had followed the tracks for another half-mile, to see that the party of three were clear out of the neighbourhood.

There were not many tales told that night around the fire, and yet it was well into the night before they fell asleep, their heads in their saddles, and their blankets around them. It was the first of many such nights; but rarely afterward had they so pleasant or secure a camping ground.

CHAPTER XX

CAPTAIN BUCHANAN'S STORY

MORNING IN THE bush! Early morning, with the sweet, fresh breath of the newborn day chasing away the night mist, and already drinking up the dew; shafts of light flashing above the treetops, and the healthy, exhilarating aroma of the morning bush everywhere.

A plunge into that clear, cool lake, and a brisk rub down until the flesh glows with health, and the eyes sparkle with vigour, and every muscle hardens with a sense of its powers and activities!

'Look here, you fellows!' cried Hartley, as he emerged dripping from the water. 'It's a pleasure to be alive such a morning as this; but make the most of it. Heaven only knows when there'll be a chance to wash one's self again.'

He swung his arms backward and forward to expand his chest; then dressed himself leisurely, carefully scrutinizing each garment for any inquisitive or secretive ant, until Holdfast called out:

'Look alive, Hartley! You are doing yourself up as though you expected to mash a girl!'

But Hartley would not be hurried with his toilet, and at last approached the fire, where the others were breakfasting, radiant and polished from top to toe.

'Don't throw that fat away, Dawson,' he called out, as Sir Charles cut off the fat end of a mutton-chop.

'Why?'

'To clean your boots in the desert,' said Hartley.

'Now,' said Holdfast, 'what's the good of keeping up appearances like that when you are camping out every night?'

'Well, I will tell you,' replied Hartley. 'A man with clean boots, washed face, and combed hair retains his self-respect, pays a compliment to his travelling companions, and has useful occupation for his spare time.'

A hearty laugh greeted this remark.

'That's all right enough. But how are you going to wash in the desert?' queried Holdfast.

'You wait and see,' said Hartley.

'You won't be able to get a bushman's bath, anyhow,' said Holdfast.

'What's that?' asked Buchanan.

'A roll in dewy grass,' said Holdfast. 'And a very refreshing bath it is, too, if there are no snakes about.'

'Ah, there's nothing equal to this, however,' said Sir Charles, looking regretfully at the lake. 'I have a good mind to have another dip before we leave it for good. Anyhow, we shall remember our first camp. If there was nothing worse than this, it would be a regular picnic party.'

There had been no trouble with the horses, and our four adventurers broke camp quite early, and rode along in the still, fresh morning, the dew wet upon the grass, blowing clouds of tobacco smoke as they jogged along after

Holdfast, who was tracking in front of them – following like a sleuthhound the trail of the party of three.

Hartley and Buchanan rode next, driving the packhorses, and Sir Charles jogged along meditatively in the rear.

They looked a formidable party, with rifles slung across their shoulders, and revolvers sticking from their belts. In their slouched hats and flannel shirts, and shooting jackets, they might have been taken for a party of diggers prospecting new country. Indeed, that was the character which they had agreed to assume, should it be necessary for them at any time to give an account of themselves.

'I believe it's the climate which gives the Australian buoyancy of character. I was as flat and sad as a bit of last week's damper overnight, but I'm hanged if I don't feel quite perky this morning,' said Hartley. 'I'd like nothing better than a good gallop after Dorna.'

'You'd better mind yourself, old man,' said Buchanan; 'that girl will run you in yet, as you Australians say, and then goodbye, you know, to good luck.'

'I always did admire a woman that could ride well,' said Hartley; 'and your town-reared girls never can. You see, they learn in riding schools, on tan tracks, and that sort of thing; but see how these country girls sit their horses and handle them! You see, they begin as babies, and it becomes second nature to them, and the only bad thing about it is that they never know when to stop; and if they get the run of other people's horses, they will simply ride them to death. A man will stop when his horse begins to tire, but a woman——!'

They spelled for an hour at noon, and shortly after came upon the gorge.

'There's only one word to express the appearance of this place,' said Hartley, – 'it's ghastly. When you turn away from the water it looks as though nature had died suddenly, after having been clean shaved.'

They laughed at this, but it was not disputed. They followed the trail of Stoneham's party to the edge of the desert, where it struck off into the sand; but there was no speck on the distant horizon to mark their presence, and Holdfast took the lead in the direction of a spring, a couple of miles on the way to the path of Zoo-zoo, where he proposed they should camp for the night.

As they stretched themselves around the fire after the evening meal, they grew more talkative under the influence of comfort and firelight and the soothing weed, and, with the exception of Buchanan, were positively merry; but the captain reclined and smoked like a man with something on his mind. Hartley had several times rallied him on being so preoccupied, but he only smoked the harder. At last, however, he put down his pipe, and reaching over for a bottle of whisky, which had been brought out by Holdfast 'to kind of celebrate their farewell to civilization', as he put it, he filled for himself a bushman's drink, and drained it, and then spoke.

'There are times and seasons in men's lives,' he commenced, 'when they will lay bare secrets which, perhaps, might best be forgotten. We are going where we are bound to meet with a man whose life has marred the lives of many; and better men, ay, and women, than himself, but his eye never pitied, and no cry of distress or plea for compassion stayed his hand. May the same be meted out to him in this lonely desert,' ejaculated the captain, bitterly, as he clenched his hand; 'it is all I ask, neither more nor less. But I will tell you, friends, the story of Aaron Stoneham, and you shall judge for yourselves.'

All this had been spoken under evident excitement, for it was an effort for a man like Buchanan to speak of matters personal to himself. But there were brief expressions of sympathy from each of the group, for they felt that he would be relieved to have the burden off his mind, and he continued, in a quieter key:

'Aaron Stoneham is my mother's brother. They were the only two children of a worthy couple of north of Ireland Presbyterians, of Scotch descent. Aaron was born during a remarkably religious movement, which convulsed the half of Scotland, but unfortunately his birth took place during a remarkable episode in my grandfather's life. For nearly twelve months the latter groaned and laboured, and upbraided himself as being the vilest of sinners. The preachers of that time referred to it as a remarkable case of religious conviction. But during these dark months of spiritual agony Aaron was born. It seems as though, by some remarkable heredity, the dark mood of my grandfather's life was transmitted to his offspring. Aaron Stoneham seemed to have been born in sin and shapen in iniquity, which showed itself in clever cunning as soon as intelligence dawned. When only three years old the child killed his playmate. It was attributed to accident; but at six years of age he committed a brutal and deliberate murder, and his father became impressed with the awful truth that he was the progenitor of a triennial homicide, and that every three years at least, and possibly oftener, he would do a murder. This terrible effect of this knowledge was heightened by the fact that after this long period of heart-harrowing self-upbraiding, my grandfather had passed into a state of peace and serenest religious felicity, during the first raptures of which my mother was brought into the world. They grew up side by side, but as different as light from darkness: she, loving and pitying, and desiring to excuse and save her dark-passioned brother; he giving dissembled affection, that he might the better hide the blackness of his soul. And yet in those days of youth and early manhood he dissembled so successfully that he was generally regarded as a fairly reputable young man.

'But both his father and mother knew enough of his real character to darken their lives, and bring down their prematurely grey hairs with sorrow to the grave.

'They both of them regarded him as the victim of heredity, and shielded and interposed themselves to save him from the consequences of his crimes, as though he were not personally responsible for them.

'I cannot prove it, but I believe that at least in each three years he has killed someone. My mother, after her marriage, became perfectly terrified of him; she would say nothing but we believed that he had threatened, or attempted, on more than one occasion, to take her life. He would sometimes be away from home for weeks at a time; and in distant parts of the country there always would be outrages and robberies and murders. But he was never associated with them; he always explained his absence successfully, and grew to be looked up to in the country town in which the Stonehams lived. He learnt engineering at the neighbouring seaport, and, notwithstanding his passionate temper, advanced rapidly in his profession, until he was generally known as one of the most successful engineers in the north of Ireland. He developed more of the gentleman in travelling to and fro, and meeting with men of influence and wealth; but there was that about him which men dreaded and disliked. How he won the affections of beautiful Mabel McCarthy no one knew, but they were married when I was quite a child.

'Within a little more than three years after his marriage two daughters were born to him. They were Marjory and Dorna Stoneham.'

Buchanan stopped at this, and reached his hand across to the billy of water and the whisky bottle. Hartley pushed the billy can and pannikin near him, and Dawson the whisky; but none of them spoke, and Holdfast looked with steely eyes, and a pained expression upon his face, into the fire.

'It was about this time,' continued Buchanan, who had taken only enough whisky with his water to flavour it, 'that there occurred the supreme tragedy of my life – the murder of my mother.'

Holdfast at these words gave an involuntary groan, and then said, hoarsely, 'Never mind me, go on.'

Buchanan was suffering too acutely himself, however, to lay much stress upon the feelings of another, and he proceeded with calm and deliberate enunciation.

'I can never forget it; the whole scene has been repeated so often before my mental vision that I believe I could reproduce every feature of the landscape, as well as the furnishing and interior of the room.

'It was a general holiday in the depth of summer, and an almost Sabbath stillness rested upon the house and garden and its surroundings. My mother had been ill, but was then rapidly recovering, although scarcely well enough to leave her bed, and for a brief hour or two I was left in charge – a child of seven.

'The room was on the ground floor, and I had talked and read until my mother had fallen asleep, and, childlike, I sat looking out across the garden through the open window, beyond the hedgerow into the meadow, where on the morrow Mike and Pat and Barney would begin to mow. The bees were buzzing audibly in the hushed afternoon as they flew from flower to flower. I wondered how long the family would be, and turned and looked at the fair white face of my mother, and something seemed to urge me to go and kiss it, when suddenly I heard a quiet step beside me and I saw my uncle Aaron in the room. He was dressed in a rough travelling kind of suit, such as I had never seen him in before. I always feared him, and on seeing him very nearly cried out; but he whispered, "Hush, don't wake her; I have only called to say goodbye."

'I was trembling with fear and apprehension, but he sat down and took me on his knee. "Now," he said, "you like sweeties, don't you? Shut your eyes and open your mouth." I thought this was said in imitation of our children's games, so I, always fearful of him, obeyed. I felt something enter my mouth, and a cloth blinded my eyes, and in a moment was tied tightly behind my head. I was gagged!

"Don't attempt to make a noise or struggle, or I shall have to kill you," he whispered quietly in my ear.

'He had fastened my hands and arms behind me, and was moving me away to the further end of the room, where there was a massive piece of furniture, to which he securely tired me. I seemed perfectly paralysed. I am not sure, if I had not been gagged, that I could have spoken, so great was my childish terror. I listened to hear if my mother would awake. Every moment I expected to hear the first sound of the bloodcurdling scream with which I knew she would greet the appearance of my uncle in the room. But I could hear her regular breathing, as well as the loud thumping of my own heart. It was as though a frightful spell had been laid upon me.

'After I was securely bound, I felt that he stepped back a step or two to look at me; then he came nearer, and turned down the covering from off my eyes and nose, and then stepped back again and looked at me. I opened my eyes! But the face I saw before me seemed no longer that of Aaron Stoneham; it had grown suddenly old-looking, and wrinkled with evil passions – it was more than personified wickedness, it was the face of a misbegotten devil, shapen in iniquity. I tried to scream, and felt a faintness coming over me, and I closed my eyes. When I opened them again my inhuman uncle was standing over the bed, leaning toward me with a fiendishly cruel expression upon his face, and placing his body so that I could plainly see that he was holding a pillow over my mother's face to suffocate her.

'I saw no more. When I came back to consciousness I was lying upon my own bed, with a servant standing near, helping to bring me back to life. In an adjoining room my mother lay dead, with my father standing over her heart-broken; my uncle had left the house to take passage for Australia. I told my father what I had seen; but he seemed to think that it was an hallucination. I heard him walking to and fro, saying to himself, "The thing is impossible."

'But before he died he, too, believed it; and one of the last things he said to me was, "It is not just or right that the man should be allowed to remain at large. He is a criminal madman, and ought to be put under confinement, or shot." That he is a criminal I have had further proof, but not that he is a madman. If I meet with him out here, he will, for the sake of all men and women of peaceful and honest lives, have to die. His crimes demand it!

'I regret,' said Buchanan, in a weary tone of voice, 'that my story is such a sad one; but what is life, or love, or aught else to me, with the memory of that scene ever before my eyes? You want to know why I am preoccupied. Now you will not need to ask me again.'

There was a long pause, after which Sir Charles Dawson reached his hand across and caught hold of Buchanan's, and said:

'We are all very sorry for you. But it's my belief that Stoneham is the victim of some remarkable hereditary transmission of brain disease, which at times turns him into a demon.'

'Why then,' said Holdfast, 'have none of his children inherited it?'

'Ah,' said Hartley, 'that may possibly be explained; but, without doubt, it is one of the most extraordinary facts ever heard of. It seems to me, however, that for Aaron Stoneham the path of Zoo-zoo will prove to be the path of retribution. A huge lonely desert such as this must be an awful place to a man with an evil conscience. Especially when he knows he has us to meet, and answer to. You see, he is, as it were, alone out here with Nature and Retribution.'

'Yes,' interrupted Sir Charles, quietly; 'but more than that, he is alone out here with God. Think of it, a murderer, a desert and a God; is it possible that such a man in such a place might find repentance?'

'I want you all to promise one thing,' said Holdfast, 'not one word of this to Marjory or Dorna. His life is forfeited by every law of God and man, and he must carry out the sentence. But it must be buried here in the desert forever.'

'Right,' said Buchanan, and the promise was duly made.

CHAPTER XXI

Buchanan Disappears

THE FOLLOWING DAY the men busied themselves with final preparations, while their horses cropped the sweet blue and kangaroo grass, which in that far country had not yet been eaten off and killed out by overstocking.

During a part of the afternoon they slept, and at sunset started upon the mysterious track which stretched away into the vast silent waste of sand in front of them. The two packhorses were turned on to the path, where they soon settled down to a steady jog in single file. Hartley and Holdfast followed after them, and the two Englishmen rode behind; and thus they started on their quest, only once halting during the long monotonous night.

At the first streak of daylight Holdfast stopped them. 'There's no water within at least twenty miles of us,' he said, 'or Susan would smell it. See!' he exclaimed, as he dropped the reins upon her neck; 'she puts her head around toward the grass and water we have left behind. We must turn them adrift here, and they will find their way back to the station all right. If we take them on any further we may lose them altogether, and find their bleaching bones somewhere on the return journey.'

'That may be,' said Buchanan; 'but if they are likely to be smitten down by heat and thirst, how are we going to get back again?'

'We can't do it with six horses,' replied Holdfast; 'they would drink all the water we have, and then not be half-satisfied. In another couple of hours the sun will glare down upon this sand as though from the open mouth of a furnace. I've brought enough meal to give each of them a mouthful; we must spare them a pint of water each, and then start them back toward home. That is, all but one, which we shall have to give a little more water to, so as to keep him upon his legs as long as possible.'

'You are not going to keep the mare, then?'

'No; she will lead the others back,' replied Holdfast.

After being turned adrift, the five horses seemed loath to leave – probably they could smell the water in the bags – but on being hunted homeward for fifty yards or so, they jogged along in single file behind Susan, who took the lead on the path back to the Western Plains. Our adventurers watched them, as they grew smaller in the distance. They had crossed the Rubicon; but even Holdfast questioned with himself for a moment whether it had been wisely done to let them go. They had travelled, from dark to dawn, about sixty miles.

'We had better prepare a camp here,' said Holdfast; 'and I hope that another night's travelling may see us over the worst of it.'

An ordinary digger's tin prospecting-dish was among their outfit, and with this the men soon scooped out a trench north and south, heaping the sand so as to give them some protection from the sun. At each end of this their guns were stacked, and a couple of blankets stretched across for shade, and the men settled down for breakfast, and afterward slept. The one packhorse left them had been hobbled and picketed, and stood munching a bit of moistened corn.

When they awoke it was hot – fearfully hot; the sun was pouring down upon them, every shaft of light like a flaming sword, and the sand so hot as to be painful to the touch. The blankets were rearranged, and, after eating, the men lay down again in the shade, and smoked and talked.

It was at such a time as this that Hartley shone. He had cleaned his boots with a bit of fat, and with his accustomed personal neatness set a good example to the rest of the party, while his flow of talk and anecdotes seemed inexhaustible.

'You make one feel quite lively,' said Sir Charles, addressing him. 'It is a good thing, though, that we are on a beaten track, and that we have some certain knowledge of what there is in front of us.'

'Yes, the White Mountains are ahead all right enough,' said Holdfast, 'and I hope that by tomorrow morning we shall have them in sight, and then another night's travelling ought to see us safely off this fearful sand.'

'It is singular,' said Buchanan, 'that we have seen nothing of Stoneham or his blacks.'

'I have been thinking the same thing,' said Hartley.

'He may have found another path,' said Holdfast; 'but if he is travelling by compass through the sand, I am sorry for him. I would sooner go ten miles further round and have this track to travel upon.'

The next night they made only thirty miles, and were compelled to leave the horse five miles before reaching their new camp. The precautions of the previous morning were repeated; but the journey seemed to be specially telling upon Buchanan – probably he was brooding over Stoneham and his anticipated revenge.

They carried their swags the next night upon their rifles, two and two, and covered about another thirty miles; but the water in the bags was nearly done. It was evident that it was drying up with the fierce heat, and that by midday they would see the last of it.

When they struck camp and started again the following night, each of the men was consumed with thirst. They sucked sixpences, but it seemed as though the heated air had drawn the very moisture from their bodies. The fact came home to them all that unless they reached water during the night, the morrow would see them in fearful extremity.

About midnight they halted for a rest; a tin of preserved meat was opened, and eaten with biscuit; but the former seemed as dry as the latter – the dry penetrating heat was everywhere.

'I never realized before how dry the atmosphere gets in the absence of vegetation,' said Sir Charles.

'It is simply fearful,' said Hartley, moistening his dry parched lips with his tongue.

Suddenly Holdfast, who was lying full stretch upon his blanket, called out, 'Hist! Listen!'

They listened, but no voice nor sound was heard upon the night wind, which just moved – and only moved – across the desert. Holdfast, however, kept his ear closely pressed upon the ground.

'Great Scott!' he shouted out in his excitement. 'Put your ear to the ground, man – I can hear the sound of running water.'

They all did so immediately, and the peculiar sound of water was distinctly audible to each.

'How far off do you think it is?' asked Sir Charles.

'It's underneath the ground,' said Holdfast; 'but, unless we reach it overground very shortly, it might as well be a thousand miles off.'

'But cannot we dig to it?' urged Buchanan, whose mouth and lips were parched and cracked with thirst.

'No,' said Holdfast; 'our one chance is to push on, and pray God that this underground river may be accessible somewhere before morning.'

For another hour they travelled on almost in silence; they had by consent left a portion of their outfit at their last stopping place. Holdfast was going first, his two hands holding the rifles like a stretcher, on which was strapped the swags, the other ends were supported by Buchanan.

'Stop!' he said suddenly, in a loud whisper, and the party came to an immediate halt.

In a few moments he had detached his rifle from the swags and pushed a cartridge into the breech. Then he pointed with his hand in front of them.

It seemed as though arising out of the semi-darkness was a company of men.

'They are trees,' said Hartley.

This proved to be the case, and they cautiously recommenced their march again, and in a quarter of an hour passed into a remarkable avenue of trees, which had thrown themselves almost in single file right out into the desert.

'Thank God,' exclaimed Sir Charles, reverently, 'we're saved!'

'Yes, I think we are,' replied Holdfast, who, however, still glanced cautiously about.

They stopped to examine the trees on entering the avenue.

'There must be water at the roots of these,' said Hartley; 'They look like a species of palm.'

'There should be some white grubs about the roots of them, such as are eaten by the blacks,' said Holdfast.

The supposition proved correct, and never was sweeter morsel eaten than one of those juicy grubs, which they found in fair numbers by digging and poking about the roots of the trees. The sound of running water was now more plainly heard.

Said Holdfast, 'These trees are like all the palm species; they flourish best with their feet in the water and their heads in the fire. But we will stop and rest here now, and travel on in the daylight under the shade of the trees. We cannot very well die of thirst with these juicy grubs about, and it's my impression we shall soon come upon water.'

The dawning light revealed a seemingly interminable avenue of curious trees, which had taken root in the moisture rising from the underground river.

'What do you make of it?' asked Hartley of Holdfast.

'Most remarkable!' he ejaculated.

'And the path leads right between the trees,' said Sir Charles.

There was no water visible, however, so they pushed on again, and dragged their weary limbs for fully an hour, when they came to another sudden halt.

Fifty yards ahead of them lay swags and rifles and other accoutrements by the side of the path.

The men instinctively got under cover.

'But,' said Hartley, 'how is it they have left their rifles behind them?'

There was no sound of life, however, and on approaching near, by creeping from tree to tree, they made out two mounds of sand and rock.

'Someone has been digging down to water!' exclaimed Holdfast.

'Yes,' said Hartley, as they stood a few minutes after around the opening. 'It's Stoneham and the blacks; and in their haste to get a drink the whole crowd of them have fallen in.'

It seemed likely enough, for the hole, which was over five feet deep, looked as though its floor of rock had suddenly given way, and broken clear off all round, precipitating anyone on it into the subterranean river.

However, our adventurers did not stop to decide that mattered then, but fastening a billy can onto a line they were soon refreshing themselves with water, which they drew up from the dark opening in the earth, cold as ice.

'I could drink a bucketful,' said Buchanan, as he dropped the can for a further supply. 'Hallo! What was that?' he called out to Hartley.

'What is the matter?' said that gentleman.

Then, as he caught the dismayed expression on Buchanan's face, he looked at his empty hands and called out:

'Well, you are a fellow! Why, you've dropped the billy can!'

'Nothing of the sort; it was snatched out of my hand,' replied Buchanan.

Hartley looked sceptical; but the four men stood around the hole and listened to the rushing water with ill-concealed apprehension. They had other billy cans, but if one or more of Stoneham's party were alive down there, their position was not at all a pleasant one. If they had means of getting down there unhurt, they might have means of return, and Holdfast had decided to camp by the water for the night.

They had all of them loaded their rifles, when Buchanan announced his intention of going down.

'I would not do that,' said Hartley.

But Buchanan was determined. 'They have no rifles down there,' he said; 'and, after all, it may have been the current of the river which snatched the can away. Anyhow, I am determined to go.'

They made as long and as strong a rope as possible of girths and stirrup leathers and other straps which they had with their swags, and fastening it below his shoulders, he was lowered into the hole.

'Pull me back!' he cried out a moment later. 'Someone has caught hold of my legs.'

For a moment there was a sharp struggle between those above and those beneath, and then something gave way and Buchanan instantly disappeared. Holdfast believed he heard a splash, as though he had fallen into the water; but there was no cry raised and his three friends stood listening in silence.

'Buchanan!' called out Hartley down the hole. The others also called, but there was no reply. Whatever had happened to him, he seemed to have suddenly passed away from sight, hearing, and the chance of rescue.

'Good heavens!' exclaimed Sir Charles. 'It seems fearful for him to perish without an attempt at saving him. Can't you lower me down?'

'No, we can't spare you,' said Holdfast.

After this the three men stood looking at the hole and listening to the rush of the water for some time in silence. Hartley's face brightened a bit presently, as though he had an idea, and, ransacking among his swag, he got out a pair of boots and trousers, and set himself to fasten the legs of the trousers inside the boots. Then, with the prospecting-dish he got Sir Charles to fill the whole arrangement with sand. The result was a fair presentment of the lower part of a man. Around the waist of this he fastened a cord and carried the effigy over to where Holdfast stood guard above the hole, with a loaded rifle.

'I am going to lower this down,' whispered Hartley to Holdfast, 'and if you see any hands catch hold of it, fire.'

No sooner said than done. The effigy was lowered feet in, as though it were someone climbing down the aperture; but soon two hands appeared, but they were immediately withdrawn with a howl of pain.

A bullet from Holdfast's rifle was the cause, and Hartley drew up his boots and trousers again, well-pleased with the experiment.

But the fate of Buchanan was still enshrouded in mystery.

CHAPTER XXII

HARTLEY MAKES A DISCOVERY

A S MAY BE imagined, the night which followed the startling events of the previous chapter was full of disquietude. A watch was kept, not only over the excavation, but along the avenue, for both Holdfast and Hartley feared that there might be a subterranean passage along which Stoneham and the blacks had escaped, and possibly, too, an opening through which they might have made their way back into the avenue.

'Should they manage to get out, they will certainly return for their swags and rifles,' said Hartley.

Buchanan's disappearance had cast a gloom over the party. No fire was lit, for fear of its proving a guide to an enemy; and as the sighing night winds swayed the leaves and branches overhead it was as though all sad sounds and mournful memories were above and around them among the trees. Many a time they grasped their rifles with determined grip, as though an unseen foe were about to spring upon them from the darkness.

The moon arose about eleven o'clock, but at first it only made the scene more weird as the uncertain shadows of the trees slowly revealed themselves. They now arranged for each to keep a watch for about two hours; Sir Charles to take the first, Holdfast the second, and Hartley the third. But the hours dragged slowly along as they in due course relieved each other; and when the morning light at last overpowered the moonbeams, both Holdfast and Sir Charles were seen by Hartley to be wrapped in profound slumber.

Hartley, however, was never more awake; he had kept careful watch and the only living thing he had seen was a bird, which he took to be an owl. He had listened for half an hour at a time at the aperture and had heard nothing but the sound of the flowing water of the river, as it swept on in its subterranean course to the lake. He was persuaded that Holdfast's rifle shot had pretty well settled matters below, and there had seized upon him an intense desire to go down and see.

This was increased when, on searching the swags of Stoneham's party, he found a length of line which, by sundry trails from one of the trees, proved strong enough to support his weight.

The cord was long enough, he thought, to reach the water if doubled; so, having first tied it to one of the trees, he fastened a tomahawk upon it, as the best weight to hand, and with it measured the distance to the water.

It was, no doubt, a thoughtless thing to do, for had Stoneham and the blacks been in ambush there, it would have been placing a weapon right into their hands; but this never occurred to Hartley. He thought them dead, or miles away. So down went the tomahawk at the end of the line, until it reached the water. Then he lifted it a foot, and dropped it in with a splash, to be sure, and measured the line roughly as he drew it up again. It was about twenty-five feet down to the river.

'That will do,' said Hartley to himself. 'I'll go down without waking these fellows, and have a bath, and see if there is any news below of Buchanan or Stoneham.'

The very idea seemed to tickle his fancy, for he looked across at the sleeping men, who, worn out with travel and watching, slumbered as though they would never awaken again, and laughed audibly. Then he commenced to strip off his garments. He had found a pair of old slippers in one of the swags, and put them on his feet to protect them during the first part of his descent through the aperture. A minute after, he had disappeared, and there might have been heard a splash as he touched the water; but after a few minutes the strain on the rope slackened, and all was silence again, save for the heavy breathing of the sleeping men.

It was fully half an hour before Holdfast awoke. But he was soon wide awake, looking around for Hartley, and listening for the slightest sound. Not seeing him anywhere, he sprang to his feet and awoke Dawson, and briefly told him of Hartley's disappearance. Then he called out; but there was no response.

Grasping their rifles, the two men went across to the opening leading to the subterranean river, and were there confronted with the dangling rope and Hartley's clothes.

Holdfast ejaculated something which sounded like a swear; and Sir Charles exclaimed, 'What a mad-brained thing!' but just then the rope strained and tightened.

Either Hartley or someone else was coming up it.

'Stand back,' whispered Holdfast to Sir Charles; 'it may be one of the others.'

They stepped back under the shelter of the trees and watched, when presently there emerged a close-fitting peaked cap and the arm of a shooting jacket, which was thrown upon the bank. The face was turned away from them, and as more of the figure slowly emerged, both Holdfast and Sir Charles covered the intruder with their rifles.

'Good heavens! Hartley's done for!' ejaculated Holdfast, beneath his breath.

The hand of Sir Charles trembled upon the trigger of his rifle; it was a marvel the piece did not at once go off!

The man appeared to be about the size of Hartley, but was dressed in a suit of blue serge, and had heavy blunder boots on, somewhat the worse for wear. He looked across to where Holdfast and Sir Charles had been sleeping, and commenced to fumble in his pockets, as though reaching for something; a minute after, he wheeled around and cooeed, and saw confronting him the rifle of his two friends.

It was Hartley!

An exclamation simultaneously broke from the lips of all three of them; and then Holdfast said solemnly:

'Mr Hartley, you're a downright fool! You were within a trifle of being shot. What on earth have you been doing, and where did you get those clothes from?'

Hartley, however, walked up to them, pale with excitement, and putting his hands into the pocket of the jacket he wore, took from one of them a small handful of rough diamonds, and from the other a fistful of gold dust.

'There's no one about,' he gasped, as though hardly able to get his breath. 'You fellows make a fire, and get me something warm to drink, and then I'll tell you.'

And at this he staggered off to where the blankets lay, and rolling one around him, stretched himself exhausted upon the ground.

Sir Charles ran over and got him some brandy, which he drank eagerly, and then closed his eyes.

'Get some breakfast ready and then I'll tell you,' he repeated. 'I shall be all right after a little rest.'

In less than an hour the first really comfortable meal they had had for days was ready; and after the rest, and some hot tea and food, Hartley was pretty well himself again, and gave a hurried account of his adventures underground.

'You'll think it was a daredevil sort of thing to do without awakening you; but you were both sleeping soundly, and I became possessed with a desire to go down that hole and find out what I could about Buchanan, and have a bath.

'I had not calculated, however, on the coldness of the water, or the strength of the current; and when I dropped into it my breath seemed to leave me, and I felt myself swept down as in a millrace. I clung desperately to the rope, and the sensation was indescribable; but as I swayed about with the force of the current, I felt myself touch a ledge of rock – for the hole, I may explain, is quite at the side of the river, and not over the middle of it, as we at first thought. With the assistance of the rope I scrambled on to the bank. My teeth were chattering with the cold, and I felt numbed all over, so I aroused myself, and began to throw my arms about to restore circulation.

'As I moved along the ledge of rock I stumbled against the body of a man. It gave me another shock, you may be sure; but seeing that he was dead, and being naked and shivering with the cold, I helped myself to his clothes, for I assure you it's like a refrigerating chamber below there.

'Unfortunately, in getting the clothes off, the body slipped into the river, and was immediately swept down by the current; but, as well as I could see in the dim light, I feel sure it was one of Stoneham's blacks.

'I sat down after putting on the clothes, for a stupid, exhausted feeling came over me, and my head swam round; but presently I felt better, and began to look around me.

'I had somehow got a good bit down from the opening; but, on returning, I found that it was fairly light beneath the hole. The river is about thirty feet across, and seems to be very deep; but on the sides there are most remarkable ledges, which lead in steps down to the water's edge, and seem to run continuously along the side of it, as though they had been formed by the disintegration of the rock, due to long ages of flowing waters. The roof is arched and smooth, as though waterworn; but the most remarkable thing is that in the sides of the banks, here and there all the way along, are pockets containing diamonds and coarse gold dust mixed with sand. Stoneham and the blacks must have some knowledge of it, too, for, feeling in the pockets of the coat, I found these!'

At this Hartley dived into one pocket and brought out a handful of small diamonds, and then into the other for some coarse waterworn gold.

'It seems to me,' he continued, as his companions gazed at the treasures in astonishment, 'that they were washed into those pockets ages ago, before the river had cut its way through the soft strata, down to its present level; and I have no doubt the whole of the banks are lined with these pockets all along its course to the lake at Western Plains.'

The men sat for a couple of hours after this, discussing Hartley's amazing discovery. 'It's a pity,' said that worthy, 'that we cannot peg out the whole bed of the river, or take up the entire desert on a mining lease.'

Both he and Sir Charles wanted to make further explorations at once, but Holdfast urged that they should proceed upon their journey.

'This thing will keep,' said he. 'Let us go on, for the place where this gold and these diamonds come from is in front of us. If we meet with nothing better, we can come back to this again. I strongly advise you to run no risks here in underground explorations; now that we know the country, we can come back from Western Plains at any time; and it is useless to load ourselves with gold, which we cannot possibly carry any distance.'

'Very good,' said Hartley, although the tone of his voice was not exactly cordial; 'you're captain, and we have agreed to put ourselves under your guidance, so we will go on; but, between ourselves, my motto is: "Keep to the luck that you happen upon, and don't lose a good thing through reaching after something that may not be worth a straw".'

'I wish we had some tidings of Buchanan,' said Sir Charles, sadly.

'It's hopeless to go down there after him again,' said Hartley. 'Unless he escaped by a miracle, he is certainly dead!'

CHAPTER XXIII

THE WHITE MOUNTAINS

TWO DAYS AFTER the events recorded, three men might have been seen toiling up a precipitous pathway formed on the side of awe-inspiring mountains, which reared their white heads in rugged, lonely grandeur toward the sky. A light rain was falling, and here and there water rushed in impetuous streams down the mountain-side. Holdfast led the way, carrying two swags and Sir Charles Dawson's rifle, in addition to his own. Behind, Sir Charles leaned heavily upon Hartley's arm.

For the last half-hour they had anxiously looked out for some sheltering cave or rock to camp under, but, so far, had not met with any place offering the slightest shelter. The roadway they trod was still the mysterious path of Zoo-zoo, and they had suffered many hardships and passed through many adventures since they started from the camp at the avenue and subterranean river, where Hartley so nearly lost his life.

The fatigue of the journey was beginning to tell severely upon Sir Charles. Crows, and other ominous carrion birds, had been following them all the day; but neither Hartley nor Holdfast had the heart to tell Sir Charles the reason why – it need scarcely be said that they smelt, or thought they smelt, a dying man.

At last Holdfast called out cheerily for them to hasten their steps; he had found a cave a short distance off the roadway which would protect them from the rain, and where they might rest if necessary, for a day or two, until Sir Charles had recovered somewhat. Leaving Hartley to light a fire, Holdfast, whose muscles seemed made of iron, went out to shoot a wallaroo, numbers of which they had seen upon the rocks earlier in the day. Within an hour he returned, trailing a huge animal behind him, which would, if necessary, keep them in meat for several days. Nourishing broth was made for the invalid, but on the following day Sir Charles was worse, and the next he was feverish and delirious; and so a week passed, and it became evident that there was no present prospect of the Englishman pursuing the journey further, especially as during most of the time the rain had fallen continuously.

'Holdfast,' said Hartley at length, 'it is plain that the only thing for it is for you or myself to go on alone, and the other remain with Dawson. We had better toss up for it.'

'Let us talk it over first,' said Holdfast, who was always cautious in regard to his decisions.

So the pros and cons were duly set forth; but as was usually the case, Hartley's proposal was at last agreed upon, and the toss decided that the latter should remain with Sir Charles, and Holdfast follow on the pathway, if necessary, for another week, and then return.

It seemed a sad ending to their hopeful anticipations, when, the following day, amid steady rain, Holdfast set out, having beforehand supplied them with quite a store of fresh meat, in the shape of birds and game. The two watched him climb the mountain pathway until he was lost in the distance.

The mystery surrounding the disappearance of Buchanan seemed to have made a very deep impression upon Sir Charles Dawson.

'Hartley, I shall never see England again,' he said on the morning after Holdfast's departure.

'What nonsense!' said Hartley, roughly, but not unkindly.

'I mean it though,' said Sir Charles.

'But I say it's nonsense!' reiterated Hartley. 'Why, if necessary, Holdfast and myself will make a stretcher, and carry you back every step of the way to Western Plains.'

'Across the desert?' queried Sir Charles.

This even Hartley felt to be a poser, for he had asked himself scores of times how, in his weak state, they were going to get Sir Charles over those weary miles of burning sand.

'Don't let us try to cross the bridge, or the desert, before we come to it,' said he at last. 'Who knows? We are so far to the north-east, we may find it better to go on, and return by steamer from the Gulf, or something of that sort. Anyhow, I am not going to trouble myself with difficulties before we reach them. So far, we have had uncommon good luck, except for the loss of Buchanan; and we cannot say but that he will turn up again all right. While in that underground river we have found treasures enough to pretty well make us all millionaires.'

Hartley set himself, by every means in his power, to cheer his companion, and bring about an improvement in his health. He knew how important this was; and Sir Charles Dawson made a not altogether unsuccessful effort to shake off his despondency, and get into better physical condition. And so several days passed.

He was never tired of talking of the strange track which they had followed from the very verge of the desert, and which ran not more than forty yards in front of their temporary camp.

'I should not be surprised,' he said, 'to see a party of blacks treading along that path in single file some morning.'

'It is truly a marvellous roadway,' said Hartley, 'and was evidently made by some superior race to the Australian aboriginal;[10] but we shall hear more about it on Holdfast's return.'

'You are grieving that you have not gone on with him.'

'No,' said Hartley; 'he will tell us all about it. I shall see it later on, if there is anything worth seeing, and under more favourable circumstances.'

'What do you mean?'

'I am going to float a great gold and diamond mining company,' said Hartley, 'when we get back from this trip; and then I will see "*the white gates and golden*" and "*the span longer than the arms of many men*", for myself. I have been thinking out the whole thing for a day or two past.'

'Tell me about it,' said Sir Charles, lighting his pipe for a smoke – a thing which he had not done for days.

Hartley sat down on a lump of rock, and, pulling hard at his pipe, propounded the following ambitious scheme:

---

10 The idea of Aboriginal people being on a lower evolutionary level than a more ancient race of people was a common racist trope in the Lemurian novel, which drew heavily on the Victorian pseudo-science of eugenics, popularised by Francis Galton (1822–1911).

'There are four of us in this enterprise, and we must take equal shares as vendors.'

'I would sooner not go into any risky speculation,' interposed Sir Charles, lifting his hand deprecatingly.

'Oh, you need not bother; I mean to put down ten thousand or so for the preliminary expenses myself,' said Hartley. 'But, man alive! Just listen to the prospectus!' he said, in a state of genuine excitement. 'I mean to make about half a million for each of us out of this trip, if a penny.' At this he brought out a pocketbook, and, to the Englishman's amazement, read and commented as follows:

'"The Central Australian Desert Tunnel Gold and Diamond Mining Company, Limited. To be registered under the No Liability Act."

'How does that strike you now?' he interjected. 'Sounds well. Why, the very name is worth a thousand pounds! You see, it's very important to have a good suggestive name when you want to put a big thing upon the London market; but this will stagger them. I am proposing to go home and float the thing myself; it's far too good to give half of it away to insatiable London brokers. But let us read on—

'"Capital £2,000,000, in 200,000 shares of £10 each. Of this number," continued Hartley, with a chuckle, "100,000 shares will be retained by the vendors, and the balance of 100,000 will be offered to the public, payable £5 per share on application, and £5 on allotment."'

'But that's a million sterling you are going to keep for the vendors!' broke in the amazed Englishman.

'Of course. Isn't it worth it, to come out all this way, and find that blessed desert and underground river?' said Hartley. 'But that's only a portion of the purchase money,' he continued; 'you don't think we are going to give this thing away to the guileless British public? I am going to stipulate for £750,000 in hard cash, which will leave £250,000 available for working and developing the property, and for flotation expense.'

'But how will you get the British public to subscribe the share capital?'

'My dear sir, it will go off like a house on fire,' said the sanguine businessman. 'You see, we shall set forth in the prospectus that the Desert Tunnel is a remarkable natural formation in Central Australia, extending for two hundred miles below the ground, running north and south. We can value the excavation at so much a cubic yard, which, taking it at two hundred miles, will come to a pretty big figure. Then supposing the pockets average five ounces of free gold to the yard on each side of the river; we may calculate it as £3 18s. per ounce, which would be £19 10s. per yard, or say £20. Taking both banks of the river as 400 miles, and a yield of five ounces to the yard, would give a return of £35,200 per mile, that multiplied by 400 gives the magnificent total of £14,080,000, while the diamonds may be set down at about an equal amount, making the grand total gross value of the property to be, say, £30,000,000. So, you see, what we ask for it is a mere bagatelle.'

'But how can you tell that the pockets continue throughout?' said Sir Charles, who was still far from being satisfied.

'Ah, that's where the speculative element comes in, which must be connected with all mining ventures,' said Hartley. 'But it's a splendid scheme, is it not? There would, of course, have to be a railway made from the lake across the desert for the purposes of the mine; and if there are any ancient curiosities, or any good country on the other side of these ranges, we might float another big company to make the railway, and get a further haul out of that. It seems to me there are great possibilities about this part of Australia,' continued Hartley; 'and I am feeling quite restless to get back and put some of them into execution. Personally, I care very little what there is further on; this Desert Tunnel scheme is quite sufficient for the present. Why, we could get enough gold and diamonds on our way back to set the whole affair going, and send half Europe crazy with gold and diamond fever. You see, the formation is so extraordinary. The river, we know for certain, runs right through to the lake, and it runs in that underground tunnel. Why, the company might pay dividends to the tune of a million per annum.'

'Yes, it might,' said Sir Charles, sceptically.

'Ah, you see,' retorted Hartley, 'you have not had the advantage of a sound commercial training.'

A fortnight dragged wearily past. Sir Charles was decidedly better, and as Holdfast did not return, they agreed to follow him, and should they not meet him on his way back, discover, if possible, his fate.

They had accumulated a store of game and wallaroo flesh at the cave, for Hartley had on several days returned from successful shooting expeditions, and on other occasions they had been able to kill wallaroo from the shelter of the cave. Hartley's idea was to have the cave provisioned in readiness for the return journey; he thought it probable that Holdfast might wish to stay and recruit for a day or two, before facing the dangers and privations of the desert. The two men looked in capital trim as they set out on a bright clear morning, and felt the cool air grow colder as they ascended.

The path was easy to follow, although strewn here and there with branches and rocks, and other debris, swept down seemingly by recent storms.

'This path puzzles me; it looks as though it was under some kind of supervision, for I cannot understand, otherwise, how it is found in such good repair,' said Sir Charles.

'It certainly is curious,' replied Hartley. 'I have been thinking myself that it is queer, if there were no people about, that it is not more waterworn, as the path is formed on the mountain's side.'

'You may depend upon it,' said Sir Charles, 'that at occasional intervals it is put in orders by someone. And we need not be surprised at meeting wild natives at any moment. I am confident that on the other side of this barrier we shall find living men and women again.'

Soon after this they found themselves rounding a bluff rock of granite, which arose from the pathway at this base for fully two hundred feet in an almost perpendicular line. They felt themselves dwarfed into insignificance as they crept around its huge majestic bulk, and discovered that they were entering a defile or gap between the mountains, which on either side, in front of them, towered upward, clothed with a white covering of snow. While at the distance of some two or three miles in front upon the pathway, which could be distinguished here and there among the trees, there arose two great white columns or pillars, fully fifteen feet high, the summits of which glittered in the sunlight, causing them to appear like masses of snow and gold. They held their breath, however, for, moving upon the pathway, they could make out a number of persons who were evidently approaching them; but what was their colour, or the nature of their attire, it was impossible at the distance to distinguish.

'We are in for some stirring incidents at last!' ejaculated Hartley.

They had been so long cut off from their fellows, however, that the sight of men in any form was a relief, although they were far from feeling sure that those approaching would prove friendly.

'The White Mountains are plain enough now,' said Sir Charles, as they presently lost sight of the approaching people.

'Yes, that is snow upon them, right enough; but what do you make of the glistening white and gold pillars?' said Hartley. 'I have it!' he ejaculated; 'those are the white and golden gates referred to by the legends of the boomerang.'

They decided to await the party, which they could occasionally discern still descending.

'I do not somehow think we need apprehend danger from them,' said Hartley. 'If they are white people, it will be all right; if hostile natives, our rifles are more than a match for a dozen of them. However, it will be as well for us to place ourselves to good advantage, and be on our guard.'

As the party eventually drew nearer they saw the tall form of Holdfast among them, his rifle upon his shoulder; and by that they knew he was with friends, or, at any rate, friendly disposed natives.

Holdfast greeted them with subdued cordiality; he evidently thought it was wise not to be too demonstrative before the natives. They were each carrying a small, but what seemed a heavy, burden supported with pliant wands, after the manner of the Chinese.

They placed these on the ground as Holdfast stepped forward, and stood waiting at a respectable distance.

'Who are these chaps?' said Hartley, motioning across to the waiting natives.

'Some of the people of Zoo-zoo,' replied Holdfast.

'You don't say so!' exclaimed Sir Charles. 'Then it is all true!'

'What have they got in their swags?' asked the matter-of-fact Hartley.

'Gold and diamonds – an offering to the departed ones,' said Holdfast.

'Are those two blessed columns up there white quartz and gold?' blurted out Hartley, who was fairly losing his breath with gratified astonishment.

'You've hit it,' replied Holdfast. 'But that's nothing. In some parts of the country, further on, it glitters like a jeweller's shop. I never saw anything like it before.'

'Cannot we go on and have a look at it?' asked Hartley, eagerly.

''Twould not be safe. These people are friendly now, because they believe us to be descendants of "those who are not"; and the gold and diamonds which these natives are carrying are, as I have told you, a present to those beyond the great waters, who may one day return. But they are naturally suspicious, and have only agreed to accompany me until I reach those who waited for me. See, they are impatient now to return; but they will first carry the presents beyond the sentinel rock, which stands as a boundary to their country, at the entrance to this pass.'

At this Holdfast gave a signal, and his escort took up their weighty burdens again and preceded them in silence in the direction of the rock.

They were evidently a far superior race to the ordinary aboriginals, being taller in stature and more intelligent, and seemingly stronger limbed. They were not nearly as dark as the Australian black, and were dressed in a quaint kind of tunic, richly embroidered. One of them wore a large polished diamond strapped upon his right arm, which seemed a badge of authority, and shone with effulgence in the sunlight.

On turning the corner of the bluff rock the burdens were laid down by the side of the pathway, and the six men saluted Holdfast and his companions, and then stood waiting, as though they stayed for some response. Holdfast gravely bowed to them, and smote his forehead lightly with his hand, Sir Charles and Hartley imitating him.

The natives of Zoo-zoo did the same, which was the common form of salutation among them, and then turned their faces homeward, and were soon lost to sight as they passed around the rock.

'Can you make a pot of tea?' was the first request of Holdfast.

'Yes,' said Hartley. 'We will camp for the night here, at the base of this rock, and you shall tell us of all that has happened to you.'

Holdfast's story was a singular one, and its narration, with the addition of Dawson's and Hartley's comments, carried them far into the night. They had made up two great fires, however, and so arranged themselves as to be protected from the winds and warmed by the glowing heat, for the night was cold.

And there, on the side of the White Mountains, the existence of which they had all of them at one time been somewhat sceptical, they smoked and talked; and there Holdfast told them the story of his adventures beyond the white and gold gates of Zoo-zoo.

CHAPTER XXIV

Zoo-zoo

'ONE WORD,' INTERRUPTED Sir Charles, as Holdfast started to begin his story. 'What is Zoo-zoo?'

'An enormous snake,' replied Holdfast.

'Now, we won't ask any further questions until you are through,' said Hartley, settling down to listen.

'You remember,' said Holdfast, 'it was raining when I started from you. I travelled rapidly on as far as this rock, and then rested and ate some lunch, and turned into the gap. I had travelled for over an hour, when the clouds parted for a few minutes and the sun shone down upon the golden summits of those white quartz pillars which mark the entrance on this side to Zoo-zoo land.

'I was fairly dazzled for a moment; for the wet, glistening mass of white quartz, studded with shining yellow metal, was very near to me, and broke out through the mist like something supernatural. But I soon had all my wits about me, for I saw in the sunlight that the lower part of the columns on each side was a writhing mass of black and other snakes. I had intended to climb up those columns and make sure that it was gold, and not a lot of pyrites, but those snakes effectually guarded the treasure. They seem to have their holes in the base of the pillars, for as I stood and looked at them they writhed and hissed at me in such an uncomfortable fashion that I was very glad to pass on. I looked closely at the gates, as we have called them, and saw that they were a mass of pure white quartz, studded thick with gold. If I had been sure of my surroundings I should have put a charge of shot into my rifle, and done some damage to those snakes; but I did not know who might be about, so I went on, leaving the snakes unmolested. That mysterious boomerang might well say, "Beware of the white gates and the golden!"

'After passing through, the pathway begins to descend, and is kept in admirable order. It was evident to me that I had entered a country with inhabitants; and shortly afterwards I found myself surrounded by a small band of natives similar to those you saw with me. They seemed more surprised than afraid, and did not offer to molest me, but simply moved along in the same direction, keeping in a kind of circle, so that there was no possibility of my escape.

'You know I had a copy of the facsimile of the inscribed boomerang with me, and after a while, as the espionage was becoming irksome to me, I stood still and beckoned one, who seemed to be a leader among them, to come near to me. On his approaching, I handed him the drawing of the boomerang. You should have seen him!

'He took it from me, and made a humming sort of sound with his lips, at which the others closed in upon me a bit, and then stood at ease, and waited while their leader intently examined the inscription. It must have given him some trouble to read it, for he took fully ten minutes to satisfy himself. Then he came respectfully near to me, and taking my hand in his, placed it on his forehead, and then upon the crown of his head. Then he wanted to take my rifle and swag from me.

'They evidently had not the slightest knowledge of the use of firearms, and his intention was simply to relieve me of carrying them. I made him understand, as well as I could, that I preferred to keep them.

'After this he motioned along the road, as though to let me know that a short distance ahead we should find rest and shelter. The others then fell behind me and their leader, as though he had explained to them that I was someone of dignity and importance.

'We travelled like this for several hours, and passed through a country which I believe to be perfectly alive with minerals. Great masses of malachite cropped right out upon the pathway, and the very sandy barrenness of the place was sufficient to suggest to a miner's eye untold wealth.

'Before dusk we reached a fairly grassed country; and what astonished me beyond measure was the sight of a great bridge; in fact, it was more of a viaduct than anything else, and was of a dark greyish stone, similar to that of which so many of the public buildings are built in Melbourne.

'It was, no doubt, "*the span longer than the arms of many men*". By the side, a large watchhouse was erected of the same material, and here it was that I found they expected me to remain.

'They brought me food, and skins to lie upon; but I found that I was watched. And the next morning, when I attempted to cross the bridge, two or three of them barred the way, and firmly, although respectfully, intimated to me that I must desist. I was kept there for over a week, and as I missed two or three of the party, I inferred that they had gone to bring someone to interview me, and I awaited events (to all intents and purposes a prisoner) with some anxiety. I had not discharged my gun during all this time, for I was anxious to do nothing which would alarm them.

'Toward the close of day, I happened to be looking along the roadway leading from the bridge, when I saw a number of people approaching with what appeared to be a long pole upon their shoulders, while in front walked a venerable-looking man with a sort of whitey-brown complexion, and with a long white beard. On each side of him were men carrying spears and boomerangs; coloured pennants fluttering from below their spear points. As they drew nearer, I saw that the long thing supported upon their shoulders was an enormous snake, which moved its head to and fro, and gazed around with its beady eyes as though comprehending the whole situation. They crossed the bridge, and passed me without the slightest recognition, and entered and took possession of the guardhouse. I judged the snake to be at least twenty-five feet long, and nearly as broad round as a man.

'Shortly after their arrival, the native captain waited upon me and spoke the name Zoo-zoo, and motioned for me to let him again have the facsimile of the inscribed boomerang, to be submitted to Zoo-zoo's self, in the person of the snake. Things were becoming decidedly complicated, and I cannot say that I altogether appreciated the situation; but there was no help for it, so I camped out beside the house under a tree, sleeping on some skins which they brought me, and wrapped around with my blanket, awaited events.

'The following morning I was invited to an audience with Zoo-zoo. I found the huge reptile surrounded by its bearers, and attended by the venerable person, who held in his hand not only my copy of the inscribed boomerang, but a scroll of parchment inscribed with similar characters. The two were submitted to me, and as it seemed to be their wish, I made my obeisance to his majesty the snake, and then examined them. The letters and words of their parchment were evidently ancient, but the characters were an exact counterpart of those upon the ancient boomerang thrown at Captain Cook.

'That evening the priest or prime minister of Zoo-zoo came to me beneath the tree where I had made my camp, and sitting down by the fire, to my astonishment pulled out a curiously carved pipe and commenced to smoke. I sat and smoked as well, this being, as I thought, the best proof I could give of my friendliness, for it never occurred to me to address my visitor in English.

'Presently, to my utter astonishment, he began to talk in very good English, but with a Scotch accent.

'"The desert you have trodden is the grave of white men, and those with them. You and your companions have reached this land in safety, but in five days you must return, and the waters of the desert will be your grave."

'"I am glad to hear my native tongue again," I said very gravely to him, "although the character of your speech, sir, is not reassuring. May I ask your name, and the circumstances under which you, a Scotchman, became resident in this remarkable country?"

'He smoked away as solemnly as though he had been in attendance at some kirk session, and for some time made no reply.

'"Eh, mon!" he said at last, "ye ken that I'm a Scotchman."

'Then he stopped short, as though he were pulling himself together a bit, before he continued, in a more guarded tone, and with less of the Scotch accent.

'"It matters naught to you whence or how I came to take up my abode with these people. They are my people now, and to the utmost of my power and knowledge I shall defend them against such as you. The legend of the sacred boomerang has saved your life, and the lives of those with you, for my people believe you to be the 'come-back ones' of those who centuries ago departed to the land of the rising sun. In five days they will send you back in safety beyond the gates of Zoo-zoo with treasures and offerings for the departed ones; but you and those with you will never return, or, maybe, I would reveal to my people the deception."

'"I have deceived no one," I protested. "If your people have taken me for one of those who are not, that is their lookout."

'"Hoot, mon," said the greybeard, relapsing into Scotch, "dinna anger me; it is for gold and diamonds you are come, and you shall have them, for these things we have in plenty; but, be warned, you have made your last journey, and I shall let you depart in peace and honour, because it will please my people, and be for you, perchance, an easier death."

'"You are a Job's comforter, sir," I said.

'"Don't speak to me of scripture, prophets, or patriarchs," he said fiercely. "I live in the land and among the people who bow before the wisdom of the Snake."

'I began to suspect by this time that the man was mad, or partly so; and now that I remember his general conversation, I feel sure that this must have been the case. He, no doubt, found his way to Zoo-zoo land from the north-west, and may have been for months travelling alone in the bush (an escaped convict, probably) before he found his way among these singular people. He told me that his title in his country was the Honourable Defender and Feeder of the Snake, and said that three days' journey off he lived in a spacious house adjoining the palace of Zoo-zoo, and that gold and diamonds were baubles to them. Then he rambled off, talking partly in English, partly in Gaelic, and partly in the aboriginal dialect. I gathered that the natives are a remnant of a great nation which came there from some part of the mainland of Asia. They had been builders and cunning artificers and agriculturists, but now most of these arts had been lost. They were content to live by and for themselves, and, save for occasional tribal wars and incursions upon the aboriginals who live on the borders of the desert, were peaceably inclined. "There were treasures", he said, "and strange relics of a bygone people", which my eyes no doubt wished to see; but if I once crossed the seven-spanned bridge, I should be made a prisoner, and, if not executed, would never be allowed to return. He had come there to warn me, but he had no wish to hear of or from me more. He had turned his back forever upon those who were once his people; he owed them nothing but hatred and contempt. He warned me, so that trouble might be prevented; but "You will die, you will die!" was the old man's parting utterance.

'I wanted to know how he managed, and had a lot of questions ready to ask him, but the disagreeable old chap arose, with all the dignity and brevity of a Highlander, and in a moment was gone.

'I saw the Honourable Defender and Feeder of the Snake at the head of the royal bearers the next morning, but only for a few minutes as the extraordinary procession reformed itself, and passed over the bridge and disappeared in the distance.

'It was intimated to me by the natives that when some messengers came back from the capital I would be permitted to return. In due time they appeared; the gold and diamonds which we have here were laid at my feet as a present for the departed ones, which I graciously accepted, and also this inscribed parchment, and I found myself free to return. This morning, with my attendants, we passed out of Zoo-zoo through the gates of quartz and gold, and in due course I met with you.

'I should think the yellow metal they have given me for a present is worth ten thousand pounds, and the diamonds may be one hundred thousand more. The inscription of the parchment is evidently some message to their departed friends, of whom they regarded me as the representative. I tried to explain to them by my fingers that two others had journeyed with me. It seems to me, however, that they were suspicious, and wished me gone again. I do not think that any of them had previously seen a white man, with the exception of that half-crazed Scotchman, who seems to manage the snake and run the show. It's a very extraordinary thing altogether.'

CHAPTER XXV

A Mountain Storm

HOLDFAST'S STORY WAS followed by an examination of the offering.

The gold was in fair-sized nuggets, and among the diamonds were some large and very valuable gems.

'By George!' exclaimed Hartley at last. 'This discovery of ours will revolutionize the continent of Australia. There will be a fall in diamonds, and not another word about the appreciation of gold! We'll every one of us be jolly old millionaires; but the worst of it is, it is spread over such a great tract of country. You'll have fifty thousand people around here within the next year or so, and no chance now of hitting upon what will be the site of the township.'

It is wonderful how bright and fanciful the visions of the future become to men with newly found mineral treasures sparkling in their hands by the light of a bush fire!

The rain had cleared off again, and the stars shone brightly and coldly down upon them. They had made themselves comfortable in bushman fashion, and the bright glow of the great tree trunks cast both light and heat.

The men were too excited to sleep. Hartley handled the gold, and estimated its weight and value, and gave Holdfast the details of his Desert Tunnel Gold Mining scheme. They forgot the dangers of the return journey, and, for the time, the fact that it was impossible for them to carry more than a very small portion of the gold with them across the desert. Holdfast was the first to think of this, and he suggested that they should take the diamonds, and bury the gold at the foot of the rock.

'No,' said Hartley; 'it's downhill. We must manage somehow to get it all as far as the cave; it's not more than three miles.'

After a few hours' sleep and some breakfast, they started, and laboriously made their way downward, each one carrying between fifty and sixty pounds weight of gold and diamonds, in addition to their rifles and swags.

It was nearly midday when they reached the cave, Hartley being the first to enter. He dropped his burden and swag at the entrance, however, in evident alarm and astonishment.

Upon the hearth, where they had made their fire, there were still smouldering embers!

Turning around, he pointed to the fire and ejaculated, 'They have followed us!'

It was evident that he referred to Stoneham and his companion.

Holdfast, however, had grasped his rifle, and having deposited his burden safely within the cave, was examining the tracks.

'It's not Stoneham!' he exclaimed. 'There are naked feetmarks all over the place; and they are feet which never wore boots. The cave has been visited by some of the natives, probably blacks, about whom I heard from the people of Zoo-zoo.'

While Hartley and Sir Charles prepared a meal of roasted wallaroo, Holdfast went out to reconnoitre, and came back with the news that there were traces of a considerable number of blacks in the neighbourhood, but, by their trail, they had seemingly made their way lower down the mountains.

'From what I heard of them from that old Scotchman, the Honourable Keeper of the Snake, they are a low, treacherous lot,' said Holdfast.

'I am afraid that we shall have trouble with them,' said Sir Charles, doubtfully.

'How would it be to camp here for two or three days, and give them time to clear right out of this part of the country?' suggested Hartley.

'No doubt they think that we have all gone on to Zoo-zoo,' said Sir Charles. 'By the way,' he added, 'they have helped themselves pretty liberally to our store of dried meat.'

'It's a wonder to me that they did not take it all,' said Holdfast.

They felt ill at ease, however, for they had now to count with these blacks, as well as Stoneham, and the ordinary perils of the return journey across the desert.

'I am afraid that that Desert Tunnel scheme of yours, Hartley, is a long way off yet,' said Holdfast.

'We may have some trouble,' replied Hartley, 'but that little affair is going to be pulled through, or I am mistaken in my luck.'

The rain seemed to have set in again, and from the leaden sky the downpour was steady and continuous.

High winds occasionally whistled and moaned in weird and melancholy fashion through the mountain passes, and the three adventurers began to feel decidedly damp and depressed in spirits.

One good thing for them was that the cave proved fairly watertight, and they were able to keep up a fire both day and night, for the weather was cold and uncomfortable. Fortunately for them, firewood was plentiful.

'By the quantity of fallen timber about, there must at times be very violent gales here,' said Hartley.

Holdfast had just entered and caught the remark, which had been addressed to Sir Charles.

'Step out to the entrance, and you will see something coming that makes fallen timber in these parts,' he ejaculated hurriedly.

Hartley and Sir Charles hurried to the entrance of the cave with him. They had no need to follow the motion of his hand, for in the distance, over the mountain passes, they saw a storm approaching which stilled their tongues with awe and amazement.

The rain had partially cleared off from the eastward, and the scenery around them was full of solemn grandeur. The great mountain peaks to the west were already partially enveloped by the grim blackness of the approaching tempest. Everything was hushed, and the sublimity and awfulness of the scene affected Sir Charles in a most singular manner. His face was pallid.

'We are safe enough here,' said Hartley to him, reassuringly.

'I am not afraid of the storm,' replied the baronet. 'You don't understand me. It is the stupendous majesty of nature that appalls me.'

It was indeed a sight such as is rarely witnessed, even amid the remarkable natural phenomena of Australia.

The approaching tempest was of a greenish blackness in its hue. So far, not a single flash of lightning had been seen; but in the distance the thunders muttered, as the darkening face of the storm swept nearer towards them. Now and again spectral towers of mist seemed to be thrown off from jutting promontories of the deep-massed clouds. These sprang out from the main body of the storm in fantastic shapes, as though flung forth by terrific explosions, while the main body of the armed clouds moved nearer with the silence of death.

Holdfast drew a long breath, and then said, 'It will be a wonderful sight when it breaks.'

The words were hardly uttered when the storm clouds struck some towering peaks, and immediately the whole of the great landscape was illuminated with a succession of lightning flashes, which seemed in the eyes of the half-blinded observers to be like the sudden meeting of ten thousand swords.

It was neither sheet, nor forked, nor chain lightning, but more like the sudden shooting, dancing radiance of the aurora australis, or the fire which flashes from the crossing of two swords by angry combatants.

With the first lightning flashes, however, the storm broke, and its descent was so terrible that it seemed for the moment as though nature was struggling in the throes of dissolution.

It beat down with the force of a whirlwind, the vivid lightnings being accompanied by one long bellowing roar of thunder, which echoed and re-echoed among the mountains.

The men shrank back within the cave, half-blinded with the lightning, while the storm swept everything living before it. Mighty trees in exposed places were broken down or torn up by the roots, as though mere saplings; while great fragments of rock, lifted by the winds from their long resting places, were sent bounding down the mountain-side toward the valley, crashing through undergrowth and trees in sheltered places as though thunderbolts of the gods. For the time, the very mountains seemed to tremble, and the three men stood together in momentary expectation that the convulsions of nature would overthrow their place of shelter and bury them amid its ruins.

'I have never experienced anything so terrible,' said Hartley at last, his voice hardly audible for the roaring of the tempest.

'Wait until the rain comes!' said Holdfast.

They had not long to wait.

Nothing like it had ever before been witnessed by any one of them.

It was not rain, but a deluge – the breaking of a huge waterspout. The roar of the thunder had been terrible, but the roar of the great waters sweeping down into the valley had a terror peculiarly its own.

'That desert will be turned into a sea,' said Holdfast.

All that afternoon, and far into the night, this downpour continued, after which steady rain fell for two days; and then it suddenly cleared away, and the bright sun shone forth as though rebuking the mountains for the quarrel, and the needless fury of the storm.

'I have been thinking out a plan to get this gold and stuff down the mountains,' said Hartley that afternoon, as they were getting things dry and a bit straight again.

'Out with it, then,' said Holdfast. 'It's certain that we cannot carry it.'

'It's all downhill, and I propose that we drag it on the bough of a tree,' said Hartley.

'Yes,' said Holdfast, thoughtfully, 'that's not a bad idea; you show your genius, Hartley, by the simplicity of your methods. It's the way we used to drag each other down hills when I was a boy.'

It seemed a primitive and simple plan, but it proved most effective. The gold was done up in the swags with the diamonds and their belongings, and the whole lot piled upon the thick part of a large branch.

Sending Sir Charles along in front of them with his rifle, Holdfast and Hartley followed, dragging the bough behind them by thongs which they had fastened to it.

Only those who, having lost a wheel off their buggy, have had to travel for miles with a sapling under the axle, will know the toughness and slipperiness of a thick, well-leafed gum tree branch, and as the floods of water had swept the timber and other debris off the rocky road (as though gangs of men had been employed for months to clear the path of Zoo-zoo), the method answered well.

The branch bearing the treasure had occasionally to be renewed, but the path, which was a steady decline, was mostly smooth and slippery, and after the first half-day's journeying they found that it would be quite possible to drag the whole of their great treasure behind them to the plain.

Thus day after day they slowly progressed until they reached the final gorge which led to the desert and avenue.

It was still early when they reached a point from which the desert was visible, the sun shone brightly down upon the scene, and it was again warm, but the heat seemed tempered by an unusual softness, as they turned the last corner and saw in front of them – a sea.

The whole desert was covered as far as the eye could reach in all directions; from the base of the mountains there stretched a great inland waste of water. The men looked at each other in blank amazement; they had talked about the possibility of the desert being underwater, but the sight of it for the moment unmanned them.

'I have known a thing of this sort happen in another part of Australia,' said Hartley, hoarsely, 'and it never dried up again.'

The men sat down and looked at the ocean at their feet. The desert they could have traversed; but they now seemed completely hemmed in. Behind them were the mountains and Zoo-zoo land, and east, and west, and south, the tossing billows of a great sea.

'Good Heaven!' exclaimed Holdfast, as he thought of Marjory. 'Suppose the station at Western Plains has been swept away!'

'They will all have been drowned,' said Sir Charles.

'Not a bit of it,' exclaimed Hartley, 'while Dorna was about. You forget that they have the yacht.'

CHAPTER XXVI

White Wings from the South

W HAT ARE WE to do now?' inquired Sir Charles, looking anxiously at his two companions, and then at the water which, on three sides of them, stretched away to the distant horizon.

'It is my opinion that it will disappear almost as quickly as it came,' said Holdfast. 'There must be an enormous soakage in a place like this; and, besides, remember how conflicting are the accounts of explorers; where one man finds a desert in these parts, another discovers a lake. This experience of ours will explain away a lot of seeming contradictions.'

Hartley, however, was not nearly so sanguine as he was wont to be. The flood had swamped his Desert Tunnel Gold Mining scheme most effectually. He was troubled to explain the presence of such an immense body of water.

'Where can it all have come from?' was the question he put to Holdfast again and again.

'The only explanation I can think of,' said Holdfast, 'is that this is the basin into which the rainfall from the mountains, and from thousands of square miles of surrounding country, flows. You remember that the Western Plains are higher than the desert, and no doubt this is the catchment area of the whole of the ranges to the east of Western Plains. It is impossible to say from what sources the water flows into this great desert basin. The blacks evidently give the whole of the country a wide berth, and the waterworn smoothness of the rocks about the head of the gorge may be the result of ages of such floods as this we now see in front of us.'

'I suppose such a transformation would only be possible in a country of violent extremes like Australia – one day a desert, the next a sea,' said Hartley.

'But what is to be done?' persisted Sir Charles.

'We might cross it on a raft, perhaps,' said Hartley; 'but I think the best thing will be to make a comfortable camp somewhere, and wait for a few days, and see what prospect there is of its falling, and eventually drying up.'

'Yes, we'd better fix up a camp somewhere; and near the water too, where we can defend ourselves if we should happen to be attacked by blacks,' said Holdfast.

'Do you think there is any danger of that?' asked Hartley.

'Yes, unfortunately, I do,' said Holdfast.

They were still upon the legendary pathway which dipped down in front of them – a smooth track leading straight on in the direction of the water. A few minutes afterward they skirted the banks of the river, which further on disappeared, to run its underground course into the distant lake. They caught sight of it with singular emotion. It seemed a connecting link between themselves and civilization and home.

Pushing slowly on, they entered the avenue again and followed it to within a few yards of where the broad path somewhat abruptly disappeared beneath the water. The gradual depression of the desert was made evident by the singular appearance of the avenue of trees, which stretched away in two lines of glossy greenness for miles, until they at last merged themselves into the water.

Hartley ran his eye along the two straight lines of foliage. 'Dry up, indeed!' he exclaimed.

'Why, there's twenty feet of water, and in places more!'

'We will camp in the avenue,' said Holdfast; 'you two fix things up and make a fire. There ought to be plenty of turkeys about. I will take my rifle and see if I cannot get something for dinner.'

It was well for them that there was no scarcity of game, for their flour was almost done, and a very small quantity of tea and sugar was all that remained. They had a fair quantity of ammunition, and with water at hand there was no fear of starvation, for both Holdfast and Hartley knew a good bit about the edible herbs and roots to be found in the bush.

The quick report of Holdfast's rifle several times in succession encouraged them to hasten their efforts to start a good fire.

'This avenue makes a splendid camping place,' said Hartley, 'and not a bad shelter, either, for a scrimmage with the black; you see, there's no cover, except for these trees, for pretty well a hundred yards.'

They were dragging in some fair-sized logs for firewood when Holdfast returned, carrying two fine turkeys and some smaller birds which he had shot.

He walked hurriedly into the camp, and throwing down the birds near the fire, looked behind him, and stood with his rifle in his hand.

'You had better hurry with the cooking,' he said, 'and I will go into the bush and keep an eye on the enemy; we are going to have trouble with these blacks. Cooee when the turkey's roasted.'

Holdfast doubled upon his tracks back into the bush without another word, and his two companions hurried with their cooking preparations, occasionally casting a suspicious glance around.

A turkey was cleaned and plucked and quartered in a very few minutes, and four long pointed sticks, stuck into the ground, served for spits on which to roast it.

The men had previously looked to their rifles, which, fully loaded, were placed handy.

Holdfast returned before the cooking was finished, and, sitting down, still facing the quarter from which he had come, told them of his adventures.

He had been stalking a brace of turkeys through a bit of scrub, exercising special caution lest they might lose their dinner, when he noticed the birds turn suddenly round, as though frightened at something, and run in his direction. As they came within range he lifted his rifle and fired, but at the same moment, the second bird also fell, transfixed with a spear, and through the bush there stared at him the glaring eyes of a savage.

They looked at each other for several minutes across the two birds; and then, with a sudden yell of terror, the black turned, and disappeared in the bush.

'We shall have the whole tribe of them looking for us presently,' said Holdfast, 'and they will find us too, for there is no way of escaping them. We are not going to leave the treasure, and we cannot go any further towards Western Plains on account of the water.'

They made a hearty meal, and as the sun drew nearer the white tops of the distant mountains, and creeping shadows darkened the higher passes, the men hurriedly completed their preparations for the night. Holdfast carefully extinguished every spark of fire with water, which he brought in one of the cans from the lake.

'What is that for?' queried Sir Charles.

'It will be a dark night, and we do not want to give them a light to spear us by,' said Holdfast.

Before the light failed, the last speaker managed to get an hour and a half of sleep, while Hartley and Sir Charles kept guard; he had the gift, common to Australian bushmen, of commanding sleep at almost anytime and anywhere.

He would, if necessary, sleep for an hour or two upon horseback; or, rolled in a blanket, would close his eyes and fall asleep by the mere strength of resolute will.

On awakening, he brought up two cans of water and placed them at the foot of one of the trees. He seemed to be taking special notice of these trees and moved the treasure and swags nearer to them.

'Now, you two had best go to sleep as soon as you can, I will look after the n-----s;[11] you may not have more than an hour or two.'

Hartley and Dawson lay down, wrapped in their blankets; but sleep was not nearly as compliant as it had been at the behest of Holdfast, and they lay for several hours conveying in whispers.

Holdfast, as still is a statue, leaned, rifle in hand, against a tree. It was about midnight when he awoke them.

---

11 Editors' note: We have taken out this offensive term (commonly used in colonial Australia) from the original text, out of consideration for contemporary readerships.

'Leave your swags and blankets there,' he whispered.

They hurriedly followed him a few yards, and, with their rifles in their hands, swung themselves noiselessly up into the low branches of a tree, then climbed higher among the foliage.

'Don't go to sleep,' said Holdfast, 'if you can help it.'

An hour and a half passed in silence, and suddenly Holdfast grew rigid, and grasped his rifle, and gave a quiet signal to his companions.

Once or twice they heard a stick snap, or something very much like it, then a whizzing sound was heard, and a thud; another, and another, and another, followed; but it might have been a bird or the dropping of a twig.

'Hist!' said Holdfast. Then he whispered, 'Fire! anywhere!' and the three rifles were instantaneously discharged.

Yells in startling proximity accompanied the reports; then followed the same deathlike stillness, except for the cry of startled birds and animals, as the echoes of the reports were caught up and thrown back by the adjacent hills.

'I think they will leave us for tonight, after that,' said Hartley; 'but we are safest where we are.'

When the grey light of the morning made objects visible again, Holdfast pointed to the blankets which had been left by Hartley and Sir Charles when he aroused them from sleep; they were each of them transfixed by several spears.

'Now we know what we have to expect from them,' said Holdfast.

As it grew lighter it became evident that the three men were surrounded by hostile natives. They were in great force, too, by the numbers which were to be occasionally seen on the higher ground among the trees.

During the day several were shot by Hartley and Holdfast, and beyond the throwing of a few boomerangs, no serious attack was made.

'They will wait for the darkness,' said Holdfast; 'or, possibly, just surround us, and starve us out.'

Under cover of their rifles they made the fire and cooked the second turkey and brewed their last pot of tea. They ate the meal almost in silence. Hartley had been to look at the water; it was no lower than on the previous day, in fact, if anything, by the mark he had made, it seemed to be rising. Certainly there was no prospect of any sudden disappearance of the water.

The day passed without any attack, and Holdfast again expressed it as his opinion that they were reserving themselves for the night.

'We had better camp in one of the trees nearer to the water,' he said.

To their surprise, however, the long night passed without any sign; but in the morning the smoke of the fires which encircled them plainly showed that the blacks were playing the waiting game. The firearms had evidently frightened them – probably more of their number had been killed or wounded than they imagined – and the rest thought discretion the better part of valour, and waited for hunger to so reduce their strength that they might fall an easier prey. At any rate, this was the light in which Holdfast and his companions regarded it.

The third day found them hungry and desperate.

'It will never do to stop here and get so weak that we can do nothing,' said Hartley. 'We must make a rush for it.'

'But where are we going to rush to?' said Holdfast, 'with probably a couple of hundred blacks around us, too.

'We should have to leave the gold and diamonds behind us,' he continued; 'and if we force our way up the mountains, we are only going further from home. I have been thinking whether we could not adopt Hartley's suggestion, and construct a raft, or something of that sort.'

'All the wood about here is too heavy,' said Sir Charles.

Early that night the natives made a furious attack upon the camp; a perfect shower of blazing darts, boomerangs, and spears fell around them. More daring savages crept from tree to tree, and the whole place seemed alive with the savages; but for the repeating rifles of the party, it would have fared ill with them. The attack was with difficulty repulsed, and, having at last sullenly retired, the great fires were kindled by the blacks, which made the intended rush in the darkness almost impossible. Holdfast would have risked it, however, but for the persuasion of Sir Charles, who feared that they might use up the whole of their ammunition or find themselves cut off in some place without water.

The position was a desperate one; hunger and want of sleep were already weakening their physical strength, and while determined to sell their lives dearly, it was evident that all three believed themselves not far from the mysterious bourne from whence no traveller returns.

'They will torture us if they take us alive!' said Holdfast, grimly.

The fourth day dawned, and they were preparing themselves to force a passage somehow through the watching crowd of blacks, if only to obtain food, when their attention was attracted by a number of natives, gathered on a bit of rising ground, gesticulating and, seemingly, now and then pointing across the water.

'We cannot spare the powder,' said Hartley, 'or I'd take a shot at the beggars.'

'Look!' said Sir Charles, excitedly pointing away toward the southern horizon. 'There's a sail!'

It was true. Like a white bird on the distant water, there was a sail approaching, and they watched it for a quarter of an hour, like men half-dazed, as it steadily grew more distinct.

'We are saved!' shouted Hartley at last, leaping up in his excitement, and shaking his fist at the crowd of gesticulating natives. 'Those beggars will be disappointed of their anticipated feast, after all! That boat is the *Marjory Holdfast*, with her namesake and Dorna Stoneham on board!'

He only gave expression to what they had all known for some time.

'Thank God!' said Sir Charles, reverently.

The excitement was not confined to the three adventurers, however. Pacing to and fro, and up and down the rocks, were the crowds of excited natives, watching what they thought to be some new bird or animal approaching.

Holdfast suggested that they should fire one or two volleys to guide those on board the yacht towards the avenue. Whether it was this, or simply good fortune, they were presently delighted to see the yacht sail right along by the avenue, and with a fair wind make its way straight in the direction of the camp.

Hartley was beside himself with excitement, as the boat gradually grew larger as it bore steadily down upon them. 'Bravo, Dorna!' he cried out; and then overcome with the prospect, and also probably with being so long without food, tears came into his eyes and he broke down unreservedly, and, as he said directly after to Holdfast, made a regular fool of himself.

It seemed hours to the men before the yacht came within such a distance as to be clearly recognized; but there was no mistaking her.

'We had better get everything down to the water's edge,' said Holdfast. 'Those black devils may rush us as soon as she comes to shore.'

'Who is that at the bows?' said Sir Charles.

'It's Marjory,' said Holdfast.

'Dorna's steering!' ejaculated Hartley.

'Steady!' called out Holdfast, as the yacht drew near the land. 'Put her nose right up to the bank. There will just be water enough to float her off.'

The girls handled her splendidly, and she was brought up bows on near to the pathway.

Dorna and Marjory leaped on shore, the former with a rope in her hand . . . The few moments which followed were memorable in the lives of every one of them.

The sharp whizz of a spear, however, soon recalled them from their joy at meeting to the dangers which still beset them.

The shower of spears was answered by the whip-like crack of repeating rifles, and several of the dusky cannibals[12] bit the dust.

The two women and Sir Charles then hurriedly removed the swags and gold and diamonds to the yacht, while the blacks were kept at bay by Holdfast's and Hartley's rifles; and within half an hour the whole of them were safely afloat, and out of any further danger from the natives.

---

12 This is a racist cliché often encountered in colonial frontier novels.

Refreshed with food and sleep, the three men awoke late in the afternoon to find themselves sailing smoothly over an immense sea of water with the White Mountains nearly lost sight of against the northern sky.

CHAPTER XXVII

The End of the Chapter

I T WOULD BE difficult to depict the astonishment of Marjory and Dorna when they heard the marvellous narration of what had transpired, including the mysterious disappearance of Buchanan.

The horses had returned safely to Western Plains; they were found feeding outside the station fences and were brought in three or four days after they had been turned loose by Holdfast.

Marjory and Dorna had judged from this that Holdfast and his party had safely crossed the worst part of the desert, and knowing that they had good leadership, the sisters had not been very anxious about their safety.

'They will return all right,' said Marjory. 'John is a thorough explorer, and few men have a more perfect knowledge of bushcraft – besides, there are four of them.'

Marjory now confessed, however, that she had her misgivings, especially when the floodwaters began to cover the desert. At first this had been very gradual, but afterwards the water rose rapidly, and they found the ridgy country on which the station homestead was built surrounded on all sides, by which their escape was effectually cut off.

'But how came you to think of sailing out after us?' asked Holdfast.

'It was Dorna that suggested it,' replied Marjory, looking the while in the direction of the fast-disappearing mountains.

At this Sir Charles raised himself – for he had been lying upon some cushions to rest – and said with some emotion:

'We must thank you, then, Miss Stoneham, for your forethought; only that you came as you did, and when you did, we should certainly have lost our lives. It makes me shudder now to think of the desperate position we were in.'

'I am indeed thankful that we came; but I don't exactly think that it was the result of much forethought on my part,' said Dorna, looking at her sister with a queer, half-ashamed twinkle in her eye. 'It was by a happy chance, I think, that we came just then. We started on the verge for the sake of Mr Crumbs and his friend, the minister.'

'I beg your pardon; what was the gentleman's name?' said Hartley, at once thoroughly awake and deeply interested.

'Jeremiah Crumbs,' replied Dorna, demurely.

'Remarkable name! Are you quite sure that it was Crumbs?' ejaculated Hartley.

'Positively sure,' said Dorna.

'Why, he's one of the richest men in the west,' said Hartley.

'But what brought him out to the Western Plains?' inquired Holdfast, mischievously.

Dorna gave him a look which, interpreted, said, 'You are a mean thing.'

'He came with a minister,' replied Marjory, who felt that she must come to the rescue of her sister, but in doing so unfortunately made matters worse.

'A minister!' ejaculated Holdfast.

'Probably the minister expected to perform a ceremony,' said Hartley. 'Nothing less than a wedding would have brought a parson all those miles out into the bush.'

'Yes,' said Dorna, quietly, looking with her large calm eyes full into Hartley's face, 'he came to marry me to Mr Jeremiah Crumbs, of Clifton Park station, a man who had travelled nearly a thousand miles through the bush to win me, and who was prepared to settle fifty thousand pounds upon me, and a station, if I would have consented to be his wife.'

'He must have been both very rich and very much in love,' said Sir Charles, smiling pleasantly across at Dorna.

'May we inquire what you said to him?' said Holdfast, quietly.

'I asked him to forgive me for having partially misled him,' said Dorna, blushing. 'Then he wanted to get away again very badly; but the floods were out, and I really felt sorry for him. The minister's parishioners, too, were being neglected; so, as the water had covered all the plains, we sailed across the south end of the desert, and landed them at the foot of the ranges. Then we decided to come on and look for you.'

Hartley had listened intently to Dorna's simple account of this incident and watched her keenly for several minutes.

She was aware of this scrutiny, however, and resented it. Yet in her very resentment there was something very much akin to love. What right had he to judge her conduct in regard to Mr Crumbs? But the very question suggested that he had some right.

They had already told the two sisters the story of Buchanan's unfortunate disappearance, and Hartley's search for him, and discovery of the gold and diamonds; and somehow Holdfast always managed to give Hartley a full meed of praise.

Hartley certainly felt changed towards Dorna. At last he was thoroughly in earnest, and the incident of Mr Crumbs and the minister suggested to him that he might lose her. He knew that they all of them owed their lives to her skill and daring.

The yacht had arrived in the very nick of time. The whole thing was courageous and fortunate; and as it is easy to be very much in love with a woman to whom you owe your life, he decided in his heart there and then that he really loved Dorna, and he determined, before he left Western Plains station, that he would ask her to marry him.

At sunset they had a discussion as to whether it would be safer to anchor for the night; but, after taking soundings, they agreed that there was very little fear of their running aground anywhere, and they decided to sail on, making a course due south.

There was quite a bit of rough sea on, after nightfall, through a strong westerly wind springing up, and the yacht lay over to it, and swept through the water with foam under her bows and quite a wake behind.

'It is wonderful,' exclaimed Sir Charles to Marjory, 'to think that we are at sea in the very centre of Australia and sailing over what only about six weeks ago was a waste of burning desert sand!'

'Yes, it is very wonderful,' replied Marjory, who, however, thought the most wonderful part of it was that she had her husband safely by her side again, after such a series of hairbreadth escapes.

Dorna was forward at the bows (on lookout duty), and somehow Hartley was with her. His long sleep had greatly refreshed him.

The sisters had arranged that the menfolk should take another watch below; but Hartley would not hear of it.

'Let Sir Charles have another sleep,' he said; 'he is delicate. But you and your sister want a rest. Just think of how you have been worked night and day to bring the yacht all this distance!'

'We had a fair wind,' said Dorna; 'and both of us were able to get a little sleep.'

Hartley placed his hand on Dorna's, and somehow it was allowed to remain there.

'Dorna,' he said, 'had you any thought of me when you started out to rescue us?'

'Of course I had,' replied Dorna; 'I thought of you all.'

'Did it rain heavily at Western Plains?' asked Hartley, abruptly removing his hand, and changing the conversation.

'Not at first,' replied Dorna, and there was no change in her voice to indicate that she had noticed either the 'Dorna', the pressure of his hand, or his sudden change. 'The water crept up at first under a perfectly clear sky, but after, it rained continuously for two or three weeks.'

They all slept a little that night except Holdfast. He was continually pacing to and fro with the lead, trying the depth of the water.

'We are certain to run aground somewhere,' he said.

Nor were his fears altogether groundless, for toward morning they several times ran over banks, where the water was extremely shallow.

'If we get stuck here we shall stand a chance of being starved,' he said.

'It's a pity that they did not bring the dinghy with them,' said Hartley.

'That would have been no use,' said Holdfast, 'it would only have carried three; and who would have gone away leaving the rest behind? We must only hope that the good fortune which brought the yacht over will see her back again.'

The day wore slowly by; in the afternoon, however, trees began to show themselves, and they presently knew by the contour of some hills that they were approaching the gorge; they had made the voyage back to the lake in safety.

Late that evening, just after sunset, they found themselves in a swift current, which rushed with great force toward the lake; once the yacht struck something, causing the slight craft to quiver from stem to stern. All on board held their breath; a grating sound was heard, and shortly afterward the swiftness of the current noticeably decreased – they were in the lake.

The wind still held fair for them, but they presently cast anchor.

'Better to wait until morning,' said Holdfast, 'than run upon some of those rocks or islands in the dark.'

That night they enjoyed their first unbroken rest for many days.

Holdfast and Hartley were stirring early in the morning, and before the others were awake the yacht was again under way – bound homeward.

Hartley was steering; Holdfast stood beside him, watching how the sails drew, when suddenly the attention of both of them was drawn to something ahead, floating in the water.

Hartley brought the yacht up a point or two nearer to the wind, so that they might pass it more closely.

'My God!' exclaimed Holdfast, beneath his breath. 'Look!'

The yacht swept past, and the floating mass riveted the gaze of both of them.

The men turned pale with horror; as well they might, for it was a sight, once seen, never to be obliterated from the memory.

'Thank Heaven that they are asleep!' said Holdfast. 'It will be better never to mention it. The man was the girls' father, and Buchanan was Dawson's friend.'

What they had seen were two swollen, bloated, disfigured corpses, with livid faces and dull glaring eyes, floating side by side; they were Stoneham and Buchanan, and the death grip of the latter was still fastened in the collar of the other's coat.

Buchanan was revenged!

'They must have fought and died together in the subterranean river, and then have been swept out into the lake,' said Hartley, hoarsely.

The sleepers shortly afterward joined them, but not another word was said. Except to the men, the fate of Aaron Stoneham and Captain Buchanan was enshrouded in mystery.

~

In a quiet home, amid pleasant scenery, thousands of miles away from Australia, a gentleman sits, after a late breakfast, looking over the columns of the *London Times*. In appearance, three years has not changed Sir Charles Dawson very much. He is now married to the sweet-faced woman he saw in his waking dreams when in Australia. The baronet is wiser, wealthier, and probably a stronger and happier man than when we saw him last.

He laughs heartily now and then while he reads his paper, until his wife, from the other side of the table, insists upon knowing the occasion of his mirth.

'Here is a double-column advertisement of Bright Hartley's Central Australian Desert Tunnel Gold Mining Scheme,' he said at last; 'and upon my honour it's almost word for word as he sketched it out to me in that cave on the White Mountains! Of course his name does not figure in it, as he is the vendor; but John Holdfast, Esq., is one of the provisional directors.

'Instead of two million sterling, I see they are floating it for one. They propose, too, to make a railway across the desert; and the prospectus is so inviting that really I feel inclined to make application for some shares myself.'

'But Charley dear,' said Lady Dawson, 'there are gold and diamonds there.'

'Certainly, love. Those we brought back with us were genuine enough; and the adventure with poor Buchanan, and Hartley, and Holdfast, on the path of Zoo-zoo, has added very materially to our wealth. I suppose, too, if they float this mining company, they will be overwhelming me with a portion of the purchase-money; for both Hartley and Holdfast are the very soul of honour in regard to engagements with friends. But I wonder whether the desert has been flooded since. It must be dry just now, or they would not attempt to form this company.

'By the way, Madge, did I ever tell you how at the last Hartley got Dorna Stoneham to promise to be his wife?'

'No; I have no recollection of your having done so.'

'Proof positive, then,' said Sir Charles, laughing, 'that you never heard the story.

'You must know that Dorna refused Hartley twice after he landed from the yacht at Western Plains homestead. He really got quite thin-looking and miserable over it, and we all felt sorry for him. After the water had gone down off the plain, and the country was fit to travel, it was settled that we should all of us go back together to Brisbane, leaving the married couple and station hands to look after the place.

'We were all of us riding. Holdfast had brought half-a-dozen packhorses, to carry the luggage, and several black boys, so we formed quite a formidable party. We were of necessity travelling slowly, and Hartley persuaded Miss Stoneham the first afternoon to take him around to see the last of Western Plains from the Bald Rock on the range. I suppose he guessed that she wanted to say "Yes" to him, but that her wilfulness would not let her.

'It seems they were sitting quietly in their saddles, looking, as they thought, for the last time upon the far-reaching landscape, which had been the theatre of so much adventure for us all, when it occurred to Hartley to make another effort to get a favourable answer.

'"Dorna," he said, pointing to the distant scene, "it was there that I first loved you as a man may love a woman, and I hoped that there in the wild lonely wilderness you would let your heart plead for me."

'At the very moment he was pleading his suit so eloquently, a shower of spears fell near them, one transfixing Hartley's horse, which suddenly reared, throwing its rider, and then staggered and fell, a few yards off, seemingly dying.

'As Hartley rose to his feet and grasped his rifle, a black leaped in front of him to brain him with a waddy; but Dorna was too quick for him, and shot him clean through the wrist with her revolver as he held the waddy above Hartley's head.

'"Quick!" she called out to Hartley, firing several shots among the startled blacks. "My horse will carry both of us.

'"You foolish man, of course I love you," she said, laughing through her tears of apprehension at his narrow escape.

'In a minute – before the blacks had time to rally and make another onslaught – the two of them were gone.

'I believe that Mrs Hartley tells her friends that blacks are always troublesome creatures, and that but for them she never would have married.

'But she is happy enough, and, to my mind, her betrothal was not out of keeping with the rest of her adventurous career.'

~

It may interest the reader to know that the goldmining company was floated to the enrichment of all three adventurers, however the 'guileless public' may have fared.

What later discoveries may have been made by gold and diamond seekers in the land of Zoo-zoo the writer of this narrative cannot say. Doubtless the mysterious pathway and the ancient inhabitants of Central Australia, ruled over by the Honourable Keeper of the Snake, are still in existence, and may any day be heard of, for the unexplored portions of the continent of Australia are attracting much attention.

It is needless, perhaps, to add at 'the end of the chapter' that the Western Plains are still green in the memories of John and Marjory Holdfast, and Bright and Dorna Hartley, or that amid their wealthy and prosperous surroundings they sometimes look back lovingly along the vista of that old bush track; for it was there, amid the wilderness, and on the great waters of that strange temporary inland sea, that they experienced some of the heartbeats which, no matter when or where, make hours and places sacred in the annals of men's and women's lives.

THE END

GRATTAN STREET PRESS PERSONNEL

Semester 1, 2018

Editing and Proofreading
Grayce Arlov, Ellie Atack, Luke Fussell, Jessica Hall,
Stephanie Lightfoot, Beth Wentworth

Design and Production
Ellen Dutton, Angela Iaria, Alexandra Robson, Beth
Wentworth

Sales and Marketing
Jessica Allan, Brooke Munday, Audrey Kearns

Social Media
Cherry Cai, Georgia Gallo

Submissions Officers
Ellie Atack, Laura Bianca Cesile, Katie Hollister, Sunniva
Midtskogen

Website and Blogs
Georgia Quirke-Luping, Laura Bianca Cesile, Katie
Hollister, Sunniva Midtskogen

Academic Staff
Mark Davis, Katherine Day, Aaron Mannion, Sybil Nolan.

ACKNOWLEDGEMENTS

This semester we raised the bar by publishing two books in the Colonial Australian Popular Fiction series simultaneously. Congratulations and thanks to the students involved in its editing and production, who rose brilliantly to the challenge: Ellen Dutton and Alexandra Robson (production editors and typesetters); Grayce Arlov, Luke Fussell, Jessica Hall and Stephanie Lightfoot (editors and proofreaders); and Angela Iaria (design and paging). Thanks also to the rest of the Grattan Street Press team, who checked OCR scans against the original texts and made corrections.

We are grateful to academic staff in the Master of Publishing and Communications who assisted the project: Mark Davis (who created the original design for the series, and gave helpful advice on its implementation), Aaron Mannion (who oversaw GSP last year, and gave us valuable advice on workflow), and Katherine Day (who always seemed to be there when editorial help and advice was needed).

We are also grateful to our new Head of School, Professor Jennifer Milam, for her support; to Beth Driscoll, David McInnis and Maria Tumarkin, and other academic staff who gave advice and assistance; to Annemarie Levin who helped us on an almost daily basis to process sales through our website and to source services; to Amanda Morris at the Australian Centre, for advice about the launch; and to GSP alumni Bianca Jafari and Wes Whitfield, who helped out in various ways before and/or during semester.

Thanks also to Ken Gelder and Rachael Weaver for their responsiveness as series editors, and their continuing interest in both the colonial fiction project and the Press itself. And last but not least, thanks to Debbie Lee, Rushelle Lister, and the rest of the staff at our printers, IngramSpark.

Sybil Nolan, Coordinator, Grattan Street Press

ABOUT GRATTAN STREET PRESS

Grattan Street Press is a trade publisher based in Melbourne. A start-up press, we aim to publish a range of work, including contemporary literature, trade non-fiction, and children's books, and to re-publish culturally valuable works that are out of print. The press is an initiative of the Publishing and Communications program in the School of Culture and Communication at the University of Melbourne, and is staffed by graduate students, who receive hands-on experience of every aspect of the publication process.

The press is a not-for-profit organisation that seeks to build long-term relationships within the Australian literary and publishing community. We also partner with community organisations in Melbourne and beyond to co-publish books that contribute to public knowledge and discussion.

Organisations interested in partnering with us can contact us at coordinator@grattanstreetpress.com.

ABOUT THE AUSTRALIAN CENTRE

The Australian Centre is based in the School of Culture and Communication at the University of Melbourne, with Professor Ken Gelder and Professor Denise Varney as its co-directors. It aims to develop innovative research projects in the Australian arts and humanities across a range of disciplines, including Art History, Theatre Studies, Literary Studies, Cultural Studies, Media and Communication, Cinema Studies, Indigenous Studies and Creative Writing.